GONE
DARK

ALSO BY KIRK RUSSELL

A Grale Thriller

Signature Wounds

Ben Raveneau Mysteries

A Killing in China Basin

Counterfeit Road

One Through the Heart

The John Marquez Mysteries

Shell Games

Night Game

Dead Game

Redback

Die-Off

GONE DARK

KIRK RUSSELL

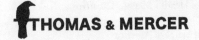
THOMAS & MERCER

Text copyright © 2018 by Kirk Russell
All rights reserved.

Published by Thomas & Mercer, Seattle

www.apub.com

Amazon, the Amazon logo, and Thomas & Mercer are trademarks of Amazon.com, Inc., or its affiliates.

ISBN-13: 9781503952218
ISBN-10: 1503952215

Cover design by Mike Heath | Magnus Creative

Printed in the United States of America

For my sister, Lydia McIntosh

Prologue

The night before the attacks, they did a dry run into the heart of Los Angeles. Not with the actual bomb vehicles but with a rented ten-foot U-Haul truck carrying twenty-five eighty-pound sacks of Quikrete to simulate the one-ton weight of each bomb. The U-Haul followed the route one of the three bomb trucks would take. It came off the downhill, made the right turn, and drove slowly past the electrical substation. A homeless man camped under plastic on the sidewalk looked up at the faces of the driver and passenger as they went by.

The homeless guy came up in the meeting the next morning. The goal was to *kill no one*. The one who would call in the bomb threat read aloud the warning a 911 operator would hear. Everyone agreed it was clear and explicit, and yet a palpable nervousness lingered in the room.

Acquiring materials had required stealth. Figuring out a detonator, building and shaping the charges, and transporting the bombs chewed up most of a year. The first small test bombs were a thrill celebrated. But this was different. This was the point of no return.

The bomb maker leaned back on the couch. He was a big guy and usually quiet. Others in the room thought of him as a little on the spectrum. He listened and took it all in. He heard worry and fear. He gauged the three bomb-truck drivers sitting together, the gate-crew ride alongs also on the same side of the room.

Their leader picked up the same vibe the bomb maker had and made a passionate speech about where they had come from and what they would make "from the ashes of the old order." But that was a much too familiar speech for the step they were about to take, so the bomb maker stood.

He awkwardly faced them, and his voice broke several times as he spoke. Then he seemed to find himself. His words were heartfelt. He didn't talk about the ashes of the old order. He talked about why he'd taken on learning how to make bombs, what it took, and the close calls that scared him. Recounting those got him a few inadvertent laughs that eased the tension in the room. He talked about why he'd joined with them and the dream of what could be, and ended with a challenge that got the room stirring.

"Throw down," he said. "It's time. It's our time. Let's go."

1

That morning from the Las Vegas FBI Field Office, I called a friend who works in the Cyber Division out of FBI headquarters in Washington. I didn't know if Carol would talk to me, but I trusted her. If you turn on TV news, a panel of experts will tell you an enemy nation-state working with hackers is behind the cyberattacks on the US electrical grid, and the two-week lull that's followed the first attack was the enemy waiting to see if we can find them before launching a full onslaught. Could be true, but no one really knows yet and that's with the NSA, CIA, FBI, DHS, ATF, the Department of Energy, and everyone else capable fully engaged.

"Grale, are you there?" Carol asked, her voice quiet yet clear.

"I'm here," I said.

"I'm on another call. Are you okay waiting on hold a few minutes?"

"Sure."

"What's up?"

"I want your opinion."

Hackers took control of Seattle City Light's systems control center two weeks ago on April 4 at 3:05 p.m., and Seattle lost power for twenty-three hours. Seattle was ground zero, day one. On day two, cyberattacks expanded to San Francisco, Atlanta, New York, and

Houston. Domestic-terror sleeper cells activated with attacks on cell towers. More sleeper cells have since activated. That's where I fit in.

Five minutes later, Carol was back, asking, "Are you still on the Vegas domestic terrorism squad?"

"I am but transferring to the LA office domestic terrorism squad on a TDY in a couple of days. I leave Vegas tomorrow."

A TDY is ninety days of temporary duty. She didn't need or want to hear the reasons for the transfer, more likely she was assessing my creds should she get called out for talking to me. I'd worked with her on an interagency grid-security task force the past seventeen months. It's how I knew her, and she knew enough about me to take the chance.

"The secrecy is ridiculous at this point, but technically I can't say anything," she answered. "So what I say stays with you. What are you working?"

"Sleeper cells, bombings, and the more sophisticated physical attacks. I'm teamed with two domestic terrorism agents out of California."

"They never hear my name."

"Okay."

"Here's what you need to know. It is a foreign power and probably Russia. It's worse than we thought. Much worse. That's why no one is talking. Bugs and viruses got in through the Internet of Things, devices communicating with other devices at plants around the world. Most of the US electrical grid is infected. Think Stuxnet, how we disrupted Iran's Natanz nuclear facility and took control of the centrifuges. Same game. Nothing can be done quickly enough. It could get real ugly where the utilities haven't invested in cyberdefenses."

"Some haven't had the money for it."

"Their reasons why really don't matter anymore," she said. "The age of talk is over. It's good to hear your voice, Grale. I miss you. I'm glad you're out there. You're my rock. Go find them."

In LA I'll work with Mark Hofter out of the FBI office there. With us, but working from the San Francisco FBI Field Office, is a third agent, Kristen Blujace. Jace is bright, young, and skilled. We've worked other investigations together. I'm glad she's in the mix. Hofter and I will report daily to the Joint Terrorism Task Force on Wilshire in Los Angeles, Jace to the JTTF office in San Francisco.

I'd rather work from Vegas, but there's no way to avoid California. It's the big target, the one state in the US among the top ten economies of the world. It's geographically large so also difficult to protect.

Phone and Internet chatter we've picked up suggests someone in the LA area is trying to teach themselves how to make ANFO bombs—AN, ammonium nitrate, and FO, fuel oil. With just four small test bombs at remote electrical and cell-tower facilities in Nevada they got a lot better. I investigated those in March. I'm a career investigator but also an SABT, a special agent bomb tech.

After talking with Carol, I spent the day in the office. I tightened up my caseload so I wasn't leaving a mess for agents here to deal with when I left for LA. That night I attended a cocktail fundraiser with my girlfriend, Jo. The fundraiser was very important to her work, but standing in the crowded room I got restless and walked outside to a terrace.

Paving stones still radiated the day's heat. Landscape lighting threw soft shadows. Across the valley, Las Vegas looked normal. The Strip blinked with colored lights. A plane descended into McCarran Airport with another not far behind as I turned at the familiar click of heels.

"City still there, Agent Grale?" Jo asked.

"Looks like it."

"But you're keeping an eye on it."

"Just getting a little air. Jo, do you remember as the towers came down on 9/11, the feeling that things would never be the same again?"

Jo didn't answer. She moved up alongside me and stood close. She didn't want to do angst tonight. She wanted to be together and hold tight for the few hours before I was gone. I put an arm around her. I felt the smooth curve of her upper hip beneath the cocktail dress and told myself, *Stand down. Be with Jo. You aren't going to solve anything out here tonight.*

"How did it go with the big donor?" I asked.

"Would you believe he wrote a check that'll carry our research into next winter?"

"That's great."

"It's huge, Paul! We can run the longer clinical trials we've put off."

The owner of the house, the brightly lit glass ship behind us where the cocktail party was, had lost a ten-year-old son to cancer. Jo was a practicing physician and a cancer researcher at UMC Hospital in Las Vegas. On the research end, fundraising was a constant. She did what she had to do to keep it all going. Dr. Jo Segovia was also my girlfriend, my best bud; we'd grown close after a rocky start a few years ago. We don't overthink things as much anymore.

It's rare either of us is at a cocktail party, but this one mattered. I held her a beat longer, just long enough that before we turned we saw the lights of Vegas flicker. There, gone, and then back on again. They flickered once more, and I counted thirty seconds of darkness before they returned.

Somewhere nearby, masked by landscaping, a diesel generator coughed and kicked to life to provide backup power for the house. The outage ended the fundraiser. A stream of guests left under a glow of pale brown light.

Jo and I stayed and stood near each other in the darkness. She squeezed my hand and we waited. She leaned into me and I held her tight. I looked at the clean black line of mountains across the valley, then back at Las Vegas as casino backup systems fired up and their lights returned.

Our FBI field office had backup power, so did McCarran Airport, the fire and police stations, hospitals, Nellis and Creech Air Force bases, and several casinos. Enough power for critical services, but nothing like the real deal.

"Let's go," I said.

"We need to go in and say good-bye first. I want to thank him again."

Jo crossed the room and said her good-byes as I read a text from Hofter.

Bomb threat just called in for three LA electrical substations. Two gates breached, bomb vehicles inside. Caller claimed trucks booby-trapped. Evacuating.

I called Hofter.

"Two vehicles are inside substations," he said.

"Inside?"

"Yeah, got through the gate and the other bomb vehicle is parked alongside a fence. With that one they tried to get in but failed. Still, if the bomb is of any size, it's going to do a number on that substation. The bomb vehicles are older Southern California Edison trucks that were sold at auction but repainted to look new."

"We know that already?"

"Yes."

"Text me a photo of the type of truck. Which substations?"

"Olin, Lake, and Anza."

"What about surveillance video of the bomb vehicle deliveries?"

"I've seen video taken by surveillance cameras at the Lake substation. The driver and passenger pulled up to the gate like they owned the place. They wore masks and hoodies. I didn't see any skin showing, hands included. The passenger's job seemed to be opening the gate. Start to finish just under five minutes. At the Olin substation, where they couldn't get in apparently, they abandoned trying at four minutes thirty seconds."

"So they probably rehearsed this," I said. "Where are we with ATF?"

Alcohol, Tobacco, Firearms and Explosives had a good bomb unit. They'd want in, although we had primary jurisdiction.

"They're taking the Olin substation, where the truck is up against the fence, and we'll work the two inside the city if this isn't some sort of hoax. For now, we wait. The 911 operator was told 11:59, so we're inside forty minutes and counting down. The areas have been cleared. Everyone has backed off."

"No one is trying to disarm the bombs?"

As far as Hofter knew, no one was. I've argued with our joint terrorism task force office here that we needed to lean harder on the utilities to replace ineffectual fencing, gates, locks, and camera-surveillance systems with higher quality product. I'd run the same by a telecom exec last week who'd shaken his head and said, "It always amazes me how little government employees know about what it takes to get things done."

"Right, but here you are again running to us to protect you because you've done so little to harden and reinforce your facilities."

"I know some people well up in the FBI," he'd shot back. "I may mention you to them. You seem to have forgotten you work for the American people."

Jo and I walked to my car. We were the last to leave and could see the red taillights lining up below at a four-way stoplight that wasn't working. Drivers gingerly made their way through the intersection, and given the line of cars, there was no reason to jump in ours yet. My mind raced as we stood in the cooling night listening to sirens.

Jo said, "I'll admit I'm scared. There are no bombs, but we're going to war, aren't we?"

"We are."

"Doesn't that scare you?"

"It should," I said.

But it didn't. It just made me determined and angry. Sirens in the distance blended and became a wailing, rising and falling. The sound conjured up the voices of the dead, or terrible weeping and mourning. I don't consider myself superstitious, but it felt like an omen.

2

JULIA

Nick swerved hard back into their lane, throwing Julia against the passenger door. Her head bounced off the window. The driver they almost hit was way down the road but still honking. It was that close.

When she touched her cheek it stung, which made her even angrier. Why was Nick so obsessed with a car behind them, and why did he keep coming at her about UG, her uncle Grale?

"You're driving like a jerk," she said.

"And you're drunk."

"Drunk, no, sorry, not drunk, or frightened by some guy who wants to pass us. I just don't want to die because you're so scared."

"I told you to wait. I said I'd do the meeting then come get you. Instead, you get hammered on vodka with those girls. You're like, what, two months from nineteen and you act fifteen or sixteen."

"Where did you really go at the party, Nick, and where was this meeting you supposedly had?"

Nick checked the rearview mirror again.

"I think we're done," he said. "Like, over with, as in we break up tonight."

"That's one of the two reasons I'm here," Julia said.

"One of two, huh?"

He smirked and looked over like that was funny.

"What's the other reason?" he asked.

"To make sure you know you're not going to get away with it. I know what you did to me. I started remembering on Wednesday. You put something in my beer when we got back to your apartment and I was in the bathroom. You and Joel drugged me, didn't you?"

"How many vodkas, Julia?"

He reached across and aggressively held his hand close to her face.

"How many fingers?" he asked.

When she didn't answer, he swerved hard again, and they passed the truck he'd been tailgating. He was maybe a few inches off the left corner of the truck's bumper when he went around it. You wouldn't know it looking at him, but he had these super-fast reactions.

When she'd first met him he'd showed her this box of medals, from shooting competitions he'd been in when he was eighteen or nineteen. He didn't let her look at them but tipped the box so she could see the stack. Later he said he didn't let her see them because they embarrassed him. That was a lie too, probably. Everything about him was a lie. Everything she had thought about Nick had changed this week.

Julia stared through the windshield at Las Vegas in the distance. She'd told her friend Samantha "Sam" Clark that she and Nick might be together forever. That was so off.

"Hey, Nick, I have a question."

She didn't turn her head, didn't want to look at him.

She continued. "Do you know how much prison time someone can get for date rape?"

"Don't know, but I've heard it's hard to prove." He looked over and asked, "Are you for real?"

He was smiling. That was the cruel streak in him. It showed in the way he smiled at certain things. She remembered waking up last Sunday morning lying on the rug near the TV next to Nick's friend Joel wearing only a T-shirt. She kind of knew what he'd say now, but it would be another Nick lie. Yesterday, she'd remembered Joel undressing her with Nick standing there making a video.

"Here's what went down," Nick said. "Deal with this because basically it's why we're breaking up tonight. Last Sunday morning early, I woke up and you weren't in bed. You were spooned up against Joel, bare-assed, wearing only a T-shirt, out on the rug by the couch. That's no bullshit. Ask him."

"How about if the police ask him?"

"When I saw you lying there with Joel Sunday, I didn't know how to deal with it, so I took a walk. It's been eating my gut out all week. We're over."

"Nice, Nick, and you sound so real. Have I ever told you you're the best at lying? You're better than anyone I've ever known."

"Last Saturday night I would say you were pretty close to pass-out drunk."

"Another lie."

"Ask Joel."

"I'll bet you really think you're going to get away with it, but I'm telling you right now you're not."

Nick was twenty-seven and had lived in different places in the world. He saw her life as unsophisticated. She'd always lived in Las Vegas, and for him she was just someone to have fun with. *That's all I ever was,* she thought. It hit her that her falling in love with Nick was a joke to his friends.

He checked the rearview mirror again, then said, "Let's just say we broke up because it was time. We had fun for six months and it's over."

"Whatever drug you gave me, Nick, you didn't use enough. You screwed up."

He shook his head and didn't say anything for ten minutes or so. *He knew,* she thought. He knew it would be almost impossible to prove, her word against theirs with no evidence. She'd waited too long already, but she hadn't remembered anything until late Wednesday night. Another thought: *He gave me to Joel because he was done with me.*

"I remembered both of you undressing me."

"Didn't happen," he said.

What had been so cool-looking about Nick wasn't anymore. He'd grown a raggedy scraggle of beard, and his little bun was falling to the side of the back of his head. He wore the same stinking blue sweater all the time. He liked to lecture people about what was really happening in politics and America. He talked like he somehow knew more than everyone.

"You were never who I thought you were," Julia said. "You're a paranoid freak who always thinks he's being chased. What you did to me is disgusting. When the cops come for you, are you going to try to pin it on Joel?"

"The cops that come for me better be kick-ass good shots."

"Oh, you're going to shoot cops now."

That made her think about his box of medals again.

"The guy I met last fall was totally made up," she said.

"Nope, not made up. That guy just thought you were more open and smarter than you are. You were invited into a community and you pretended not to understand. Mommy and daddy and brother got killed. It's been years but you can't deal with it. You're frozen in time, a permanent teenager."

Years? Yeah, true that. It was April, so July Fourth would be three years, but Nick had no clue. He'd told her he hated his family, so even though she lost hers, she was lucky because she knew what it was to care. He talked big about how strong he was, but how hard is it to be strong if you don't feel anything? *Not too hard,* she thought.

"If I were you I'd forget about your little made-up drug-in-your-drink story. Breaking up with you, I should have done it a long time ago. You've got a killer body but you're just . . . I don't know, not there or not enough there, and your little pacifist thing is lame and kind of embarrassing to be around when you explain it to people who get the world."

"That's so you, Nick. Tear down anyone who calls you on your bullshit. You'll trash me to everyone, because that's how you roll."

Up ahead, Las Vegas changed. It got duller and looked like a pale smudge of brown light.

"Power is out," Nick said. "Cool."

He said "cool" in a totally different voice, like he'd just switched to some different person. *He wasn't worried at all about what he did to me,* she thought, *and now had something more fun to talk about.*

Nick and his friends and the other people she hung with were fine with the power grid getting trashed. They all said the same thing: the old world is dying. Like some *Game of Thrones*-y type thing, like they weren't going to need electricity anymore. She understood the vibe when it was about smaller, local, off the grid, and with battery storage, and the person talking about it knew something about renewables. Nick really didn't. Nick talked political theories and threw complicated phrases around to make up for not having any ideas of his own.

If someone agreed with him, he would say, "Exactly, you totally get it," then put his joint down and high-five the guy. If it was a girl and she was cute, he'd flirt.

They bounced hard in a pothole, and she flashed on Nick walking toward her and how she was barely able to breathe and her face flushed in the first weeks last September after she'd met him.

He'd walked into the ice-cream store and said, "Sam Clark, who's someone I trust completely, said there's this unbelievable woman you've got to meet. Are you Julia Kern?"

Julia remembered being instantly attracted to him and thinking if Sam sent him he's got to be completely real. That felt very distant now. So much had happened in the last ten days. What was the date-rape drug? Ketamine? Some name like that. Who could she even talk to about this? Maybe Jo. Jo was a doctor.

The lights in Las Vegas came back on. The car Nick thought was chasing them had passed the truck, but everyone was passing the truck. The guy still behind them was probably just some dude coming home.

A wave of crazy sadness came over her and moved through her body. She'd been stupid and naïve.

"Let's talk," Nick said as they reached the outskirts of Vegas. "I want to take back what I said about you and pacifism. It's actually real cool even if it's disconnected with what's happening in the world. And breaking up sucks, right? But I think we both knew it was coming. You're better off without me. I'm too selfish and caught up in changing things. I didn't give you any date-rape drug or anything like that. I would never do that, so I'll just forget that you said that. I hate to say this, babe, but you've got an alcohol problem that messes with your memory. I know we're going to run into each other, so I want the split to be chill."

She was drinking too much, but nothing like he was saying, and definitely not last Saturday.

"We're done and you acted first," he said. "I can be cool with that. One of us had to do something, right? I'll get all your stuff together in my apartment and get it to you. The box in the back of your car you're going to have to drop off for me. You down with that?"

"You're so screwed up, Nick."

"You don't want to mess with me on this, Julia. There are a lot of ways you don't want to mess with me. You really don't." He kept talking but wouldn't look at her. "It never happened. You've got personal issues and need to see a—"

He never finished the sentence. The inside of their car lit up as someone pulled out right behind them. Nick sped up and turned onto a street with houses. The car behind was going just as fast. They went around the next turn hard and knocked a mirror off a parked car with a loud bang as they skidded.

Nick blew through a four-way stop heading toward an intersection where the light was already yellow. He sped up even though it would turn red. She screamed when a man ran into the crosswalk. It was way too late to stop.

3

My cell rang. I told Jo, "It's Julia." I put her on speakerphone and heard background noise that sounded like police radio.

"UG, we were in a car accident," Julia said, and I heard agitation, fear, and worry. "We hit a guy. Not straight on but we broke his legs. An ambulance just got here. Two undercover cops were chasing him. Nick was driving because I had a couple of drinks at a party we were at. Nick ran away before the police arrived. I don't know where he went."

"Are you hurt?"

"Bruises."

"Where are you, Julia?"

"North Fort Apache and I don't know the cross street." Her voice broke. "Hold on."

I heard her talking to a cop and overheard him give her the cross street.

"We're ten minutes from you," I said. "See you very soon."

From a quarter mile away we saw police flashers. We parked and walked up, and two Las Vegas Metro officers intercepted us.

Jo touched my back and said, "I'll wait here for now but get me across. I want to make sure she's not hurt."

I showed my FBI creds, and the younger of the two officers looked at those as I looked at my sister's former car, a green four-door Subaru. Two tires were flat, and the driver's side was raked where they'd sideswiped cars. Her mom's car was a sanctuary for Julia, a tie to her life before, but at its age and with this amount of damage, the insurance company would likely total it.

"Do you know the boyfriend, Nick Suthers, Agent Grale?" the younger officer asked.

"I do."

I spotted Julia over near an unmarked police car. She'd lived with me since her parents—my sister, Melissa, and her husband, Jim—and her younger brother, Nate, were killed in a terrorist bombing here in Las Vegas almost three years ago. Julia's bomb shrapnel wounds were still healing when we packed up the clothes and things she wanted from her bedroom, then moved her to my house.

Much has been written about the stages of grief and moving forward, but I like Jo's view as a physician. It rings truest to me. Jo says there is no normal with grief. It's different for everyone. In Julia's last two years in high school, she withdrew and her grades fell. I got her counseling. I tried different things yet felt powerless.

"We found Nick Suthers' wallet on the street with four driver's licenses inside. Same photo but different names, and all kinds of credit cards in various names," the officer said. "Detective Allred has the wallet."

"You're saying multiple false IDs?"

"Yes, sir."

I looked for Allred and saw him as he spotted me. He lifted a long arm to acknowledge.

"Who's the young man they hit?" I asked.

"He pushes pills for a gang here. We know him."

The older veteran officer who'd been quiet interrupted and asked, "Are you bomb tech Grale?"

"Yes."

"And that's your niece who was the only survivor of the Alagara bombing?"

"Yes. Julia Kern."

"To most everyone in the department, everything you did then was right."

"Thank you."

"Better get her straightened out," he said.

In the months following the Alagara bombing, America kept track of the orphaned teenage survivor. This country has a big heart, and people wanted to know how she was. Media tracked her progress with headlines like "Alagara Survivor Returns to School," "Julia Kern Heals; Stars at Soccer."

That changed in her senior year, when she was asked to speak to a local Rotary group on the topic of her choice. In her speech, "Violence and Us," she argued that we like war and that if one doesn't come to us we find a way to make one. She touted pacifism and labeled several of our invasions imperialism.

The Rotarians are a thoughtful, kind-hearted body who can embrace a young person's questioning, but the speech got picked up by other media, and you can pretty well guess what happened in current America. "Lone Survivor Anti-American." Trolls arrived and set up camp. That's not to say she didn't hit back. This pacifist isn't passive. She went at them head on.

"Agent Grale, can I talk alone with you first?" Allred asked and then continued talking as we stepped away. "After the power came back on, the stoplight worked but cameras didn't," he said. "Witnesses say your daughter's car was traveling at high speed and may have run a red."

"What do the undercover officers say?"

"They're not sure. They say their focus was on Mr. Henry Cataula hotfooting it away after trying to sell them fentanyl, and I don't know if I'll be able to determine whether the light was red when Mr. Suthers, if that is his real name, drove through it, but we'll get a pretty good estimate on his speed." He let a beat go by, then asked, "What can you tell me about the boyfriend?"

I could tell him I didn't particularly like Nick Suthers and that was a source of tension between Julia and me. I found Nick disingenuous and condescending. But Julia had fallen so hard for him that I continued to make an effort to like him.

There were no boyfriends before Nick that I knew of. In her senior year Julia had visited churches and graveyards and intensified her study of pacifism. She met a Catholic priest in his late eighties and struck up a friendship with him. They talked philosophy. Whether the embracing of pacifism was the twisting force of grief, teenage idealism, or true inner belief that had surfaced I couldn't tell you. I do know Julia still visits chat rooms where war and peace are topics.

Coming on nineteen, she's grown into a willowy, strong young woman with a presence. She no longer bows her head. She's straight at you. She's confident about her beliefs. Mine are wrong. Hers are right. When we disagree about politics, she takes it very seriously. It's another thing that has strained our relationship, but that'll change. I see aspects of my sister's personality in Julia: a strong will, a need to live to her own code, a way of being, and a certainty and righteousness when angry. In some way, that's prepared me. I have this feeling sometimes that Melissa is watching and laughing as Julia lectures me.

"How is it that your niece is the girlfriend of a guy with four driver's licenses with the same photo of himself and different names and credit cards to go with them?" Allred asked. "I guess I'm asking how can it be your niece is living with you but dating a dirtbag?"

"He fooled me."

"He fooled you?"

He repeated it as if saying, "That's your answer?" Allred then nodded at a guy standing alone.

"The fellow there with the untucked shirt and belly, who's been drinking somewhere tonight so is questionably credible, says he saw another car that was either after them or with them. Could have been road rage. Type of car, any other detail, he doesn't have it. Julia claims she and Nick broke up tonight just before the accident. Were you aware they were having trouble?"

"No."

"Do you talk to her much? I'm asking because someone needs to explain to her that it's in her interest to help us. If her boyfriend is a credit-card scam artist and she's known it and doesn't tell us, it makes it look like she's part of it. But I don't have to tell you that."

He sighed as if he didn't want to be in this position.

"Here's what I have so far," he said and ticked through a list using his left hand to count starting with his little finger. "She went to a party with her boyfriend but doesn't know if he drank. Some unknown car for unknown reasons was chasing them. He's got false identities falling out of his wallet, and she doesn't know anything about them. He ran. She doesn't know where. They coincidentally just happened to break up tonight."

He'd run out of fingers, so he dropped his hand and said, "I've got more, but you get my drift."

Allred was tall enough to look down at me, and I'm six foot one. His long face was somber. He wore size eighteen shoes and was known for them. Other than that, I knew little about him. He got Jo across the tape then left us alongside his car with Julia, who bowed her head and wept silently. Allred, who was probably thinking about Julia's bruises, had left a rear door open. Julia got in and Jo slid in alongside her. She didn't care about the blood on Julia's jeans or what it would do to her dress. She pressed close and held her as I walked back to Allred.

"I'll get into the fake IDs tonight," Allred said, and then added, as if the two thoughts connected, "Julia claims she has never looked in her boyfriend's wallet."

"Do you look through your wife's wallet?"

"Only if I'm missing money, so yes, and often. Julia gets to go home tonight but wants to start helping me no later than tomorrow morning. She doesn't want to become an accomplice."

"You can't begin to make that jump, Detective."

"Try me," he said.

4

Julia, Jo, and I were still at the accident scene at 11:59. When my phone rang seven minutes later, I knew the bombs had detonated. The call wasn't from Hofter, though. It came from Ted Mara, my supervisor on the Vegas field office domestic terrorism squad.

Mara can move investigations like an air traffic controller, but when stressed, his voice tightens and speeds. That was there tonight.

"The LA bombs detonated simultaneously. Damage is substantial," Mara said. "There are fires that may spread, but LAPD is holding the fire department back until they're sure there are no shooters. So far no reports of anyone killed, but the bombings were less than ten minutes ago. LA is in a rolling blackout. They were unable to reroute in time. LAX is down. Fly into Burbank or Ontario or drive. They want you there tonight. Give me the name again of the agent you work with in LA."

"Mark Hofter."

"Do you go through him, or do we need to send the LA office an electronic communication?"

"I don't think you need to do anything. It's less than forty-eight hours before my TDY starts," I said.

"Report in here until we hit that mark."

Mara is strict on FBI procedure, so it wasn't worth arguing. During the TDY, the temporary duty, I'd report to Rodrigo Fuentes, who runs the domestic terrorism unit in the LA office, rather than to Mara here in Vegas. I'd have a desk in the bullpen of the LA office and a place to bed down on government per diem. How the rest of it was going to work was unclear.

When another call came in, I told Mara, "That's Hofter, I've got to take it. Talk to you tomorrow from LA."

"Two of the bombed substations, Anza and Olin, have fires," Hofter said. "The fire department is on one of them and about to get on the other. All three substations are gone. They're do-overs, and the basin is on rolling blackouts."

"The city is, or everywhere?" I asked.

"The whole basin."

"Okay, I'm on my way soon. I'll call from the road."

I looked at Julia's heaving shoulders and again at my sister's former car. In the first year after her family was killed, I'd sometimes find Julia sitting outside in the car crying. She'd told me that when she sat in the car, she could feel her mom and her little brother, Nate.

"I'm headed to the Anza substation," Hofter said. "Look for me there." And then almost in a stream of consciousness, he added, "My wife is freaking out. She heard one of the explosions, and there's no rolling blackout in our neighborhood. The power is out, and the kids are scared." He laughed an odd way. "We're still in America, right? Call me when you cross into California, Grale."

JULIA

Julia heard Uncle Grale talking quietly to Allred. In her head she saw Nick scurry away ratlike, then pull out his phone. He must have called somebody for a ride. She didn't know anything about different IDs and credit cards in different names the detective had asked her about. She was still getting her head around Nick as a credit-card scammer. She had no idea, and the detective didn't believe her. She'd had more drinks than she'd said, but that was going to change tonight. She was going to be different about a lot of things.

Detective Allred had said, "Your boyfriend was drunk, wasn't he?"

"He doesn't drink much, so I doubt it. He smokes a lot of weed."

"So he was high?"

"I didn't smell anything tonight," she said.

"You're saying he could have been high."

"I'm saying I don't know because I didn't see him much at the party."

"Do you know where he is?" Allred asked.

"I still don't, and we did break up. I don't know if he'll call me."

"You don't seem upset that he left you here to deal with this."

"I hope I never see him again."

She said that last bit in such a hard way the detective took a step back. He left her and started talking with UG as she thought about her friend Sam, Samantha Clark, who had told Nick last September, "Go to Spring Mountain Organic Ice Cream and meet Julia Kern. You two are made for each other."

That was nine months ago, and it turned out Nick was phony, yet Sam had vouched for him. Sam didn't really know Nick. Just thought she did.

Allred jabbed a finger at UG, who shook his head. Julia watched that and remembered Nick making fun of UG. UG was here. Nick ran. That kept going through her head. *Nick ran.* She looked across the intersection at the two police officers who'd found Nick's wallet and showed her the different driver's licenses almost as though they thought it was funny, asking her what her favorite name for Nick was.

UG started toward Jo and her. When he arrived he said, "Let's go through your car and clean it out before we leave."

"Really, right now?"

23

"Yes, right now, and let's talk because I'm headed to LA. The car is going to go to a yard and sit. Everything valuable should come out."

"Why?"

"Things get stolen. I've got a bag in my trunk you can put the smaller things in. I'll get it. What's the box in the back?"

"Nick's stuff. It was in the garage of the house where we went to the party," Julia said. "He had some stuff stored there that the people who own the house wanted to get out of their garage. It was one of the reasons to go to the party, but I don't know what's in the box. Just some crap of his, I guess."

"Have a look in it before we do anything. Maybe it can stay in the car."

Julia's right knee hurt. Her shoulder was sore and her face stung where she'd hit the window. The driver's door was open and the window broken on the passenger side. She was careful about glass fragments as she felt down along the floor and under the seats. UG reached and handed her the bag through the broken window. He was on the phone when she emptied everything out of the glove compartment. She finished with under the seats as UG raised the rear door and slid the cardboard box toward him.

"I'll take a look in Nick's box," he said.

"Go for it." A moment later she said, "We were arguing when we drove back. We're over with. We were over with before they found his wallet and the false IDs."

UG didn't say anything to that. He opened the box.

"Nick said we were being followed. I didn't believe him, but when we got to Las Vegas this other car jumped out and was chasing us."

"Are you sure the driver was chasing you?"

"He was right on us."

"That doesn't sound like an undercover cop or any law enforcement I can think of. Are you sure it wasn't just another driver who got angry over something?"

"No, it wasn't like that. I told Detective Allred, but I don't think he believed me. He thinks Nick was high or drunk or both and speeding."

"Was he high?"

"I don't think so."

"I'm glad you're okay and that the guy that got hit will make it."

He said that, then peeled the tape off the box. It made a ripping sound, and UG reached in and pulled out a carton of something. He put on glasses and read the label on the carton. He pulled one, then another, then another. It didn't make any sense. What was up with the cartons? UG looked inside three or four, then put the one he was holding down and straightened.

He glanced at Detective Allred like he wasn't sure, then took photos she could see he was zooming in for, so something in the writing on the boxes. He texted the photos to someone, then typed something longer and turned toward the detective again, who was talking with Jo. UG raised his right arm. Her heart skipped a beat as he waved for Allred to come over.

I knew Allred would want to leverage anything found in the car, so I had some hesitation, but there really was no other way. But I was also close to telling him that if he kept pushing Julia to admit colluding with Nick, I'd make sure she lawyered up tonight.

As he walked up, Allred said, "I'll be straight with you, Grale. I don't buy the breakup story. Most likely—"

"Let me show you what's in this box. It's full of bullets. Three types. The bottom two layers of cartons are armor-piercing bullets. Sniper ammo. Military grade. Those will punch through a half inch of steel from a mile away. There's no legitimate way for Suthers to have them in his possession. I've texted serial numbers to our office and asked for a run on these. The others are standard, 5.56 × 45 and 7.62 × 51 millimeter. Do you remember a hijacking of an ammunition shipment two months ago outside Grand Junction, Colorado?"

"I was aware of it," Allred said.

"It was a shipment of ammunition, bullets, and an interstate hijacking, so we got involved. That and they were military grade, and some of those bullets started showing up here on the black market. I've texted one of the agents working that hijacking. She's on her way here. If the bullets check out, our agents will take them as evidence and you'll get a lot more help locating Julia's ex-boyfriend. They'll go out with a fugitive warrant as early as tonight."

"I'd like that. But with what name?"

"We'll list them all and go out with his face."

He nodded but was silent, which in truth was a relief.

"Some of that hijacked ammunition was offered to a Las Vegas gun dealer who then called us," I said. "We worked with him to set up a buy, but whoever was selling got spooked, so it never went down. I haven't heard of any arrests, so if these bullets trace back to the hijacked truck it's a big deal. But it'll be our investigation, not yours."

"Your niece is involved, so you're out."

"No argument there, I'm not part of it."

My phone buzzed. I read the text message and showed him.

"That's Sue Egbert, one of the agents working this. She'll be here in fifteen minutes, and I have to leave soon. There were three bombings in Los Angeles tonight at electrical substations. I'm headed there and will be working out of the LA office for several months. I'll be in and out of here as well, and I don't want to leave tonight until I know Julia is going from here to home. Something else you need to know is that Julia may have a job offer in LA. She's already had one phone interview."

"Don't try 'she's got a job' bullshit with me, Grale."

"I'm not bullshitting you, and the problem you're going to run into is that Julia was a passenger not the driver."

"If these bullets are what you think they might be, then they were being transported in her car. How could she not see the box? She's protecting her boyfriend. Most would."

"She told you she broke up with him."

"A half an hour before the accident they broke up? I'm supposed to believe that?"

"Do you know the defense lawyer Erica Roberts?"

"Really, Grale?"

He shook his head and looked past me into the night.

"I never liked Suthers," I said, "and I tried. I really did. She was so head over heels in love I tried hard. I'm telling you Julia's world got flipped over tonight. If she said she broke up with him, she did. She will help you, and Roberts is no showboat. She's real. And our agents will work with you. You'll like Egbert."

"Aw, fuck me," he said.

I shook his hand to make peace for now. Half an hour later, the serial numbers on the bullets were matched to the stolen shipment, and I was running hard toward LA.

5

Los Angeles, April 19th

In east LA, down the street from the Anza substation, I pulled on a HAZMAT suit and was back in my role as a bomb tech. I'm good at it, although the LA FBI bomb squad was close to finished here. I took in downed electrical lines, transformers shattered and leaking oil, rows of broken windows blocks away, fragments of glass in the street reflecting morning sunlight. A few transformers might get salvaged, but Anza substation was otherwise a toxic mix of oils, downed wires, and torqued metals.

The prelim was ANFO. A dog had scented Tovex, a common igniting primer. Ammonium nitrate, an oxidizer used as fertilizer, was the major ingredient in these bombs. The fuel-oil component may have been something more stepped-up than diesel. From the look and a faint acrid odor, my guess was that it was.

DHS, the Department of Homeland Security, was here as well and not happy with their role. Like ATF—Alcohol, Tobacco, Firearms and Explosives—they had a good bomb investigative unit. The problem was we all had different techniques and labs. Mixing it up on the same bomb site led to problems, but something would get worked out with Homeland.

Employing decommissioned Southern California Edison trucks sold at auction then repainted and cleaned up was a clever idea, although maybe too clever. Even assuming false buyer names or shell companies, money changed hands. So, as Hofter suggested, there'll be a trail. We could trace bomb ingredients and pull DNA even after the blast, something bombers often didn't realize. We had surveillance video from the substations.

Somewhere in the neighborhood, a video camera on a business or apartment may have captured the getaway car. An Edison truck lumbering through a neighborhood didn't go unnoticed. People would call. Tips would come in, and evidence would accumulate.

When Mark arrived, I was out of the HAZMAT suit, and we left soon after to interview a witness named Alicia Juarez, who'd seen the bomb truck delivered and "a skinny white dude doing a cameraman thing."

Her apartment was on the third floor of a four-story apartment complex two hundred yards from the substation. Ahead of the blast, an evacuation order went out. Juarez ignored it, and turned her lights off and stayed in her apartment. It was all over the news that the bombers claimed three bombs would detonate at 11:59, so she got well away from the windows before then.

Residents still weren't allowed to return home until the buildings were declared safe. Hofter found two structural engineers walking the perimeter of Juarez's apartment building and was told the building was safe and we could go up. We stepped through broken glass to where Juarez had stood with a glass of wine, looking out the windows. She saw the bomb truck arrive.

"This truck drives past with two people in it, stops at the gate, and one of them gets out on the passenger side. I can't see him very well. I'm not even sure it was a man. He messed around with the gate for maybe five minutes, then they left the truck where it was. It didn't make any sense to me because the utility people must have seen them on their video cameras. But then, no one really works there. They run it all from somewhere else."

Hofter tapped at his phone and then held up an image of an Edison truck for her to verify."

"Same as that one," she said.

On a side street but within her view, a car had slowed to a stop. The pair left the truck, crossed the street, and hurried to the car. Alicia watched them get in and go. We went through every detail with her several times, and I liked her all the more for her patience and effort to get her facts right.

"The car left with the two who'd been in the truck, then I saw a man with what looked like a big video camera filming. He made me think he was making some documentary-type thing."

"Tell us everything you remember about him," I said.

"Tall, skinny-armed, long, the kind that's narrow from the side, all spidery with a little bit of pointy beard. A white guy." She turned to me. "He was closer to here than they were with the truck. He came this way before he went up the sidewalk there. I saw him go under the streetlight."

We'd get a sketch artist to sit with her. From this distance she didn't see much of his face, but the body type was less common so worth a try, I thought. Looking at the destroyed substation I couldn't help but think about a briefing on the US cyberattacks yesterday.

The attacks on the US power stations bore a striking resemblance to 2016 attacks in Western Ukraine. There, attackers overwrote firmware and were able to shut down substations one after another with the click of a computer mouse. Ukraine uses the same serial-to-Ethernet converters as US power stations and were susceptible same as ours to the malicious software, BlackEnergy3, that we've found here. BlackEnergy3 opens a backdoor that after a series of steps allows the overwriting of firmware, at which point they can do whatever they want.

No bombers and bomb trucks, an attacker thousands of miles away in front of a computer, perhaps with a cup of coffee, turning the lights off in a foreign city. I felt for a moment as if I was looking out Juarez's shattered windows at the past.

When we left Alicia, I picked up a message from Julia recounting her interview this morning with Allred. I called her back.

"Julia?"

"Yes?"

"Did you call the lawyer, Erica Roberts?"

"Friends say I don't need a lawyer."

"They're wrong. You need one, and Roberts is very good. I'll help pay for it."

"I've got to go, but I'll call you later. I'll think about the lawyer."

I'd left a message for Roberts with Julia's cell phone number as I'd driven to LA. It frustrated me that she resisted or didn't grasp that Allred would have to go through the lawyer. Roberts was more graceful than combative and, more to the point, she knew the rules of evidence cold.

Julia texted me later, Thank you, but you're not paying for any of this. Also looking for another car. The insurance guy went by this morning. He's going to call this afternoon, but it's probably like you said, a total.

I texted back, Call Roberts. She's honest. You'll like her. We'll figure out the rest.

The Los Angeles FBI Field Office, much like the rest of the LA Basin, was coming to grips with how important electrical substations were. I was coming off seventeen months of the grid-security task force, where I'd learned just how vulnerable the grid was, but what really woke me up happened in April of 2013 at Pacific Gas & Electric's Metcalf transmission station along the outskirts of Palo Alto, California.

Metcalf supplies power to the Silicon Valley. Who attacked it is still unknown. It's an open case at the FBI. What is known is the attackers knew their way around. They cut the telephone lines and followed with nineteen minutes of shooting that took out seventeen large transformers. PG&E averted a blackout by rerouting power, then spent nearly a month, twenty-seven days, getting Metcalf back on line.

Nineteen minutes followed by twenty-seven days. Fifteen million in damage and no suspects arrested. And that's just one transmission substation. At Metcalf they'd used military-style weapons. They shot well. They left no fingerprints. No shell casings were recovered. No arrests made. No one was ever charged in the single most significant attack on the US electrical grid.

Or rather, used to be the most significant. The substation bombings in LA changed that. Another thing Metcalf taught me was how vulnerable electrical and telecom facilities were to bullets. I think about that a lot.

The bullets used at Metcalf were lightweight compared to the sniper bullets in Nick's box in Julia's car. When I see bullets like that or a Stinger missile that's traveled halfway around the world to a closet in a house in Las Vegas, I have to remind myself that most people buying these things lack the skills to use them.

That said, the San Francisco FBI Field Office received a worrisome call yesterday about a shot-up cell tower in Northern California. Kristen Blujace fielded it and talked to a tower consultant who said he was looking at a shot-up cell tower where the shooter had used sniper ammo. Jace knew I'd investigated in March five cell-tower shootings in remote locations in Wyoming and Nevada where armor-piercing sniper bullets were used.

"Could be your shooter has migrated west," she said. "Want to take a look at the tower here with me tomorrow?"

"Yeah, I do."

"It'll be a long drive tomorrow to Butte County and back."

"I'll fly up tonight, though it's not going to go over well with Fuentes, the DT supervisor here."

It made no sense to Fuentes. "You just got here and three bombings just about blacked out LA. Why would you burn a day in Northern Cal looking at a dead cell tower?"

"The grid has stabilized," I answered. "The bomb site evidence is in and we're waiting for results. Those results will affect where we go with it. I'm back soon, and this may be a sniper I've looked for since March. Mara told me he talked this through with you before I transferred."

"That was about two or three of your ongoing investigations."

"This sniper is one of them."

"When you get back we'll revisit this."

From the airport I talked with Julia, who called to say she was meeting in half an hour with Erica Roberts. She also said, "My first real guy was a credit-card scam artist named Nicolas Knowles. That's pretty crappy."

"It is and it's over. When did you learn his real name?"

"An hour ago from a fraud investigator back east. They were already onto Nick being here. That's why he was always watching cars behind us. The fraud investigator said it was one of their people driving the car that chased us. He was tailgating us because he wanted us to pull over. There was another investigator behind him, and between them they were going to try to block the road, trap us, and then call the police."

I read a text from Jace after the call ended with Julia. Pick you up Marriott Emeryville at 5:00 a.m. tomorrow. Black coffee? I texted, yes. Then texted Mara,

Check out the telecom attack arrests nationwide so far. Six arrested for cell tower vandalism. Five were terror related. Suspects arrested were Americans. Their stated goals were "to free America," "to remake the economic dynamic," "to throw off the yoke," "to start the country over," "to force change that the powers who control us will never allow," and more with the same commonality.

Cyberattack speculation still centered on Russia, given the level of sophistication and the similar chutzpah as the election meddling in 2016. They thought things could be hidden through hackers and it would all be fine. That one they got away with. This one will come back to haunt them. The grid attacks have already cost billions, so who knows what will happen if the needle settles on Moscow.

There may be a demand for reparations, but they'll never confess so we'll never collect. But it won't be forgiven. There will be retribution. I don't remember who, but someone once said the United States is slow to anger but vicious when aroused.

6

JULIA

That night Julia sat in the cool dark of UG's kitchen holding herself, arms wrapped around her chest, as if by holding tight enough she could make everything that had happened go away. She needed to eat but wasn't hungry. The meeting with Erica Roberts, the lawyer, went fine, but like UG warned, the bullets worried Roberts.

This morning Detective Allred had asked almost out of curiosity, not challenging her, "How could you not know something was off about Nick?"

And Allred didn't even know what Nick had done to her. Crazy suicidal thoughts crept in. She pushed those away and walked through the house. She ate crackers with peanut butter. She needed to get another car. She needed to prove she had a job, not just an offer, so a judge wouldn't order her to come back to Las Vegas. That's what Roberts had told her.

"You can say you were planning to move because you were. But then you need a reason. It can be school if you're accepted somewhere. It can be a job. Judges like to hear it's a job. They like jobs."

Julia had told her she'd been accepted to the University of Arizona but had deferred to figure some things out.

"Like what?" Roberts had asked.

"Like whether it's worth the cost. Millennials are the most indebted generation in the history of America."

It was a little bitchy. She wished she'd said it differently, and she liked Roberts, who didn't seem to mind at all. Her phone buzzed as a text came in.

What's up, Julia? it read. Need to see you tonight. Home?

Tonight? she thought. What was up with "need to see me" and were any of these friends really her friends? She turned on the kitchen lights and texted back, Who is this?

Shanna. You home?

Why?

Gotta talk. Pick you up outside like last time. Same place half an hour from now.

So it's about Nick, Julia thought, and texted back, Nope.
You have no choice, came back a few seconds later.
Julia texted, Why don't I?

Explain when I see you.

Julia laid her phone down. It's about Nick, but no way with the police looking for him will he be there. She went back and forth, but before the hour was up left the house and walked in darkness to the dry little park. Shanna's car was already there.

"What's up? Come on, get in, let's talk," Shanna said.

"What's to talk about? You're going to tell me what Nick wants and why I should do it because it's good for everybody?"

"Come on, girl, let's take a drive and talk, but first I've gotta say this. Val, me, everyone, we really like you; we don't want to lose you. Nick is a weird guy, but he does some good works sometimes. You split with him, but we're still your friends."

"He told you we broke up?"

"He said he broke it off and you're trying to deal with it."

"That's such bullshit."

"Duh, but you've got to deal, right. He needs his wallet back and wants you to deliver some box you know about. You've got his wallet, right?"

"Nope. The police have it, but all he has to do is go to the Metro main police station and ask for it. They'll help him."

"Ha ha. Come on, let's drive."

Julia got in, and Shanna pulled away, then got her serious voice going. "I'm supposed to tell you some stuff that might make you really angry," she said. "So that sucks, but that's what's happening."

"Don't tell me he got a credit card in my name."

"He has a video of you and Joel Shepherd that he could post."

"Tell him I'll go to the police if he does that. He drugged me, and tell him also it's not date rape, it's rape."

"Dude, he showed me."

"I don't want to hear about it. He slipped something into my beer. They drugged me."

"Why would he do that to you?"

"Why would he have four driver's licenses, Shanna? Because he's bullshit, that's why."

"He said you were drunk and you've always thought Joel was hot."

"If I drank all the alcohol in the world, Nick would still be a bad guy and I would still never sleep with Joel Shepherd. Nick is going to pay for what he did to me."

Shanna said, "Or maybe you just forget about it and let it go."

"What do you get for doing this tonight?"

"It's about all of us."

Shanna picked up a piece of paper lying next to her phone.

"That's where you deliver the box that's in your car. You'll get a text when to take it there."

"Why does he think I still have the box? The car is in a wrecking yard."

"He knows where it was taken. I know where it was taken. I went there and looked in it. The dude who towed it said everything got cleaned out of it and what's the big deal anyway? He just wants to get his stuff back. Why do you care? What are you going to do with it?"

"My ex-boyfriend is about to post a video of his roommate raping me after they drugged me and you're asking why do I care if he gets his stuff back? Don't say another thing to defend him, Shanna. Not a word."

Julia rattled the piece of paper.

"Seriously, he gave you this to give to me? These are instructions."

Julia lowered her window, held out the paper, and let it go.

"Tell him I dropped it out the window. Tell him I'll deliver after I have the video and proof all copies are destroyed. And he and Joel are going to sign something a lawyer writes, so if he posts anything I can sue him."

"Good luck with that."

"Or they can forget about the box," Julia said.

"You're making a big mistake, girl."

"Not as bad as falling for him. Take me back to the park, Shanna. You know what, forget that. Pull over and let me out."

"This is not a good place to get out, and we need to talk more. You need to think about this."

"Stop the car!"

"There's nowhere to walk from here."

40

"Let me out."

Shanna finally did and came back twice after Julia started walking. She walked miles along the empty desert road not really caring what happened to her. She was thirsty and tired when in the moonlight on the shoulder she saw her mom and dad and Nate. They shimmered in silvery light, and her father waved her forward. When he did, she straightened and stood taller. In her head she heard, *Do not forget who you are. Never forget.*

She walked through the spot where they had been. A police car sped by with its lights flashing and was tiny in the distance when it braked, turned around, and came back. The officer questioned her.

"I got in an argument," she said. "I didn't want to be in the car anymore and didn't realize how far I was from home."

"I'll take you there, but you're lucky. There's a sexual predator we've hunted in this area for a year and a half. We just caught him. They've got him in cuffs in the back of a car. They don't need me. I'll take you home."

She'd been around friends who were so hard on cops that his kindness was unexpected and moved her. She choked up as she thanked him when he dropped her at UG's house. Inside, she curled up on a couch. She'd always thought of herself as strong like her mother and aware and on top of things, yet she'd been hanging with people who tore her down. Nick had belittled her whether teasing or angry, and listen to Shanna tonight, laying down what she had to do, telling her what to forget. Threatening her.

Julia turned these things in her head and returned to her dad's impatient wave urging her forward. She knew his gesture. She knew what he was saying. *These people don't own you. You're Julia Kern. Do you hear me? Stand tall.*

7

Jace was parked in front of the Emeryville Marriott hotel at 5:00 a.m.
I got in the car and asked, "Waiting long?"

"Not too long."

"When you start dating again, make sure the first question you ask
is whether he likes to get up early."

"Best time of day. Here's your coffee. Let's go."

We pulled onto I-80 east. I looked across the dark bay to the lights
of San Francisco, then we were on our way. We work well together—
older agent, younger agent. I don't tell her how to think or investigate,
but we do bounce ideas hard off each other. She's the rare skeptic who's
not negative, something I admire.

Two and a half years ago, Jace's fiancé was in a motorcycle accident
that left him without higher brain function. When the question of
whether it was best to let him go came up, Jace had said yes, that's what
he'd want.

Gene's mother said no and brought him home to Sausalito and a
two-room caretaker's cottage beneath a stand of eucalyptus at the rear
of her property. A nurse was available 24/7 for his needs.

During one of Jace's weekly visits, Gene's mother made a request
Jace still struggled with. She'd explained that a seer had felt the presence of a negative energy that came and went from Gene's cottage. The
seer had then determined it was Jace who was preventing Gene's full

recovery. Gene's mother told this to Jace, who was thirty-one at the time, and asked that this visit be her last.

The Jace I know works long hours and has no life at home. But I've seen changes in the three years I've known her. She's coming to acceptance in her own way. If she ever wants to talk about the motorcycle accident and losing Gene, maybe I can help. I know some things about loss.

"Read consultant Gary Farue's report," she said.

"I'm reading right now."

"He's in tight with the tower companies, and now he wants to be close with us. They let Farue crawl all over the cell-tower site yesterday morning before notifying us of the attack. He dug out slugs. He contaminated everything then called me all chatty brothers-in-arms wanting to help us figure out who did it. He said he knew the second he got there it was a serious shooter. Have a look at his website, look at his background."

On the website was a photo of him in combat gear sitting near the open door of a helicopter. It was on the opening page, so maybe that was how he saw himself. Beyond the helicopter were high snowy mountains, as if Farue was part of SEAL Team 6 on his way to Tora Bora. Another page said he'd seen combat in Afghanistan.

"Farue is looking out for number one, but it does sound like he knows his stuff," Jace said. "He calculated the arc of the bullets and concluded shots were fired from Buckhorn Ridge across the valley."

She glanced at me and continued.

"We're not here because Farue called us. We're here because someone made an anonymous call to the Butte County Sheriff's Office. That caller heard dozens of shots and saw a lone adult male in a green Jeep descending a dirt track from Buckhorn Ridge after the shooting stopped. Farue called me late in the afternoon just before I called you."

I read more of Farue's report. He'd concluded the bullets recovered were military-grade, steel-jacketed, high-velocity rounds. Twenty-three of the sixty-one shots he'd counted had a second bullet within an inch of the first. If the shots came from across the valley as Farue believed, that degree of skill was in high-level sniper territory. Every significant working piece of equipment on that tower was dead. Farue used the phrase "a complete kill."

I turned to Jace. "If this shooter was US military and that good, we'll get names. I know an Army lieutenant colonel I can ask. I've talked snipers with him before. He used to teach in sniper school. He's still connected."

"Why, with Russia looking like the source of the cyberattacks, would we assume it's an American sniper?"

"I'm not saying it is. But if the shooter is American and that good, he'll be known, especially with the two bullets close together style. Someone will recognize that, so it's worth checking." But I wasn't done. I'd been dwelling on this and added, "Granted there haven't been many, but every arrest so far tied to an attack on a telecom facility has been an American."

I scrolled for his phone number, then sent a text to Roy Anders. He would frown when he saw the text and debate for nearly a day whether to respond. It was outside standard protocol, but he would respond to the simple question: Gary Farue. Any record of him as a sniper?

8

Butte County, California, April 20th

When we crested the road up to Tower 36 we saw Farue on his phone standing near the chain-link fence surrounding the facility. A clean, waxed, black Suburban not unlike an FBI vehicle, a Bu-car, sat under firs growing downslope though tall enough to shade a corner of the clearing.

"Every time we get close to one of these big towers I think cancer," Jace said. "Cancer. Cancer. Cancer."

"On the ground, the radio frequency signals are well below federal safety standards."

"If you believe them," she said.

"I believe them." I pointed at the metal-rung ladder attached to a tower pole. "Climb that ladder and they get stronger and start heating up cells in your body.

"RF signals fall between FM radio and microwave spectrums, so it's a little bit like a microwave. That's why cell phone manufacturers say hold a cell phone a half inch away from your ear."

"Yeah, well, who does that?"

Farue wore stained leather boots, jeans, and a long-sleeved shirt with cuffs rolled halfway to his elbow. He looked like he was closing out his thirties, barrel-chested and fit, six foot two or close to that, bowlegged and blue-eyed. I looked at his hands, dirt on his fingers and under the nails, blood on his thumb as if he'd rubbed it over a bullet hole in metal and cut it on a jagged edge. That was the kind of cut I might get.

I shook his hand, saying, "Thanks again for sharing your report with us."

"Wouldn't do it any other way, sir."

"It's Paul Grale, not sir, or Agent Grale if you're more comfortable with that." I handed him a card. "Why did you wait a day to tell us the tower was shot up by a sniper?"

"I talked to Agent Blujace yesterday."

"After you'd already been here all day."

He looked exasperated, then glanced at Jace as if this was her failing.

"My client wanted me to take a look first to confirm what had caused the damage," he said.

"How long did it take you to figure out it was a sniper from across the valley?"

"Could have been as much as five minutes."

So Farue was a bit of a smartass as well.

"You knew right away," I said.

"I trained at the Army sniper school. The shooting here reminds me of why I couldn't hang with the truly good ones." He pointed at the ridge across the valley. "He shot from over there."

"Do you think he was military trained?"

"Where else would you learn that?"

We walked the bullet-pocked cell-tower facility listening to Farue as we videotaped and took notes, then I put on gear, clipped in, and climbed a steel ladder behind him. Higher up, we got a clearer view of Buckhorn Ridge to the east. Its slopes were treed, but there was also a long face of open rock.

Between Buckhorn Ridge and us was a valley green with the spring. A creek curled through a meadow, and a red-brown ribbon of dirt road cut across it. Snowfall in California was heavy this past winter, and the Sierras looked like a white cresting wave in the sunlight.

The anonymous caller—who we were also looking to identify—had reported a Jeep coming down off Buckhorn Ridge after the shooting. That didn't prove anything but might corroborate Farue's conclusion that the ridge was the shooting platform. Farue's coming out alone yesterday to examine the damage followed a pattern we'd seen with several tower companies. Many insurance policies excluded terrorism coverage, so the tower owners sent their consultants first with the unspoken goal of finding damage to be vandalism.

That wouldn't work here. With his "five minutes" comment, Farue had acknowledged that, and up here it was hard to miss the repeaters and transceivers with the two-shot pattern, one bullet hole with another bullet hole very nearby, as close as an inch or less.

When we finished at the tower, we drove down to meet the Butte County sheriff, John Callan, and a deputy of his in the valley below. Farue followed and wanted to come with us up Buckhorn Ridge, but the sheriff said no.

"What's your problem with him?" I asked as we drove away.

"He shows up uninvited at crime scenes. I don't like him."

We bounced through the meadow ruts and then rattled over a narrow wooden bridge before switchbacking up on a dirt road through trees. Branches dragged along the Toyota 4Runner's sides. Above the trees the slope turned to loose rock, and the narrow track made a steep climb over a hump onto the ridge. Farue was right. The ridge was a well-positioned shooting platform.

Ninety percent of ex-military, law enforcement officers, hunters, and criminals are mediocre shooters. Some hunters can hit a rabbit running through grass at a hundred yards. TV and movie actors can hit anything. And then there are the truly gifted who have also been trained. That training is, as Farue had said, most often military.

Callan got on his radio, and Jace and I walked the rocky dirt track that ran out the spine of the ridge. We scoured the area for any signs of where the sniper might have shot from along the brushy rock face looking west at the gray cell tower.

Jace pushed on ahead, and I studied the brush. I wasn't pretending to be a buckskin scout down on one knee reading the signs, but the three small broken branches—twigs, really—could mean our shooter pushed through the brush here to get into the open.

When I caught up with Jace she said, "If we'd found a pile of shell casings, that would be one thing. We're wasting time here."

"Let's walk it once more. I found a broken manzanita branch and a few twigs recently snapped."

"Awesome. Snapped twigs. We've got him cornered now."

"He's carrying a gun, ammo, a tripod or some stand, and he's going to leave a mark wading through brush."

My opinion: FBI agents depend too much on computers. They were a mainstay when I joined the FBI and have become more and more important. I love mine. Whole investigations take place in front of a computer screen. But when you add something, you usually take something else away. What I see diminishing are the powers of observation in investigating agents.

Somewhere here in the early morning quiet the sniper had waited for the sun to rise. He'd want clear light, no sun on his scope. Sunrise was close to 6:30 a.m. The tower equipment went offline at 7:46 a.m. That marked the general timing and said something about where he chose to set up.

I looked out at the tower, then back at the rocks and turned as Jace called, "Hey, come take a look at this. Those two spots right there."

I walked over and agreed they could be tripod legs.

"And the gun would be here," I said.

The more I looked, the more I believed. I looked downslope where a shell casing could have bounced down.

"I'm going to take a look," I said.

I had the sun overhead, so I might see the reflected glint of a shell casing between rocks. I tried to be patient and started low and worked my way up.

"I see one," I called up to Jace.

"Deer hunter," she yelled back.

Nope. Too big for that. I took photos, bagged it, and half an hour later we recrossed the wooden bridge into the meadow. When we had cell reception again, a string of texts and voice mails came in. I scanned texts and reread one several times, then showed it to Jace.

Farue was one of ours. Got unhappy. Blamed equipment.
Applied for something else.

"Okay, so Farue was good but not good enough," she said. "That's pretty much what he told us. What's the next step?"

"We get a short list of who is good enough, and we make no assumptions."

We pulled into a mini-market, and I gassed the car as Jace went in to buy a couple of coffees and something we could eat. Most likely peanuts—that's what she liked with coffee, that and a piece of chocolate. As I finished filling the tank, Farue pulled up.

"Small town," he said.

"Looks like it." I pushed the button to get a printed gas receipt and added, "Let's keep talking, and thanks for all the help today. I appreciate everything you did to get us pointed the right way. I wish you'd called the day before when you realized you were looking at a top sniper. But we'll let that go."

"I had to sort it out myself," Farue said.

"I can understand that. I like to do things my own way first. I'll call you in the next few days. What's up with you and the sheriff?"

"Aw, it's a long story. He's a territorial fucker. I'll tell you over a beer sometime. Watch your back, G-man. If I hear anything I'll call you."

"We'll be calling you."

He smiled at that, then waggled my card as if to say he knew how to reach me. I caught him looking in his rearview mirror as Jace came out of the store. She handed me a coffee. "I don't know about that guy," she said. "But we will hear from him soon and often."

She couldn't have been more right.

9

I flew back to LA midmorning the next day and got a call from Julia as I reached the FBI office.

"There's something I should tell you," Julia said. "It's about Nick and it's pretty random. You're probably getting millions of tip calls, but do you remember when Nick and I stayed with friends of his in LA for a couple of nights at the start of March?"

"Sure."

"We walked up Mount Lee while we were there, to the back of the Hollywood sign, but also up to the radio tower. There's a way to walk up from Griffith Park that's really pretty and not too hot. It was great, but then it got a little weird. At the radio tower he got super serious about taking photos, but he didn't want it to be 'all him on their surveillance cameras.'"

"His words?"

"Yes."

"So you took photos?"

"I did, but lots of people take photos there. Where it got weirder was when he wanted to walk down the other side even though our car was parked near Griffith Park. Walking down he said we were on a scouting mission looking for security vehicles. I guess they go up and down to the tower from that side, though we didn't see any. Nick also said the tower handles all radio traffic for LAPD. True?"

"Yes." I paused a moment. "So what do you think now?"

"I didn't know whether he was serious or not."

"Is that true?"

She didn't answer for several seconds, then said, "It's not true. I knew he was serious, I just didn't take him seriously."

"Have you been around other talk like this?"

She was quiet again before saying, "I always leave the room."

"But with the bombings you're wondering?"

"Sure, I'm wondering about a lot of things and I'm angry. I'm really friggin' angry, but the good news is Erica Roberts called today. She said since I wasn't the driver and the bullets are an FBI investigation to go ahead and move but make sure I let Detective Allred know what address I'm at and how to reach me."

"Good, I'm glad."

"Got to get going, UG. Talk soon. Bye."

I spent the next hour with the website the Bureau built to map the electrical grid and cell communication tower attacks in the US. It had been around less than a week but was already useful at tracking where, when, and method of attack. It gave us an overview and updated daily.

With the map we could see the cell-tower sniper with the one-two shot patterns had moved east to west. We had photos, videos, investigative notes, and interviews, but to see his movements on one screen made it easier to look at his patterns.

The most recent tower he'd attacked was a critical linking tower. Cell towers are like bubbles touching each other. Interrupt that in the right location where there's no real redundancy and you create a gap. Our sniper was working through open country, rural areas where the county might be as big as an eastern state but the population less than a quarter million. He was systematically creating cell-network gaps.

We'd speculated the unpopulated areas were practice ahead of attacking cellular infrastructure in cities where millions would lose communication, but maybe that was wrong thinking.

His attacks shadowed electrical transmission pathways. Did his pattern have something to do with those? Astronauts can see those pathways from space. They cut through forests and over mountains. The National Academy of Engineering once termed the US electrical grid "the world's largest integrated machine." That's still apt.

But there are really three grids. Some say four. In the west, dams generating hydroelectric power and long electrical transmission pathways to transfer it are the backbone of the grid. Could it be that decimating telecom communication near electrical transmission pathways was a way to soften them as targets?

I floated that idea late morning with Jace, Hofter, Fuentes, and Mara. Fuentes sat across from me in the conference room as we did the call. He was probably a decade younger than me, black haired, brown eyed, with an expressive face. They all deferred to him around here.

I watched Hofter nod as Fuentes said, "Millions of people in the LA area are dealing with rolling blackouts, so why, after wasting a day touring a dead cell tower, are you burning more time today on hypotheticals?"

I didn't have a quick answer for that, nor did his tone bother me. We needed to think differently. Many were calling for a full rollout of the National Guard and US Army troops to protect the grid. That would happen. It was already happening, and an emergency war-funding bill was working its way through Congress, but the grid is too big to protect. That's what I learned in my seventeen months on the grid task force. The grid can swallow an army. The only answer is to find the saboteurs.

Find the cells here, then confirm the enemy behind them, and even as they deny any involvement, hit them very, very hard. No calibrated response, no world court, no warning, no talk of sanctions that'll end up watered down—just take it to them. They wouldn't have tried if they didn't think they could get away with it, so in turn we owe them a response they'll never forget. Dark thoughts, but enough was enough.

10

Allred called early the next morning.

"Courtesy call, Grale."

"Where are you?" I asked.

"I have a search warrant for your house, and we're about to knock on the door. Is your niece home?"

"What's the warrant for?"

"Possible storage of stolen ammunition and information leading us to Nicolas Knowles."

"That's an FBI investigation. How did you write yourself into it?"

"I have absolutely no quarrel with you, Grale, and I don't like going into your home. At issue is whether your niece was manipulated by Knowles, helped him move contraband, and is storing stolen materials that could lead us to him. She might not even know she's doing it."

"You're going into my three-bedroom, one-story ranch house looking for boxes of bullets?"

"I've talked with the agents working it. They don't like the idea, but they acknowledge it's cleaner than them entering a fellow agent's house. Anything bullet related I find I turn over to them."

I could understand that, but I knew he didn't expect to find bullets. There was no basement or crawl space, just a concrete slab, no attic, and no room in the garage.

"Here's what I think. You're still trying to tie Julia to Nick Knowles' criminal career."

"No, I'm trying to find him," Allred said.

"Julia was working in an ice-cream shop when he walked in and introduced himself last September. They went out for eight months. His criminal career predates that by you tell me how many years. You know better than I do. But okay, you've wrangled a warrant and you're going in. Julia should be there."

"We'll leave the house the way we found it."

"This is not right, Detective, and you know it."

"Get her to talk to me and quit protecting Knowles."

Julia was working two summer jobs when Nick walked in. He'd lived around the world and told jokes in four languages. He was handsome and funny. He came back the next day and asked her out. It was storybook stuff unless you looked at him as a credit-card scam artist using yet another false name as he dodged fraud investigators and preyed on younger women.

I stewed on it, then flew home that night. Mara wanted a follow-up meeting on some of the cases I'd handed off before starting the TDY in LA. We could do it over the phone, but he wanted to meet in person early tomorrow.

When I got home, the house was locked up and quiet. Julia probably heard me moving around but was in her room. I sat outside on the back patio in the cool of the night under the stars and unwound next to the lap pool. I slowly drank a beer and thought of Carrie, my wife, dead, gone for more than a dozen years, and how different life was before. There are times when I wake and forget she's gone, as if part of me has never accepted it. I listen for her bare feet on the tile in the kitchen, thinking she'd gotten up to get a glass of water or walked outside into starlight.

Something in me died with her. It was the end of that and the start of something different. True loss changes you, but I know more and I'm more accepting, and life is even more precious.

My thoughts turned back to Julia. The east-coast insurance fraud investigator who'd identified Nick Suthers as Nicolas Knowles had connected Knowles to thousands of false credit-card applications and a hack into the Visa system, which Visa preferred to absorb rather than see publicized. That was the fraud investigator's opinion; it was nothing Visa had confirmed.

I got that yesterday from the agents working the Colorado ammunition-truck hijacking. The fraud investigator called Knowles "highly skilled, a top hacker with conceptual vision," whatever that is. "Knowles manipulated credit-card software and generated thousands of cash advances made to bogus cards that went undetected for six weeks." The fraud investigator gushed at his ability to avoid detection.

And then there was something much darker. Knowles was the only child of two career US State Department employees who'd spent their adult lives abroad. They sent him to college, then retired to Malawi. In Malawi someone nailed the doors of their house shut and torched it with them inside. Locals saw a young white man, but a twenty-two-year-old black man who'd done previous jail time for theft was arrested and later released. A police request made to US law enforcement to interview the son of the murdered couple had gone nowhere. That request was still made yearly.

At dawn the next morning I made coffee, then heard rustling in the front room and walked out to Julia sitting on the couch with a blanket wrapped around her and her legs drawn up. The blanket was over her head, hiding most of her face as if she wished to disappear.

"Hey," I said.

"Hi, UG."

"How are you?"

"I'm okay. I'm not really okay, but I'm figuring it out."

"I'm making coffee. Do you want any?" I asked.

"Sure, I'll come to the kitchen in a minute."

"Stay there. I'll bring you coffee and let's talk. Did you sleep?"

"Not really, I keep thinking about everything."

"Do you want milk?"

"I do, but I'll get up," she said.

She came into the kitchen, and we walked back with our coffees and sat across from each other, Julia on the couch again. The sun was still behind the mountains, but through the windows I saw the red-orange burn of dawn.

"Anything more changed since we last talked?" I asked.

"You mean with the bullets?"

"Yes."

"Detective Allred says he has a witness who saw me help carry the ammo box with Nick to my car. Supposedly that person also saw me tape the box shut in the garage of the house. They said I was wearing plastic gloves. Why would anyone lie like that?"

"If they're friends of Nick and he asked them to they might. It could just as easily be a mistake, and they saw a different woman wearing gloves helping carry the box. Didn't you say you were with the same people the whole time you were at the party?"

"Not the whole time. I went to look for Nick."

"Did you look in the garage?" I asked.

"I looked everywhere and couldn't find him."

"When you looked in the garage was anyone there?"

"No."

"Who might have seen you look in the garage?"

"I don't know. There were a lot of people at the party, the kitchen was crowded, I was angry Nick disappeared, and I had a couple of drinks in me. I worked my way through to a door off the kitchen into the garage. I didn't move any boxes at the party. I didn't even notice it when we drove away. It was dark. Why is this happening?"

"It's not all just happening to you, though you make it sound like it is."

"Great. Thanks, UG."

"No, really, you're putting yourself in situations where things can happen. Like being a couple of drinks into a party with a boyfriend who disappeared when you got there."

"How about we just say I've screwed up a whole lot in the last eight months and need to get it together," Julia said. "I haven't stolen anything. I haven't done anything illegal. I know you think I hang with the wrong people. But you know what, they actually care about the world and what happens to it."

"Is Nick one of those?"

"I thought he was, but he's not."

I left that alone and took a drink of coffee, but Julia was like her mom. I saw that more and more. She wasn't disrespectful, but she wasn't done.

"At least my friends aren't pretending climate change isn't happening so they don't have to do anything. They know there isn't going to be any social security system left when we get there, but there will be a big debt and a lot of old people wanting to be taken care of."

I nodded and asked, "Is moving into that house in Long Beach the right decision? I'm asking because of the connections to Nick and Samantha Clark."

"How come you don't call her Sam like everyone else does?"

"Samantha is how I first heard her name."

"Let's be real, UG. You think I'm moving because Sam Clark has so much influence over me that if she thinks it's a good idea I'm doing it. Actually, one of my friends from high school is living in the Long Beach house."

"What about renting an apartment first and getting to know the people in that house before moving in with them?"

"What are you so worried about, and why should I live alone? I don't want to live alone," she said. "Let's face it, Sam started Witness1 and you have problems with it."

"I think Witness1 is a great idea. It's just gone a little sideways."

"Right."

She put her coffee down on the table and folded her arms the way she does when we disagree. Julia's friend and sometimes mentor, Samantha Clark, had started Witness1 several years ago when she was nineteen. She'd gotten some serious press coverage for it. The idea was that if you witnessed a serious crime like a shooting, let's say an unarmed black man killed by a police officer in a disputed incident, you'd video and write out your eyewitness account, and then post to the Witness1 website. It was an idea made for its time. It took off.

Julia had $180,000 that came from selling her family's house, a small life insurance policy Jim had, and what Jim and Melissa had saved. It was earmarked for college, but she could rent an apartment in Long Beach then figure the rest out.

"I have a question for you," she said. "Did you know Nick was bad news for me? I mean from the start."

"You seemed happy. I didn't think it was my place to say anything. He fooled me too."

"Did you think he liked you?"

"Not really."

"Nick despises the FBI, UG. He said if you work for the FBI, you do bad things every day, and I would learn the truth and turn against you. I had to prepare myself to hate you."

"How's that coming?" I asked.

"I'm working on it. Thanks for the help this morning."

She smiled and I smiled, and it broke the tension.

"Actually, I love you," she said, "even though you put yourself in bad situations."

"Like giving you advice?"

"Yeah, like that." She smiled, but in the next instant tears ran down her cheeks. "Nick made a video that supposedly I'm in. I think he drugged me and his friend Joel raped me, or I had sex with him because I was drugged. Nick sent someone to tell me if I don't get that box to him, I can watch myself on the Internet. He'll post it after the drop. I know him."

"Can you talk about what happened?"

"He or they put something in my beer when we got back to Nick's apartment after a concert. Or that's what I think. That was on Saturday, not this past Saturday but the one before. I started to remember on Wednesday. I'm going to talk to Jo when I'm ready."

"Report it to the police. I'll go with you. They can question Joel now and use whatever they learn when they catch up to Nick."

Julia shook her head. "I've thought about it. Nick and Joel will have their version down by now. I told Nick I knew. It was the only reason I was with him that night. To tell him I knew and to break up. I've thought about what I can prove or not. Too much time has gone by."

That was possible, but I said, "I can think of any number of investigations where we had two suspects with a bulletproof story they'd worked out together, and then we separate them and tell one what the other guy is saying about him, and pretty soon their stories come apart."

"I'm not sure what I'm going to do yet, UG, and I can't move until I do the fake delivery to Nick."

"What fake delivery?"

"The dummy bullets with the GPS tracker. What do you mean? Do you not know? Susan, I mean Agent Egbert, is working on it."

"I haven't talked to her," I said. "She's not going to tell me what they're planning."

"Well, it's going to happen soon, and when Nick finds out it's not the sniper bullets, he'll post the video."

"Post it where?" I asked.

"I don't know. I don't want to know. He'll post a link and people will go there. He'll post it no matter what. It's time for me to move out, UG. I can't be here when he does that, and it's just time anyway. I have to get figured out on my own."

That I could understand. I paused and took her in as a young woman rather than Julia, my niece. Then I asked, "What do you think your mom would say?"

"She would say if you're going to make a new life, do it well. If you screwed up, get clear on what happened then put it behind you. People who don't make mistakes never really live. That's something she always said. If you haven't made mistakes, you haven't really lived. I've thought about what she would say. It's time, UG. It's time for me to move. Give me a hug."

I gave her a hug, then headed to the meeting with Mara.

11

I came in the back door of the Vegas office and went upstairs to Mara's office. He was at his desk on the phone and pointed at a chair. I looked at the chair but didn't feel like sitting. My thoughts were with Julia.

When he hung up, Mara said, "The Speaker of the House just released a statement saying foreign enemies are waging economic jihad. In the Senate they want the Director to testify tomorrow at a closed hearing and detail what we're doing to stop these attacks. I want anything you can contribute to that."

"Tell me that's not why we're meeting," I said.

"It's not. The agents who have taken over what cases you had left have asked for an hour with you before you return to LA. I told them right after our meeting."

"Okay."

"Fuentes isn't happy about the amount of things you're working outside the LA field office area. That's another reason we're talking this morning. We've agreed to modify your temporary transfer such that you report to him anything in his territory. Anything outside it you'll report to me and copy both of us. I've gone to the top here. I've asked the special agent in charge to make the request, and I'm not even sure where it went, possibly the executive assistant director's office. I'd have to ask the SAC where he sent it. Either way, we should know this week. Normally, it would never get approved, but now isn't normal. This is the best idea we can come up with to give you flexibility, but you still need to let go of most of your extraneous leads and investigations outside of LA FBI territory."

"I can do that, but I'm not walking away from the cell-tower sniper."

"Which brings us to Gary Farue. He was in—and it's not certain he's out—an Idaho militia called the Northern Star Freedom Brigade or NB. If you're a member, you're a soldier and you're sworn for life."

"He sure talks like he's out, though mostly to agent Blujace. He told her the Brigade is after him. He told me the opposite, but there could be something to it. He's got a house in Ukiah but lives in hotels. It's believable to me he's watching his back. He also said to Jace it's Ashton Croft, the guy heading the Brigade, he worries about. He deeply offended Croft somehow. He hasn't told Jace the why of it yet."

"He's the kind of recruit the militias look for long term," Mara said. "He's got actual combat experience. Be careful with him."

"We are being careful with him."

"How much do you know about them, Grale?"

"I've read three or four reports an FBI agent out of the satellite offices wrote. He was working out of Kalispell, Montana, and reporting to the Salt Lake field office. He tried to penetrate and get recruited, but the Brigade didn't take him, and I didn't learn that much from his report other than Ashton Croft is really the one who decides everything."

"Few militias are dangerous. NB is dangerous. Most are all talk. No killings have ever been traced to the Northern Brigade, but they're suspected of several."

Mara knew more about American militias than anyone I'd met in or out of the Bureau. He was mixed race and sensitive to the reality that militias got a big recruitment bump when America elected a black president. It hurt his heart that he could do what he does here every day and race was still a big issue in America.

As I got ready to leave him and sit down with the agents here, he said, "Hey, some of the higher-ups would like you to fly to Washington and talk grid security with them. They'll put you on a business-class flight tomorrow."

"Business class."

Mara smiled broadly, and we both laughed at the idea. He was working eighteen-hour days, and I was moving around like a wanted man. It was a good way to end the meeting. Three hours later I skipped through TSA as a LEO, a law enforcement officer, and caught a flight to LA.

12

JULIA

Julia liked the first car enough to buy it. The guy selling gave her online access to all the servicing, repairs, and warranty records. After they agreed on a price, the seller hit on her, asking if she wanted to take a ride in his new Audi.

"Another time," Julia said. "I'm moving to California and packing today."

It felt strange yet good to say that. It definitely chilled the dude's interest in her. She transferred the money with the Venmo app and went home to pack.

Packing her room triggered the feeling of when she was much younger and she'd go to Uncle Grale's house. He was the uncle who was around for holidays and barbecues and then sometimes gone mysteriously for a long time. Mom had loved him like crazy, and he'd been Dad's best friend before he met Mom. She knew Uncle Grale's wife had died and that he was alone. She didn't really remember his wife, though Mom would ask her sometimes if she did. UG also carried a gun, which her little brother, Nate, had thought was so cool.

When she moved here, UG started acting more like a parent. She got it, but it was kind of weird, and then he sorta figured it out and turned pretty chill, except for not connecting with Nick. She'd resented that. For a long while it made her angry, but now everything was turned upside down.

She would miss Jo. They never argued, and Jo knew about a lot of things. Julia had screwed up more things in the last year than in her whole life, but she would fix that too.

UG had said she didn't have to put things away in the closet or take the whole room apart, but that wasn't right. She wasn't ever moving back. She took the posters off the walls, then vacuumed, washed the sheets, and remade the bed with a flutter in her stomach because it was late afternoon. The call would come soon from Agent Egbert.

She didn't have to leave tonight. She'd told UG she probably wouldn't because Agent Egbert had said don't load the car up yet. Don't show them anything about what you're doing next. She got everything packed and at the front door, so when she did load the car it wouldn't take long.

As she waited she wrote a note that became a letter for UG. She'd thought about the things he'd done for her since her mom, dad, and Nick were killed. Her mom had taught her how to drive, and she had a learner's permit. UG showed her how to spin a car and regain control, how to change a tire, what to carry in case things really went bad, how to shoot, how to defend herself and hit back, but mostly how to keep composure and think things through. That was it. It was that last part that really mattered. He said it's about knowing who you are.

She was nervous about the fake bullet drop, but she was ready because of UG. *Straight up, that's true,* she thought. There was the drop and then what Nick would do after. Ten minutes later, when she was still at the house, a call came from Shanna.

"I'm going to give you directions," Shanna said.

"Don't bother. It's not going down that way."

"Okay, then Nick uploads the video."

"If he uploads, I drop the box in some Dumpster. You aren't dictating how this goes down, Shanna."

"Nick is telling you. He's going to call you."

"Tell him not to call me. Tell him I hope he falls dead in the street."

"This is Julia Kern the pacifist talking?"

"Everybody dies, Shanna, even you. I'll text you where. I'll text you what time. Check with Lowlife then call me back. He doesn't call me. You get an hour from when I hang up, which is right now, so pick up your pretty little pink phone and look at the time."

Julia broke the connection and looked at her phone screen: 6:38 p.m. Agent Egbert would call soon. Egbert promised her she wouldn't be alone. The FBI would listen in on all the conversations.

Egbert called her a few minutes later, saying, "You were awesome. You've got steel in you, girl."

"What do you think will happen?"

"They'll go for it. We knew they'd want to do the drop at night to cut down on anybody watching. We'll have you covered. Night makes it harder for us to follow, but we'll deal with it. Where are you going to be until this goes down?"

"At my uncle's house. I'm going to hang here until it's time. I'll have my phone."

She turned on the TV but watched the clock on her phone. When it got down to twenty minutes to go, her heart pounded. Her chest felt tight. She forced herself to breathe deep and hold it, then let the air out evenly, but it wasn't working. She was angry at Nick and pictured finding him and calling him out on everything. On TV they were showing supermarkets stripped clean, and long lines at gas stations in Los Angeles. People were freaking.

Her phone rang. She didn't recognize the number. Another burner phone probably. Could be any one of the people she knew. Half of them used burner phones and switched around all the time.

Egbert had said, "Answer like normal."

There was a pause, then Nick said, "Hey, babe, I—"

Julia hung up. The phone rang twice more and she didn't answer. Then Shanna's number showed on the next ring.

Shanna said, "What's up, girl? Where's it going to be?"

"At a shopping mall. I'll text you the address. You go around back. You'll see a pole by itself with a sign on it. I'll leave it at the base of the pole. Why did Nick just call me?"

"I told you he was going to."

"And what did I tell you?"

"You were talking big, so I didn't tell him."

"Talking big?"

"Yeah."

"Don't ever call me again, Shanna. We're done."

Julia hung up, then texted UG, It's happening tonight.

13

On February 28 this year, a trucker hauling a shipment of military-grade ammunition took a break for food and coffee at a truck stop just east of Grand Junction, Colorado. When he returned to his truck, another man was with him. There was no appearance of coercion. Surveillance cameras captured both getting in the cab and driving away.

The following morning the trucker was rescued 110 miles west in Utah along a freeway shoulder on I-70. He had no coat, no shoes, no phone or ID. He claimed the other man, another trucker, a friend of a friend, had pulled a gun on him and directed him to a freeway exit, which led to a road where three men in two cars were waiting. They hogtied him and heaved him into a car trunk.

It was hours later, he wasn't sure how long he was in the trunk, two and a half hours he guessed, before he was freed way out on a dirt road without his shoes. He'd walked ten miles to get back to the freeway. They left him with a bottle of water and a promise to kill his two daughters, Kayla and Kylie, if he talked to police.

A Good Samaritan picked him up along I-70 at dawn and drove him to the nearest hospital. That led to a county deputy hearing his story and witnessing him call his trucking company. The company was skeptical, but what could they do but support him?

They checked him into a hotel, notified his family, and scrambled their top investigator because the story didn't quite hang together. At this point both the Denver and Salt Lake FBI offices were aware of the hijacking. Three days later the driver confessed to FBI agents he'd received a payment of $20,000.

I had that on my mind walking into the LA FBI bomb squad meeting, where we had a good back-and-forth on the three substation bombings. Nitromethane was a component of two of the bombs. In the most powerful bomb, hydrazine had been substituted for nitromethane. Another open question was why the largest bomb at the Olin substation was the weakest. The working theory was that when ammonium nitrate absorbs moisture from humid air, which it does readily, its explosive capability can be dampened.

The higher moisture content might help determine where the largest bomb was constructed. Since early March there'd been little to no rain in Southern California and not much fog along the coast. We could rule out surrounding desert, but somewhere the bomb makers had exposed the ammonium nitrate to moisture.

When I came out of the meeting, I got a call from Jace, who said, "I'm calling for a different reason, but do you want a thumbnail sketch of the cell-tower attack I walked today? It wasn't our sniper, so maybe you don't need to hear it."

"Tell me anyway."

"Okay. It was north of here in a watershed behind Santa Rosa. An asphalt road runs up through trees to a grassy hilltop. There's a chain-link gate at the bottom and another at the tower, both chained and locked. They cut both with bolt cutters. I know that because I found a chain with a padlock attached lying in weeds on the side of the road. No video cameras, no alarm, nothing resembling a security system.

"It was like the first five we saw, no shooting, just bolt cutters and a torch to get inside the chain link and into the backup generator shed and the main electrical-supply panel for the tower facility. They torched the main panel and all the conduit wiring feeding out. Everything shorted out. Grale, there are burn marks on the galvanized metal roof of the shed. It must have been scary as hell in there."

"One of these days they'll fry themselves," I said.

"I could live with that. I've got video of the scene that I can send you."

"Send it."

"Sorry to dump that on you. I know we're down to working the one-two sniper. And about that shooter, we may be taking a trip north, if you can do it. Farue called today about a former US Army sniper named Bill Mazarik who he says lives along the lake in Coeur d'Alene, Idaho. He knows him. He said they're good friends but don't see each other anymore."

"What's that mean?"

"You tell me, but he claims Mazarik is the guy to talk to about our cell-tower sniper."

"Spell his last name."

"M-A-Z-A-R-I-K. William Mazarik. I was thinking you could run his name by your Army-sniper-school contact. Farue says Mazarik doesn't answer his phone except when his kid calls. Otherwise, the phone is just for emergencies."

"Farue's idea is we fly there and just ask Mazarik who our cell-tower sniper is?"

"That's pretty much it. I've got an address, and if we go we can borrow a car from the Spokane office and be there in a couple hours or less. We can day-trip it."

"Did you try calling Mazarik?"

"I did. No answer and I didn't leave a message."

"I've never had much luck with this kind of tip, and we're in a dance with Farue, but let me see what I can find out."

When I texted the sniper-school instructor, Roy Anders, I again pictured him as he used to look, tall, fit, and proud. Some are born for a uniform. Roy was one, and he liked procedure, so I didn't know if he'd answer another text like the first I'd sent. He surprised me with a return call a few minutes later.

"I last heard Mazarik was in Montana then moved somewhere along the Idaho border, where he joined up with the Northern Brigade militia. I've been authorized to aid the FBI, but I can't volunteer private information. If you ask the right question and we have the answer, I can give it. Otherwise, once discharged, they're done. I can tell you Mazarik went out with an honorable discharge."

"Roy, I'm going to interpret that as you saying the Army believes a former sniper is a risk. Can you tell me if Mazarik knew Gary Farue?"

"He did."

"You're certain?" I asked.

"Absolutely. Are you talking to Farue?"

"We are."

"Farue may not have the facts, but he was in or is still in the Northern Brigade. Three ex-snipers settled in the Idaho-Montana area and got caught up in it."

"Farue, Mazarik, and the unnamed third man?"

"Yes. I don't know his current status, but I can say they all know each other."

"You told me before that Farue didn't make the grade and moved on, but what about this Mazarik? Is he skilled enough?"

"Highly skilled."

"And the unnamed third man?"

"One of the very best."

"Did the third man have a signature where he put a second shot very close to the first?"

"He had a habit that could be interpreted that way."

"Would Gary Farue be aware of that habit?"

"He could be but I can't confirm that. As I said, Farue moved on."

"What about Mazarik?" I asked.

"He would be aware."

"Farue has a cabin somewhere in Montana. Do you know where?"

"No."

"Tell me what you know about the Northern Star Freedom Brigade," I said.

"I know some things about them. I know they look for disenfranchised ex-military and in particular those trained to operate alone."

"Do Farue and Mazarik fit that?"

"Mazarik did, Farue no. The Northern Star Freedom Brigade usually goes by Northern Brigade or NB. No matter what they call themselves, they hold views inconsistent with democracy. They discuss 'canceling' various politicians and judges, but look in your Bureau files. The FBI investigated them. Mazarik and the unnamed man are highly skilled snipers."

"Mazarik isn't in our file, neither is Farue," I said. "We have hearsay on another sniper who has lived in that area on and off in the last five years. He could be Mazarik. We don't have a name on him. Brigade members are careful on the phone, or so I gather. Are you available if I have more questions?"

"Yes."

"I'll be back when I have the name of the third man. We will also request the Army give us his name immediately."

Anders replied, "I'm sorry about the protocol."

I sat several minutes after hanging up, then called Fuentes and talked through a one-day trip to Idaho tomorrow.

"Go," Fuentes said, "but I still want to see a lot more of you here. Copy both me and Mara on your report, and if you learn anything, who's reporting this to a joint terrorism task force office?"

"Agent Blujace reports to the San Francisco office."

As that call ended I got one from an upbeat Sue Egbert.

"I'm letting the guardian know his niece made the drop and is away. I also got cleared to have a couple of agents watch her house tonight, but she won't be there. She's leaving for Long Beach."

"Thank you for that."

"She was good. No, she was great. We're tracking two suspects right now, though neither is Nicolas Knowles. He didn't show."

"Thanks for calling. I'll check with Julia," I said.

I did and left a message. Half an hour later I got a text from her saying, Call you tomorrow from California.

14

I went well into the night with the LA office bomb squad. We had more data to look at and the ATF report on the Lake substation. DHS had also provided a two-year record of California ammonium nitrate deliveries. Ammonium nitrate was the prime ingredient of these bombs. We also went over a list of possible bomb makers, or rather those with known skills and radical political leanings.

That night Fuentes and I ate Thai food together and talked through the Anza, Lake, and Olin bombings before moving on to the cell-tower sniper, where I argued once more that while there might not be coordination between terror cells, we were seeing a strategy aimed at weakening communications along the electrical transmission pathways. Fuentes listened, then yawned and changed the subject.

"If we see more bombings like Anza, Lake, and Olin, we'll need you working bombings only. Between us, ATF, DHS, LAPD, we've got enough skilled people in evidence collection and analysis. But those guys are largely 'defuse and analyze' types. You're the hunter. We need your investigative skills. We need you tracking down bomb makers. Do your trip tomorrow and stay on this sniper, but if we see another wave in LA, be ready to focus on bomb makers."

"I'm not coming off this sniper. He's too good. He's doing a lot of damage."

"Then catch him and solve a problem for both of us."

Jace and I met in Spokane the next morning. We picked up a Bu-car at the FBI office there and headed to Idaho. Forty-five minutes later we were in Coeur d'Alene looking for a microbrewery. A Coeur d'Alene police lieutenant had told Jace yesterday that Mazarik had been arrested at the brewery six months ago after an argument with an ex-girlfriend who worked there.

As we parked in the lot and got out, she asked me, "How's your niece doing?"

Jace knew Julia had lived with me since the Alagara bombing, and from time to time she'd coached me on teenage girls. I mentioned in passing that Julia had broken up with her boyfriend. Jace was very intuitive. She was intuitive and she was tough. She was hard on herself and just as hard on others, but I always got the feeling she had a softness for Julia, a recognition of what Julia had endured.

"She's having a hard time," I said.

"Are there things she's not comfortable talking about with you?"

"A whole list of things. She's good friends with the prime founder of Witness1 and has fallen in with a mix of other activists, some with blurred lines. Julia has a good head and is independent, but her world got turned upside down when her boyfriend turned out to be a criminal who was likely using her. She's humiliated. She doesn't trust her judgment. I need to figure out how to reach her and to help her. I need to be more than I have been."

I turned to Jace.

"She believes she was drugged and raped. Her now ex-boyfriend has threatened to upload a video he made to the Internet. She's certain he will."

"And she has no one to talk to."

"You're good, Jace. You're right, that's a problem. It's too awkward and uncomfortable to talk to me, and she's about half in shock and trying to run from everything that has happened."

"Who wouldn't feel that way? I can totally understand."

The drive had been cloudy and blowing. We got a little rain as we crossed the lot and walked through the open door of the microbrewery. A woman called out in a cheerful voice, "Sorry, we're closed."

"We're looking for Nikki," Jace said.

"That's me." She came around from behind the bar. "Who are you?"

"FBI."

Nikki was blond and dressed as if every single day matters. Several strands of hair were damp with sweat and stuck to her forehead. With a finger she swept them aside, then we all sat down at a table. She was across from us.

"How do you even know about Bill and me, and why would you care?"

"From an argument you had with him, and an arrest," Jace said.

"That's creepy. Can you show me your ID again?"

She examined our creds and slid them back, saying, "Bill wouldn't hurt anyone. You don't have to be afraid of him. He's not some crazy guy, and what happened with us was just sad. That's all it was. Just sad. But you're not here about Bill and me. So is this about the Northern Brigade? No one around here calls them that, by the way. Well, *they* do, of course, and so does the FBI."

"What do locals call them?" I asked.

"Croft's kooks. Ashton Croft's militia. Mostly they camp, drink, shoot their guns, and listen to talk radio. But they also do military drills and troll the Internet. Those are their main skills. Bill and a couple of other ex-snipers joined so they could shoot for fun for a while and be told how good they are. The other two were more serious about it than Bill."

"What are their names?"

"I think you should ask Bill that. I don't feel comfortable giving names."

"How did Croft's kooks get their rep?" Jace asked.

"Rep for what?"

"For being dangerous," Jace said.

Nikki stared at us, then answered. "That's why Bill broke with them."

"What is?" I asked.

"Two young guys, kids, really, from California were growing pot in a rental house. They disappeared but their cars and all their stuff were still at the house. They were at a bar late at night and never made it home. One of the militia guys told Bill they were *gone* gone. I think Bill heard more than he told me. He quit that day, and Croft's guys have ridden him ever since. They bad-mouth him. They pressure anyone who hires him. Four of them showed up at his house and made death threats after he quit. It's why he doesn't answer his phone. Ask him about that. Even though they're all a bunch of losers, they don't like quitters. Go figure."

"We will," I said, and then asked her, "What happened with you and Bill?"

"Is it any of your business?"

"Not really."

"Then let's leave it there."

As we were leaving, she said, "Don't worry about Bill. He's got issues with the federal government, but he doesn't kill anything anymore. A coyote ate his cat out front, and he wouldn't shoot it. He's just so used to guns being around he's not going to get rid of them. You don't have to be afraid of him."

"When did you last talk to him?"

"Maybe a month ago. He comes in here every so often. We were together six years, and now we're pretending we're just friends."

There was a faint dusting of snow falling but sunlight on the road as we wound around the lake to Carlin Bay. We passed long piers and plenty of boat docking. We looked at houses along the water and got all the way down to Martin Bay before figuring out we missed the turn to the Carlin Bay Airport.

Ten minutes later we were on a dirt road with three houses, well spaced. None had marked addresses. The first had a big mastiff on the deck that stood up and looked at us but didn't bark. It looked to me like the dog was thinking, *It's your call. Nothing has happened yet. Decide what you want to do, and we'll take it from there.*

Outside the second house I asked a woman unloading groceries from her car which house was Bill Mazarik's. She pointed at a kit-built log house set back from the road in the trees near the end of the street.

Bill Mazarik was maybe fifteen to twenty pounds lighter than in his Army days, and from photos he was lean then. He wore sweatpants, a Denver baseball jersey, and running shoes without socks.

Jace pulled out her creds. He waved them away and she handed him a card instead.

"I know why you're here. Come on in."

Inside, the warm air smelled like wood smoke and dog. Mazarik's dog was an old black lab, who lifted his white chin to look at us, then laid it down again. His tail thumped hard several times, then went quiet.

"I have tea, coffee, water, or beer, but agents don't drink, do they?"

"I'd love some water," Jace said.

"I'll get it, and I'm making coffee anyway."

"Coffee for me," I said.

Protocol is you don't accept anything offered. You do the interview; you don't sit down over a drink. But over the years, if you're an investigator you figure out everyone is more comfortable if there's some hospitality. Even the condemned prisoner likes the gesture of the last meal. It's a human thing.

I looked around the front room as he went to his kitchen. Simple and humble, pretty clearly a man living alone, a couple of beer bottles on the wood floor next to an armchair where his long arm could reach them. A book lay open, a cork coaster keeping the pages flat. The book was a how-to primer on teaching yourself to navigate using the stars. I didn't see any political diatribes.

When he moved out of view in the kitchen, I followed, wanting to keep him in my line of sight. He was aware. A faint smile formed as I appeared in his peripheral vision.

"I have a prescription," he said. "I'm taking a pill. Does the agent with you want ice with her water? I'm sorry, what is her name again?"

"Jace."

He asked Jace if she wanted ice. She didn't, and he swallowed two pills, then filled a glass with water for Jace. While the coffee brewed, he stumbled, sloshing water out as he carried the glass to Jace. He apologized and got a dishtowel to wipe up. He refilled her water. I saw his left foot and the way he moved, his self-consciousness. He brought out two mugs of coffee, handed me one, and I no longer read the shaking as nervousness.

He looked from Jace to me and said, "Talk to me. If it's about the militia, I'm not in it anymore. The Army was here a year ago asking about someone I'd heard was in California. I'm not going to give his name unless you already have it."

"Gary Farue?" I asked.

"I know Gary. I don't like him much, but it's not him I'm thinking of."

"I feel like I'm on a game show," Jace said, but it didn't affect him. He wouldn't give us the name.

"Do you talk with Gary Farue?" I asked.

"Not often, it's better that way."

"What's that mean?"

"It means I don't need to see him ever again, and I'll sometimes take a call from him to make sure that doesn't happen."

"Are you aware of the cell-tower shootings?"

"If you're asking if I watch TV, yeah, I do. It would be hard not to know about the mysterious, highly accurate shooter. He's all the buzz in my circles."

"Then you know why we're here," I said.

"Pretty much."

"What are you hearing?" I asked.

"Let's get clear first. I made a mistake joining Croft's militia. It was just a way to target shoot, which I missed doing. I quit Croft. I agree with some of the things he says, but he's a bastard. I was US Army for thirteen years. That doesn't just go away."

"Why did you join in the first place?"

"To be honest, they admired my shooting when I didn't have much else to be proud of, so I hung out with them for a few years."

"What views do you share with him?"

"You're city folk, right?" He nodded at Jace. "Your card says San Francisco."

"Yeah, the FBI office is there. I can't afford to live in SF."

"And you?" he asked me.

"In Vegas but where I can look out in the desert from my back patio."

He pointed a finger at me and said, "You and me, brother, I know what you're saying."

"We were asking about your and Croft's views and what you share."

"I'd shut down immigration until we get it figured out. I'm not such a doofus I second-guess scientists on climate change. They're saying it's happening, so we need to prepare. There'll be wave after wave of immigrants. We've got to turn them back. If that doesn't work, we sink boats and blow up tunnels. That sounds harsh, but it'll save more lives later."

"What else?" I asked.

"I'd move the capital out of Washington and put it out west. That way we get rid of half of the deep state." He frowned, exhaled hard, and then said, "We've got to take a stand against the globalists."

He was getting ready to go further into that theory until Jace asked, "Race?"

"That was the real problem with Croft. Hell, I'm Army, we're equals. Not all the same but all equal. A lot of what they talked about turned my stomach, so I quit."

"They let you?"

"They showed up here several times. My last pickup burned in a parking lot outside a bar in Boise. After that, several of them had trouble with their vehicles, including Croft. I heard someone shot some heavy-weight slugs through his new truck engine and tires from a long way away. I don't know if that's true, but things settled down around here.

"They've made it as hard for me as they can, but I've got work with a local contractor, and I pull wire for an electrician too. I've got a son almost five years old. He and my ex are down in Missoula. I had a girlfriend here. I made a big mistake with her, but I'd just gotten a medical diagnosis."

He saw me looking at his hand, and his gaze fixed on me. Gray-blue eyes. Some of the best shooters had them. I was putting it together. He'd tripped carrying the water. His hand had a tremor.

"Reach around to that little chest behind you and open the top drawer," he said. "There'll be some papers clipped together there. Pull those out. You're both welcome to read them. Do you know what a young Parkie is?"

"I do," Jace said.

I didn't, and pulled the papers out and read about a Parkinson's disease diagnosis. I handed them to Jace.

"Whatever it is you're here about, I couldn't do it if I wanted to, but maybe I can help you."

"We flew here because we believed you would," I said.

Jace pulled photos from a manila envelope that showed bullet holes made by pairs of steel-jacketed sniper bullets punching through close together. They were close-ups that showed the pattern of the bullets on various metal pieces of cell-tower equipment. She handed them across the makeshift coffee table. Eight photos. He went through them slowly, then asked, "From what distance?"

"Half a mile," I said, and then showed him more on my phone.

"The news reports don't say anything about this pattern," he said. "Someone absolutely comes to mind with this one-two, one-two, but it doesn't feel right just to throw a name out like that."

"It must be catching," I said. "We keep getting that answer."

"Excuse me?"

"The country is under assault, but it's hard to get a name from anybody. Farue didn't recognize the pattern. Does that make sense to you?"

"What I would say about Gary Farue is that he should have married himself. There was never going to be anybody he'd love as much. Let me text somebody I know."

His index finger trembled as he texted. A response came, and he frowned and texted back and forth a few times.

He looked at me. "What if you're wrong? I don't want to get anybody hurt. This one they're calling the cell-tower sniper, he hasn't hurt anybody, right?"

"He hasn't."

"If you hunt him, it'll be with guns drawn. Cops are afraid of trained snipers, so if it gets to that point, they'll shoot first. The FBI is not much better, and as you've no doubt figured out, he's a helluva lot better shot than all of you. No one is going to take a risk once they've talked themselves into going after him. He'll get killed. I don't want to be responsible for that." He sighed. "Did they send you here?"

"Who are they?" I asked.

"The Army."

"We have two sources on you. Both said you were the guy to ask about this particular cell-tower sniper."

"Go back to Farue. You said Farue is in California, and if the news reports are right so is this shooter. The guy I'm thinking about Farue knows plenty well, but if they're in contact, Gary is getting something out of it. Guaranteed. For Farue, everything is a transaction."

"What else on him?"

"That's it."

"There was a federal judge in Boise shot and killed outside of his house. We're told members of the Northern Star Freedom Brigade have talked about 'canceling' judges. Did you ever hear any talk like that?"

I could tell the question disturbed him, but he answered without hesitation.

"Yep, the Obama appointment. The Brigade had their eyes on him a long time, and yes, they did talk about taking him out. It's hard to sort out what's drinking talk, but it could have been them. They could have gone through with it. But I'm not saying the one you're looking for was the shooter."

"But it was someone skilled, and you didn't see a lot of skill when you were active in the Brigade."

"That's right. Most of them are assault-rifle guys. Not much skill but a lot of bullets."

"Is respect for him part of why you won't give us his name?"

"Ask the Army," he replied. "They know who he is."

"We did ask the Army. They need evidence first."

"Okay, say I give you a name and he figures it out when you come for him because he knows the Army rules. Will the FBI be there for my son if something happens to me?"

"No," I said. "It definitely won't. I'd be lying if I said we would."

"I'm beginning to like you, Agent Grale, but go back to the Army. They can give you a name."

"We came a long way to talk to you. Give us something."

"He bought a cabin with Gary."

"Where?" I asked.

"Outside of Missoula."

We left several ways he could get hold of us. After he walked us to the door and was standing on his porch, I turned and asked, "How will we know him?"

"His boots. He always wears Kelley Zipper Tactical Boots. They're kick-ass boots. He loves 'em. We all do."

"Show us yours," I said.

He did, and we got in the car and wound our way back around the lake to the highway. Back in Spokane, we dropped the car at the Bureau office and moved up our flight.

After we landed and were walking out of the terminal in Oakland, I checked my messages. I read and reread a text from an unknown number with an Idaho prefix. It wasn't Nikki. It was two words.

"Jacob Corti," I said. Jace stopped and turned.

I handed her my phone. When she handed it back I typed thank you and sent the text. That night I left a message for Roy Anders. The next morning he confirmed the Army had discharged a Jacob Corti, a highly trained sniper, six years ago after five tours in Afghanistan. Current whereabouts unknown. Corti was a three-time top sniper. It was a team award, but he was the guy.

I called the Salt Lake FBI from the San Francisco field office late morning the next day. The investigation into the judge's killing ran from that office. They hadn't talked to Corti but had wanted to. They still did and wanted to be in the loop if we found him.

Not the Army, though. Anders wrote me back and I told Jace, "They're saying he's been out long enough that he's ours to deal with, not theirs. They'll help in any way they can. They're telegraphing concerns about him."

I looked at her and said, "I can't figure this out. We're ninety-nine percent certain it's a foreign enemy behind the cyberattacks, so why is an ex-Army sniper shooting up cell towers? How does a guy with Corti's background fit into that? After what we just heard in Idaho about the Northern Brigade, you can't tell me he's working for a foreign enemy. That makes no sense."

I was just thinking aloud. This was nothing Jace or I could answer today, and her response was practical. "You've got the bombers on your plate, I'll work on Corti."

"We'll both work on Corti."

We talked through our next moves in a conference room until the door opened and an agent leaned in and said, "Hey, you may want to take a look at this. They're talking about evacuating Phoenix."

15

The Palo Verde nuclear power plant in Arizona lacks the bragging rights of the Grand Coulee Dam in Washington. The Grand Coulee has the largest rated capacity in the United States at 6,809 megawatts, but that's somewhat misleading. That's a measurement derived by measuring output under more or less ideal conditions for a reasonable duration. It doesn't account for the less-than-ideal conditions, the repairs, the dry years, and off-season. It's nuclear plants that consistently produce the most power year after year. The top producer of electrical power in America is Palo Verde.

But nuclear plants also top the nightmare list. Three Mile Island. Chernobyl. Fukushima. Things happen.

"When did they pick up on the virus?" I asked an agent who seemed to know.

"Five days ago they moved into a slowdown. It had already rewritten the code for the operation of the cooling system. Two pumps started operating at unsustainable speeds. When they tried to bring the pumps back under control, they had to deal with additional pressure as well. We're hearing they need to shut everything down to wipe the computers clean but are afraid they'll lose the pumps and risk a meltdown. Don't ask me how that all goes together."

On the TV screen, CNN went to an aerial shot of bumper-to-bumper traffic leaving Phoenix.

"Voting with their tires," the agent said. "As soon as the plant went public with their problem, the cars lined up." He turned and looked at me. "The virus is replicating itself and may be hiding in a piece of smart equipment that talks to the main computer system."

I watched for another ten minutes, then stepped out to take a call from Hofter. Jace, Hofter, and I couldn't do anything about Phoenix or the large blackouts occurring elsewhere.

"What did you get from Idaho?" Hofter asked.

"The name of a top Army marksman named Jacob Corti with some current or past connection to an Idaho militia called the Northern Brigade. I'll see you in LA in a few hours and catch you up. I'm about to head to the airport."

"We've got another bomb threat called in and a vehicle parked outside a substation. It's not an Edison truck, it's an RV."

"Where?" I asked.

"North Hollywood, with the same booby-trapped threat, but this time we've got robots and drones on it. There's also a report of something going on at Mount Lee. Two men. Suspicious activity. LAPD is all over that and not asking for help, but we've asked to be in the loop. You and I have a tip to check on in Newport Beach, then we'll head to Hollywood."

We have thousands of tips. Why wouldn't we go straight to North Hollywood and the bomb vehicle and learn everything we can there? It sounded like the same approach but with a different vehicle, so good chance it's the same terror cell. But Hofter is a very competent investigator and I was in no position, with the cell-tower sniper expeditions, to be arguing priorities in LA. So I didn't say anything and caught my flight.

Hofter picked me up at the airport and we drove an hour and change to meet eighty-three-year-old Ed Harris in Newport Beach.

Harris lived on a comfortable street above the coast highway. His wife had passed six years ago. He'd had a second knee-replacement operation last year and was thinking about doing his right hip. He asked where I was from. I said Las Vegas and he frowned and pointed out a window at a neighbor's house across the street.

"I called the FBI about the RV with the bomb on TV. It's the same damn truck that was here for two days. A blond girl, good-looking, and a young man about six foot with dark hair. He was fiddling inside it all day yesterday instead of being down at the beach with the girl."

"What have you got for us, Mr. Harris?" I asked.

"Photos. What did you think I had?"

"Let's have a look."

He took three steps toward a little room we could see was his office, then turned back and asked, "Why does it take two of you to come here?"

He didn't wait for an answer and returned with photos he handed to Hofter. I saw puzzlement on Hofter's face and watched him pull out his phone. His eyes went from phone to photo.

He said, "Grale, take a look," and stepped around Harris.

And so it goes sometimes, a confluence of the unexpected and the randomness of the universe. An eighty-three-year-old self-appointed neighborhood watchman with time on his hands and anger as it turned out at a neighboring couple who rented their house via AirBnB. He'd captured the license plate of the bomb vehicle parked at Station H Hollywood and had one very important photo of the couple staying there.

Neighbors guessed the blond Caucasian female was twenty-five to thirty years old, the male's age similar. The female's hair fell to her shoulders. She was approximately five foot nine, one hundred forty pounds. The male was taller, closer to six feet. One neighbor said he looked Italian. Another said he was a mix of Caucasian and Hispanic and Jewish, whatever that is. He was dark haired. Descriptions of him varied widely, but the FBI was out to the public with artist's sketches before Mark and I reached the Hollywood substation.

With binoculars from the roof of a building, I got a look at the rented RV. It was big enough to carry a large bomb. If it was a "shaped charge," so that the blast was directed toward the substation, it would do substantial damage. Edison, the utility provider, was already rerouting power.

A robot on the ground under the RV plus two drones overhead were trying to determine if it really was booby-trapped. So far they weren't coming up with anything, and the threat warning that motion sensors would trigger an explosion did not appear true. The caller warned of a detonation near midnight. It was 10:07 now, and a debate was underway whether to approach and attempt to defuse.

"I'm okay with walking up to check it out," I said to Hofter.

He looked at me in disbelief, then asked, "Have you got a will?"

"Yes, with most of my vast estate left to my niece."

"Nothing for me?"

"Next time."

"That's hard, Grale. I would have thought there'd be something for me. How about that watch of yours? I like that watch. I'll hold it for you while you're up looking for the sensor that sets the bomb off."

I smiled but said, "I'm halfway serious. If it's another ANFO, we could disarm the detonator, and I'm getting the strong signal these bombers don't want to kill people."

"Yeah, but it's also the first we've heard of motion sensors. Fuck them. Can't wait until we get them."

I did make the offer to approach and look for a way to defuse. A "no" came down twenty minutes later, and the bomb detonated at 11:59 p.m., which said to me we were looking for the same terror cell as the first three bombings. It was an arrogant and cocky signature to detonate at the same hour and minute.

It made for great TV. An ANFO explosion expands faster than the speed of sound. The flash of light was visible across the LA Basin. It killed no one but destroyed fifty percent of the substation largely because of how well the charge was shaped. There was the roar of the blast, debris falling over and over on CNN.

But it was a local TV station that was the first to run "Blond Bomber Strikes Hollywood."

16

On Amazon you can buy a copy of the National Research Council of the National Academies report titled "Terrorism and the Electric Power Delivery System," but it won't be the same as the one I have. Mine is pre–Homeland Security review and redaction, and includes all of the warnings and recommendations. In 2004, experts assembled to assess grid vulnerabilities. They finished in 2007. But not until 2012 did Homeland Security allow a heavily redacted version to be published.

My opinion: the Department of Homeland Security, DHS, in its effort to keep critical information from terrorists, has inadvertently hidden the truth from Americans.

I thought of that as I pulled on another HAZMAT suit. We worked the warm night in Hollywood with the thrum of rented generators forcing everybody to talk louder or less. The air smelled of diesel, blast burn, and oils seeping from torn transformers. This was yet another bombing we didn't stop, but we did have two suspects, and were learning the bomb maker's methods.

At dawn I stripped the suit, filled a large paper cup with coffee, and picked up a sandwich from an open cardboard box as I talked with an Edison manager who'd been allowed inside the tape. He was solidly built, midforties, alert, a little on the hyper side, an engineer with some business school and management ambitions, here to assess.

"How long to rebuild?" I asked.

"Two years."

"That long?"

"Or longer." He pulled off his glasses and rubbed the bridge of his nose. "Around here they'll already want us to move it to a new location. There'll be hearings and neighborhood committees. Might be more like three or four years."

"You're not going to move it?"

"Christ, no, that would quintuple the cost. And where would we move it? No neighborhood wants it. They just want the power."

We drank more coffee and chatted. Then I got a call from Julia and stepped away.

"You working the bombing?" she asked.

"We're wrapping up. I'm close to heading to the LA office. Where are you?"

"Long Beach. Want to come see? I met with them last night. I'm moving in here. I like all of them and Sam came over. It was great to see her and catch up. She wants to do a joint posting on Witness1, a reaffirmation of statement of purpose. Millions of people will see it with both of our names as authors. Pretty cool, huh?"

"Sounds interesting—I'd like to hear about it and see the house. How's two this afternoon? I can give you a call when I leave the office."

"Sure, okay, two is fine." She sighed. "Doing this reaffirmation with Sam is actually a really big deal."

"I don't really know what 'reaffirmation' means yet, and I'm kind of flat from working through the night. I'd like to hear more about it when I see you, and I look forward to seeing the house."

"It means what it sounds like. I take it you don't think it's a good idea to co-author with her."

"I don't have any opinion."

"You sound like you do."

"Can we talk about it when we see each other?"

"Okay, bye."

I sat on that a moment thinking that I should get out of this pattern with Julia where how quickly or slowly I respond and with what level of enthusiasm too easily determines how the conversation will go. We needed to get on more equal footing. I mulled that over and listened to a news report on a White House press release that the president was planning a western tour to survey the damage and talk to the people. Good on him, but he should stay away. There was already enough pressure on city police departments without adding a security detail. The president would visit Salt Lake, Phoenix, Los Angeles, and then San Francisco, where he'd give a speech before flying to Seattle, the site of the first attack.

I thought about Julia's friend, Samantha Clark. Investigations are driven by evidence, but patterns of character emerge as well. Clark's character as a witness was called into question earlier this year. It was something I was aware of but nothing I'd said anything to Julia about.

On January 3, a gunman with an assault rifle shot and killed an Oakland police officer. Three days later, 361 miles south in the small city of Signal Hill, two Long Beach East Division police officers were gunned down as they left a Black Bear restaurant at 9:50 p.m. The shootings had some similarities if no evidentiary connection: a lone gunman, night, and the possibility the officers were stalked. The close timing of the killings pulled the Bureau in, although it was an LA County Sheriff's Department investigation.

For the Long Beach officers, the stop at the Black Bear was a habit but not a routine. They only made the stop if they were near the end of a shift and returning in that direction. It wasn't something they did every night, so it might point to an impulsive shooting or the dark specter that the officers had been stalked.

Then there was this. The Black Bear was nearly empty and fifteen minutes from closing when Samantha Clark came in. She wanted a window seat. All seven booths along the windows were empty. She had her pick of any and took the corner booth with the promise she'd order immediately, which she did, coffee and dessert.

From the corner booth she looked down the sloping asphalt lot at the Chevron station below and the intersection of East Willow and Cherry. She told detectives she saw the officers drive up and park. They looked beat but relaxed as they walked up to the restaurant entrance. To her, it seemed they liked each other. The male officer touched the carved wooden bear before going in the door as if he liked the feel of the wood or maybe for luck.

Inside, the witness may or may not have seen them order coffees to go. She remembered looking out the window at traffic going by in the intersection. She remembered a van and a car gassing up at the Chevron station. The McDonald's adjacent to the Chevron was open. In her first interview she said she'd never been to this Black Bear before, although she lived in Long Beach. She'd said she'd gone there that night after arguing with a boyfriend, telling detectives a Black Bear diner was the absolute last place he'd look for her.

The detectives asked to talk with the boyfriend to confirm that, but she refused to give them a name or his cell number, the reason being he wasn't really her boyfriend. That came out later. He was the boyfriend of someone else she knew. That woman was a friend of hers who would be very hurt if she learned that Sam was also seeing him.

The detectives pushed, told her it would corroborate her story, and she'd answered, "I don't have to corroborate anything. I went to a diner and ordered coffee and dessert. You need to do your jobs and figure out who killed the officers. Who I sleep with is none of your business."

When the two Long Beach East Division officers left the Black Bear, Clark said she watched them walk down toward their car. Then from the corner of her eye, coming from her right, she picked up on a man moving toward them.

Samantha Clark was the only witness to the Black Bear slayings. She'd caught the public eye when she created Witness1 and moved to California with the stated goal of "organizing." She was a Las Vegas native and had reached out to Julia a year after the Alagara bombing, when Julia's Rotary Club pacifism speech generated negative press. Julia was already aware of her and admired her.

Clark saw the shooter raise a gun. She saw the muzzle flashes and heard what she called "hard, short popping sounds." The female officer, Leung, collapsed. "As if she just stopped being," Clark said. The male officer, McDermott, died reaching for his gun.

Clark had encouraged Julia to do what she'd done, skip college and just get into life. Come up with an idea and go for it. I got the feeling Clark saw her as a protégé and liked Julia's tragic celebrity as the lone survivor of the Alagara bombing. It was Clark who drew Julia into Witness1.

Signal Hill is a small city surrounded by Long Beach but has its own police department. Signal Hill officers responded to the call of two officers down. They strung tape and contained the site but deferred the homicide investigation to the LA County Sheriff's Detective Bureau. The Crime Against Police Officers Section, CAPOS, a DA representative, two Long Beach homicide detectives, a Signal Hill detective, and the FBI all became part of the investigation.

LA County detectives had numerous issues with Clark from the outset. That the creator of Witness1, who'd made it her mission to police the police, should happen to be the lone witness in a double slaying of officers strained credulity. And despite their request that she not do so, Clark had posted on the Witness1 website after the shooting.

She took videos of the bodies lying on the asphalt until one of the Black Bear waitresses pushed her phone away, telling her it was obscene. That waitress carried the same outrage into an interview room the next day. When questioned about the apparent callousness, Clark had shrugged and told the detectives it was obvious the officers were dead. She saw nothing prurient in leaning over to video them then posting it as an eyewitness account.

There were other issues with Clark, one of which was her widely varying description of the lone male shooter. In surveillance tapes, baggy clothing disguised his body. He wore thin latex gloves. None of his hair showed and it was night, so in many ways it was unfair to take Clark to task over her descriptions.

But there was something disturbing in the casualness with which she changed descriptions, albeit with apologies, as she withdrew her prior statement and offered a new one. More than that, detectives felt she was working against them. As one put it, "She's fucking with us."

Her credibility with the detectives had done nothing but erode since, and the shooter was still at large. He'd hurried down Cherry Street along the backside of the Chevron car wash and was picked up by an unidentified sedan.

To the north a few weeks later, an arrest was made in the Oakland officer assassination. The sister of the shooter walked into the Seventh Street police station and handed over her brother's laptop. On it were detailed plans of the murder. The shooter's name was Robert Overton. The weapon was an AR-15 converted to automatic. He used a thirty-round magazine. Twenty-one of his shots missed, but with an assault rifle you don't need to be much of a marksman. The officer was struck nine times and died on scene.

In Signal Hill the shooter was highly accurate, so precise that investigators debated it being a hired hit, a pro. They looked at whether the two officers might be dirty. I read the investigative files and am always interested in shooters with unusual skill. It's so uncommon I could contemplate our cell-tower sniper as that shooter but for the fact this was a handgun, which is a different skill set.

Officer Leung was killed by two bullets dead center in her forehead. McDermott, her partner, was shot three times in a tight pattern at the right temple. Five shots perfectly placed by a man running downhill and across with his arm extended. But again, Clark was the only witness and as her credibility diminished with the shape-shifting descriptions of the shooter, so too questions were raised about her shooting account. Had the officers stopped walking? Was the killer running when he shot them, or had he stopped too? Clark might nod her head and say yes, maybe they did stop, and twenty minutes later say no, it didn't happen that way.

Clark's accounts varied enough that county sheriff's detectives decided to shake up the interview process. FBI agents out of the LA office tracking the investigation interviewed her. In those interviews, Clark was less contradictory and talked of waking up at night with flashbacks and seeing things she didn't the night of the killing. Trauma can do that, so our agents would have taken that in without judgment. Or they did at first. But they too grew skeptical.

One of them, an agent I've known a long time, Sara Decca, agreed with them that Clark was hiding something. That carries weight with me. Decca showed me video of Clark answering questions about the shooter.

"The gun was in his right hand," Clark said. "He turned and looked through the window at me and I couldn't move. I would know his eyes if I saw them again. I think he has a beard. I saw something below his lips. He's got sort of a beak to his nose. His eyes are really, like, straight at you. Fierce-like or it's the way he concentrates, so focused. His eyebrows are dark. He looked strong."

"Would you recognize him?" Decca had asked.

"I'm not that good with faces."

There was the mishmash quality to her descriptions, and there was this. Julia had once said to me, "Sam's like famous for remembering people. If she's met you before, no matter how long ago, she'll remember you. That's so cool. I wish I was like that."

I'm not part of the Signal Hill investigation, but I care about the officers killed, and the anomaly of such a skilled shooter gets my attention. I'm also looking out for Julia. Samantha Clark has been a strong influence on her. Trauma can do a number on memory. I've seen that. But listen to the detectives working the Signal Hill murders as well as our agents, and they leave you with the feeling something is wrong. Something is hidden. Something Clark knows. What do I do with that and Julia?

17

"Hey, what's up?" Farue asked.

"You've called Agent Blujace four times this morning. She's swamped with other work, so she asked me to give you a call. What did you want to talk with her about?"

"She and I have a conversation going on."

"Bring me in."

Farue paused on that, then said, "It can wait until she has time."

"We're both so busy, Gary, we have to double-team things. I'm sure you understand. Hey, I know I'm not as much fun to talk to."

"You've got that right."

"I've got something I've wanted to ask you," I said. "We got more back on Croft's militia, but I don't know if the sources are any good. Do you want to take a stab at helping unravel a tip?"

"Where did this tip come from?"

"Can't say. Promised to keep it confidential, but if you want to help, here's your chance."

"Let's hear it," he said, as if I was an underling reporting.

"Did you and another Northern Brigade member, also former Army, own a cabin together outside of Missoula?"

He was quiet long enough for me to think I should repeat it or that he'd hung up.

"I bought Jake Corti out of the cabin in 2014. Who did you talk to that's trying to make me look bad?"

"What do you hear in that question that makes you think that?"

"Look, I work my ass off to protect things. I want to know who said that to you."

"Do you still have the cabin?"

"My cabin I never get to. You want to talk taxes and upkeep, or maybe you're in the market? I thought you were so busy you and Jace have to cover for each other. But you've got time to talk about summer cabins?"

"Slow down, and explain what you meant about making you look bad."

"I don't like being gamed, but, yes, we bought it together and I bought him out. I bought him out because he changed his mind and wanted us to sell. I got a loan and it got done with no hard feelings."

"So you're good with him. Have you seen him lately?"

"No, but I've tried to reach him. I heard he was in California. What are you asking?"

"We'd like to interview Jacob Corti. The Army tells me he was highly skilled. He might be able to help us."

"You don't lie very well, Grale."

"Teach me how to."

He muttered something before saying, "I don't know where Corti is, and sure I've thought about him and everyone else I knew who could shoot that well. But why would Jake be shooting up cell towers?"

"Could it come from Croft and the Northern Brigade?"

"Anything could come from Ashton Croft."

"Why did you join the Northern Star Freedom Brigade?"

"Look at you finally getting the name right. Tell you what, I sure wish I'd never joined. I was in a bad space and influenced. When I look back I don't get it."

"So you quit."

"I told Ashton to his face I was gone."

"What did he say to that?"

"Nothing."

"Nothing?"

"Oh, his usual 'once in, you're in forever.'" He was quiet, then added, "There are stories of guys who've gone missing, or their car has died on the wrong road in a snowstorm. Shit like that."

"Do you believe that?"

"I don't disbelieve it."

"Any current contact with other members?"

"None."

"We hear Corti is still in. Can you send me the phone number you have for him?"

"Sure, but every single time I've tried to call him back, and I'm talking about right after he texts me, his phone doesn't work. It's like I'm his last call on a burner phone or something like that. But you're the FBI. You guys are so good at everything maybe you'll figure it out. I'll send you his last one when we get off, but don't call me back if it's disconnected."

"What was the thing that made you quit the Northern Brigade?" I asked.

"Some of the things getting said after Obama was elected I didn't want any part of. Look, it all started years before that in Missoula when a couple of Croft's guys bought me drinks one night. All of a sudden I was meeting up with the militia on weekends in Idaho. They sold it as just a good time and a chance to hang out and have fun on the occasional weekend. Mazarik and I were there to shoot and have fun with the guys. We weren't there for their political opinions or any of their other deep thoughts."

"What about Corti?"

"He was still there when I left. I'm a traitor. So is Mazarik."

"Our photos aren't current. What's Croft look like now?"

"He's lost all his hair, and his face is very pale and wrinkled. He's got big jowls. He looks like a used condom. I heard a rumor old man Croft tried to start his pickup with his house key, and had gotten less than a mile from home and had to have someone come help him find his way. What's that sound like?"

"Like you're still keeping in touch with the guys. So who's in charge now?"

"Let me say this before I hang up. You work domestic terrorism so you know more than me, but I know there are three hundred militias in the US. I was in one and I quit. That's legal, right? Before that I was in the Army protecting your ass. So was Mazarik and he quit Croft too. Corti, who the fuck knows with him. You and me, we're done talking about it forever. I served my country. I don't have to take crap from an FBI agent. You have a fine day, Grale."

18

"UG, come in! How do you like it?"

"Looks like a good street and not far from the ocean."

"Not far at all, and I'm buying a beater bike to get around."

The rental was a corner house probably built in the seventies, a mix of stucco and painted wood siding, an asphalt-shingle roof and brick-lined concrete approach with the desert landscaping I see more and more. Julia looked like she was trying to be happy but it wasn't quite flowing yet. She moved out of the doorway and let me inside, where it was warm to stuffy and smelled of cat urine.

The main room's windows and an aluminum slider opening to the backyard were all shut. Through the slider I saw the gas fire pit Julia had talked about. Around it were scattered sun- and salt-faded patio chairs.

"There was a break-in last week at a house pretty close to here, so they want to keep the windows shut, and they don't run the air conditioning. Sorry about the smell. The people before had four cats, and one of them had kittens."

It was spacious enough, and it ought to be fun to live with people her age. The main thing was getting on with life and finding direction. The aged aluminum slider scratched and bumped its way open, and we walked out onto a concrete patio, brick-lined like the front entry. On a rusting metal table were beer bottles and a couple of ashtrays with ends of joints poked in the sand. A redwood fence faded gray with salt and time marked the property edge. In the back and on one side were neighboring gardens.

"Nice," I said.

"This is where everybody gets together at night. The other choice was finding an apartment, UG. I don't know if I've told you, but it's always been my plan to skip college and live off my inheritance while hanging around beach towns."

"I always figured that was the plan."

"I knew you knew, so I changed it. I don't want to burn up my inheritance, so I'm going to sell drugs."

"What kind?"

"Pretty much everything. I can make deliveries on the beater bike, and if I shoplift on the way back home it'll be convenient."

"What do you do when the store owner chases you out the door?"

"Race down the bike path."

"The cops have bikes."

"Oh, I didn't know that."

This was a patter we kept that lightened things up. I'm sure what was on her mind and weighed on her soul was the video Nick had threatened her with. I wanted to ask but wouldn't. It had to come from Julia. I had questions about Samantha Clark as well, but we didn't have to go there today. I'd take my cues from her.

"I wouldn't have done this if I didn't have one good friend living here already. They're all pretty political. Two of them are hard-core. They like to argue."

"What do your more hard-core ones worry about?"

"Being targeted by the government because they're actively recruiting for Witness1. Last night they were talking about hiring someone to sweep the house for electronic devices."

"They'll pay for that but not air conditioning?"

"Priorities, dude," she said, and smiled. "We're close to the beach, so there's the breeze. Or at least that's what they said last night."

"Is everybody on board with Witness1?"

"Totally."

Witness1's controversial aspects, such as how a posted video could shape a future jury, weren't going to get resolved tomorrow. The argument against posting was that if you have a video that shows a possible crime in progress, turn it over to the appropriate legal authorities so that the evidence can be reviewed impartially. The counterargument was "Turn it over? You've got to be kidding. We're trying to shame the police into changing." In her next sentence Julia reinforced that.

"Some of the guys over here last night think the government is behind the power outages and will use them as an excuse for martial law."

"That sounds ripped out of the playbook of right-wing nuts, not your crazy liberal vigilantes," I said.

"I'm just saying. Look, I'm a spy here, UG. I'll gather intelligence, and FBI SWAT can do a huge raid on the fire pit."

"Would we get more than wine and dope?"

"You'd get a lot of that. Did I tell you I've got an interview for a job this afternoon? It would just be temporary, but at least I'll be earning money. I've got to get ready soon. Do you want to see my room?"

We looked in at her room. Small but with two operable windows and worn oak-strip flooring. There was a single bed and a desk, and she told me she was ordering things from Amazon. We finished the tour in the kitchen, which had an electric cooktop and an island bar with blue Mexican tile. Wineglasses were near the sink, and a half-empty bottle of vodka bookended three cookbooks. "These girls are bomb," Julia said. "It's going to be fun, and I'm going to seriously check out Long Beach State. After I put my room together I'll send you and Jo photos. This is the best thing I could think to do, at least for now. I'm sorry for how I've messed up."

"I'm glad you're checking out Long Beach State."

"I'm not running away."

"I know you're not."

"I told Detective Allred I'd call every day. He said I could just leave a message on his cell, so I'm doing that. The deal is he'll only call me if he has a reason. Thank you for making me call Erica Roberts. I like her. She's smart and pretty cool. I get what could happen. Everyone thinks I'm pretty naïve, but if you live around an FBI agent you pick up things."

She gave me a sly smile, and I asked, "Are you talking to Agent Egbert?"

"Yes, and she said she was going to tell you, so I think I can. The tracker didn't work. Nothing worked. They left the box out on a dirt road in the desert. There's something else, UG, I should have told you. I screwed up and loaned Nick money. Don't ask how much. Too much. Any ideas on how to get it back?"

"First we catch him. Would Samantha have any ideas where to look for him?"

"It's Sam. Everybody calls her Sam. I don't know why you have to call her Samantha, and Nick isn't her problem. He's mine."

"But she knows him and she's your friend and can talk to him. He took over her apartment lease in Las Vegas, right? And didn't you deliver some things to her from him?"

She dismissed that with a shrug, and I said, "Those are my only ideas for getting the money back unless you can get ahold of one of his credit cards."

She didn't see the humor in that. Not long after, I left. I heard the front door shut softly behind me as I walked to my car. It was an empty place to leave things. Driving away I felt I'd missed a chance to tell her how much I want life to work out well for her. I hoped this move led to good things. She and Jo were my family. I had more I wanted to say, but the timing wasn't right. Today was just about a house tour and Julia trying to assuage my concerns.

She called Jo later, and much later Jo called me.

19

JULIA

Julia had wanted to tell UG but somehow just couldn't. She sat on the couch and wept after he left. Even as she'd toured UG around, she'd known she wasn't going to stay in this house. She couldn't stay here. On the drive through the desert from Las Vegas, she'd pulled off the freeway at an overpass and found a place to park, then waited there until her body stopped trembling and she could drive again. Her face was streaked with sweat all because she was listening to news reports on bombings. Her heart had pounded so hard.

Get over it, she'd told herself as she'd started driving again, but hearing any news about the substation bombings triggered things she'd thought she was over. Now she wondered if she ever would be over them. And last night, outside around the fire pit, they were talking about the bombings, and she'd explained away the shine on her face as heat from the fire and drinking wine. She'd only had a little wine, and it was chilly. What had disturbed her was their talk, the way they sort of probed each other and looked at her, wondering aloud if a bombing was a good thing.

A good thing? *They don't know anything,* she'd thought. *They don't know what they're saying.* She'd flashed back to the Alagara and all the blood around her when she'd regained consciousness after the bombing.

She remembered they carried her out, and she'd tried to look for her parents when they went through the bar area, and the paramedic guy held her head so all she could see was the ceiling and the hole in it. He wouldn't let her look. Just remembering that made her feel sick.

Forget the power outages, the rotting food in markets, the car accidents, the clinics, schools, and businesses closed, dialysis machines that didn't work, computers down, and on and on and on. Forget all that. That wasn't what got her. It was the casualness of talking about bombings as if they could be good.

Like the hundreds of windows broken and all the chemicals released in the substation fires, like that, and cops working overtime driving everywhere, and guards at the other substations and everything electrical, all that money spent for what? To destroy something without first building or knowing what you're going to build didn't work for her. She couldn't deal with that thinking.

Above all, Julia knew she couldn't handle being around bombings. Couldn't even tell UG that she'd been wrong to move here, because she couldn't deal with making yet another mistake. She couldn't leave, but she couldn't stay and was unsure what to do. She'd written the rent check the first night, and they'd just put it on a kitchen counter and said, "Not yet." They wouldn't take it, because once they did, there was no refund. This morning it was gone, so she'd wasted more of her parents' money.

You have to be tougher, she thought. *You have to stay. You cannot cut and run. Make yourself stronger. If they talk about bombings, get into the conversation and tell them you lived through one. Tell them. It was a mistake moving in, but now you're here. Change clothes. Get ready. Go do the interview. You have to figure this out on your own.* That was it. No more Nicks. No more mistakes. No more blaming other people.

20

Los Angeles, April 26th

Late that night Jo called and said, "Julia told me what she believes Nick did. It made me quite sad. She's not one hundred percent sure of everything. Some of it is like a dream. She was out with Nick and his friend Joel. They went to dinner and were at a club listening to music and dancing. Nick didn't want to dance, so she danced with Joel, then they all went to a party in Summerlin. Julia said she and Nick were in a weird space. She drank at the party but not much. She knows she's been drinking too much."

"She volunteered that?"

"She did and we talked about that after. On the way back to Nick's apartment, they bought whiskey and beer. She and Nick had been having problems, and she was close to breaking up with him. Joel drove. She was in the front seat talking with Joel. Nick wanted to sit alone in back. On the drive, Nick was talking weird."

"What's talking weird mean?"

"Joking with Joel they only had one girl between them and then saying to Joel, 'You can try her tonight.'"

"Try Julia?"

"Julia said she turned around and got in his face. He apologized, said he didn't mean that at all. When they got to Nick's apartment, Nick put his arm around her and said he was very sorry and didn't mean what she thought she heard. You with me so far?" Jo asked.

"Yes."

"In the apartment they put on music and poured a round of whiskeys. Julia didn't want any more hard alcohol, so she poured a beer in a water glass. Now they're sitting around joking and talking. She finishes the beer. At some point later she uses the bathroom. When she comes back, her beer is half full again. Nick is drinking the rest of the bottle, and they're watching her. She can feel something has changed."

"She remembers with this level of clarity?"

"I'm telling you what she told me."

"Okay."

"They start talking again, and she stops thinking about the beer and slowly drinks it. The next thing she remembers is waking up Sunday morning on a rug out in the main room wearing only a T-shirt. She thinks she woke up when the apartment door shut, and that might have been Joel leaving. She goes to the bedroom and looks in. Nick wasn't there and, in her words, 'the bedroom smelled totally like dope.'

"She found her clothes folded on a chair in the kitchen, which upset her. She didn't understand it. She took a shower and knew she'd been with somebody and assumed it was Nick but couldn't understand why she woke up on the rug. She left. She came home."

Jo paused, then said, "I remember that Sunday morning. I had gone to the hospital early to check on a patient. When I got home Julia was there. We got sandwiches for lunch at that new deli a couple of hours later."

"Did she say anything then?" I asked.

"No, but she was very distracted. I remember that. She said today that she knew when we were together on Sunday something wrong had happened the night before. Wednesday morning she started to get little flashes of hazy memory. She remembered Nick slowly undressing her in the bedroom. She thinks she remembers him taking her hand and leading her into the front room and a soft comforter or something they sat down on. On Wednesday night she remembered Joel with his shirt off, and he may have been kissing her. The next day she remembered more. And more since then, including sex with Joel, though she's not positive about that. She remembers Nick standing over her holding his phone. She's certain she was drugged."

Jo paused again, then said, "There's more detail, but Julia asked me not to say anything more."

"I understand."

I did. I got it. Julia wanted me to hear enough details to know it really had happened.

"I'll help find him," I said. "He's planned his escape and his new life, but I'll find him."

"I can tell you as a doctor all of this would be difficult to prove unless she is pregnant, and Julia uses birth control. You know how hard it would be in all the other ways to bring charges, and it doesn't sound like she wants to. She also blames herself."

"Family trait."

"She's been told the video is her and this friend of his having sex."

"Who told her?"

"She didn't say."

"Police can get this friend, Joel, into an interview box and talk rape. I can make that happen."

"She said you would say that. She doesn't want to do that but is very worried the video will ruin her life, and not just temporarily but permanently."

I didn't answer. I was thinking about how to heat up the fugitive hunt for Nick Knowles.

"Paul?"

"I'm here."

"Let her talk to you when she's ready. It won't be long. But let her do it her own way."

"This is rape we're talking about."

"I know what it is better than you, but let her tell you her own way. Her focus right now is on the video."

"When he hears what he's going to be charged with I'll bet Joel will give up Nick, especially after he hears there's a fugitive warrant out for Knowles."

"Julia knew you'd say that and doesn't want to do anything yet. She's hoping Nick will get arrested on the fugitive warrant and won't be able to post the video. Let's hope it happens that way," Jo said.

I wasn't as hopeful.

"What do you think of what you heard, Jo?"

She knew what I was asking, and she'd heard more accounts of rape than I ever would.

"She told you she was raped," Jo said.

"What she said was, 'I think he drugged me and his friend Joel raped me, or I had sex with him because I was drugged.' I don't know if that's it word for word, but it was very close to that. She wanted to talk to you next. She didn't want me to talk to you."

"Are you telling me you were unsure if it was rape?"

"It was rape. They drugged her drink and I want her to go to the police so they can pick up Joel and start breaking him down."

"She's not ready for that. Julia is in deep distress and running from a betrayal of a grotesque kind. She needs us. The very best thing we can do is support her until she's ready to go to the police. I know you don't understand waiting and I'm not sure I do, but for now just support her. Can you do that?"

I could do that and find this Joel too.

21

In the early 1960s, after the federal push to build dams on the Columbia River, hydroelectric power became cheap. So cheap it was worth building a transmission line from The Dalles, Oregon, to the LA Basin. That line runs 846 miles and ends at the Sylmar Converter Station at the northeast end of the San Fernando Valley. From the station, power is distributed to five utilities. It's the largest, most sophisticated station in the world and floats like a ghost ship on the horizon in my nightmares.

I'd driven past it three or four times since moving to LA. Additional police patrols watched it. National Guard troops are stationed there, yet I still see gaps. I've pushed Fuentes and I'd dogged Caltrans. Caltrans has the equipment to move in heavy concrete barricades, but they're swamped with other requests, and Sylmar won't see more defensive measures installed until next week.

That afternoon, with Jace in San Francisco, and Mark and I here, we worked off a shared screen using the Bureau's map of all known electrical-grid and cell attacks. It showed all attacks in every state. After looking at nearby western states for similarities, we enlarged California. Below each of the four LA substations bombed was the word "ANFO" in black. The four were now known as the HALO attacks: Hollywood, Anza, Lake, and Olin.

I moved the map up to Klamath Falls, Oregon, and switched to split screen with a Google Earth view as well. On the Google Earth map, we followed the high-tension lines south through forest and mountains and across farmland in the California Central Valley. I scrolled until Los Banos was at the top of the page, then LA. Farther south the recorded attacks thinned.

"If we go to Mexico, I want to shop for a new swimsuit first," Jace said.

"Be patient," I said. "We're looking at where they've concentrated and where they haven't. With the National Guard deployed and local police patrolling, substations are becoming harder targets, so I'm following the high transmission lines."

"You've been pitching high transmission lines since the attacks started. Let's look at thefts of explosives before we wrap this up."

Several break-ins at mine hives, facilities storing mining explosives, had occurred in the past six months. We vetted ideas several more hours and ended up with a list that might or might not mean anything, then signed off with Jace. I felt better for the back-and-forth, but an unsettled, restless feeling still lingered.

Toward dusk, Fuentes stopped me as I returned to the conference room where I was working. Can't seem to work in the bullpen anymore. I need more space and quiet.

"You're based in the Vegas office, so you're probably more up on Palo Verde," Fuentes said. "We just heard they're evacuating all but essential personnel. Have you been following this?"

"Yes."

"What's your take?" he asked.

"That there's something else going on they're not talking about."

"Like what?"

"A virus embedded in some ancillary piece of equipment that keeps reappearing. Have you ever heard of the Aurora Experiment?"

"No."

"Idaho National Laboratory did an experiment with a cyberattack where they rapidly opened and closed diesel-generator circuit breakers. That resulted in explosions that destroyed them. I don't know if it can happen in a similar way, but something took out the second line of pumps at Palo Verde, so now they're down to battery-powered pumps as the only means of getting water into the cooling towers. The batteries are only good for seventy-two hours. If they can't get water flowing, they know what their estimated time to meltdown is. But I'm betting they'll figure something out. They'll bring in more batteries. They'll do something to buy time. They have to."

"That's all you've got?"

"Do I look like a nuclear scientist?"

He smiled and left.

22

At 4:30 the next morning a call came in to the LA FBI office reporting that a private security guard had been shot and killed in his pickup during an attack on a high-voltage transformer along the southern face of the Tehachapi Mountains. Hofter and I arrived in the early morning. We'd seen the dawn and nearer saw the smoke column from the fires.

County sheriff's deputies had secured an area surrounding the pickup. Firefighters streamed jets of water onto the fires. The power had been rerouted, the grid adjusted to account for the lost transformers. Two county detectives were there but waiting for a Bureau evidence-recovery team that was on its way. Shell casings and slugs would get collected from the transformers and from the body during autopsy.

The security guard was a vet discharged a year ago, married with a kid, and with two jobs trying to make it all work. He was slumped in the driver's seat, his shirt reddened and torn by bullet holes large enough to make me think it was the same weapon used to punch through the transformers' steel casings.

The victim's wife arrived with her two-year-old boy. She collapsed, distraught and sobbing. The boy began to cry as well. I knelt beside her. Words and tears flowed from her.

She kept repeating, "How could this happen here?"

Her husband earned fifteen dollars an hour to guard the facility at night. There was no restroom. There was nothing up here but equipment. The utility required that any independent contractor providing security had to sign papers agreeing to hold the utility harmless should anything happen. Her husband had worried over that. Anger at the utility's attitude and indifference spilled out of her.

"They don't care about anything except their money. People come up here, drink, and leave their trash. Look at it all. They don't even clean up. Mike cleaned it up. He couldn't stand it." She looked at me and repeated the question she'd asked many times. "Who would do this?"

I could tell her the shooter was caught on video approaching the truck from behind, but that wouldn't help her at all. The shooter wore a hoodie that would make identification from the surveillance footage difficult. A rifle that could be an assault rifle became visible as he reached the tailgate, followed by muzzle flashes. He retreated the way he'd arrived, down the slope behind the truck. Another security camera—this one well down the access road—recorded a Chevy Tahoe passing by twelve minutes after the shooting. It was angled such that it did not cleanly record the license plates but delivered clean images of the vehicle's left side and corner. The Tahoe's paint was likely dark blue or black.

A utility security manager arrived and sought out the victim's wife. I overheard him start to talk procedure, his back to her husband's pickup, with her numb and dead to his words and her boy crying. He moved in front of her as she tried to turn away. That was too much for me.

"Lose yourself," I said. "Find something else to do."

Black smoke from burning transformer oil rose for another hour into the clear morning sky before the fire crew shut it down. The last dark smoke folded east in the wind, and Mark and I got a good look at a bullet-pocked transformer casing. A utility manager told us it was 5/8" steel. That made high-caliber armor-piercing bullets a good choice for damaging the copper coils inside. To me that said one type of weapon was used to kill the guard and take out the cameras, and a different weapon to punch through the steel.

I suited up and glopped through oily water and foam the fire crew had used. I took photos and shot video and learned enough to say it was someone spraying bullets from a close range and without much gun skill or knowledge of electrical transformers. But enough rounds were shot—hundreds, judging from the casings—that they'd overwhelmed the transformers. Out here no one would have heard a thing.

When I waded out of the oily water and took off the mask, I met the engineer in charge of the facility.

He said, "I was told to get my ass up here, make a damage assessment, and talk to you."

By then the guard's body was out of the pickup and bagged. The mother and child were gone, and a tow truck was standing by to load his pickup. Two news helicopters circled overhead. I talked louder so he could hear me above their noise.

"Can you switch out these transformers, or are they custom made?" I asked.

"They're custom, so three months minimum to replace them. We'll work around the problem."

"And if you can't?"

"More rolling blackouts. Nothing else we can do about it."

He was six foot one, my height, and with a buzz cut that reminded me of a 1960s astronaut. He talked shop for a while, and though I couldn't follow a lot of it, I learned more, and he was generous in his explanations of what I didn't get.

When we left, the sky was the blue of a robin's egg, and the transformer facility looked small from the highway. As we got back to LA, Mark surprised me by saying, "The guard's wife loved him. My wife would never cry like that. She'd be on the phone to the life insurance company while I was still warm. Then for her friends and followers she'd Instagram a photo of me. I take that back. It would be a video."

"Catching your last breath?"

"Yeah, something like that, the last heave and a close-up of my lips turning blue. I'm serious. She's over me. She thought being married to an FBI agent would be exciting. It didn't turn out that way. I'm late. I'm not home when I say I'll be. I don't come home because some dip-shits blow up something. When I go off on some training thing, she thinks it's a vacation I got that she missed. I get home late, exhausted. I shower, get in bed, and what does she do? Does she roll over toward me? No chance. She slides the other way. She's turned mean and quick as a snake. The kids are scared to death of her."

He exhaled and sighed.

"Other than that, are you guys good?" I asked.

He laughed, smiled, and then laughed again. "Yeah, other than that we're golden."

Later I heard an NPR report on three more blackouts and one happy story with a hacker in Portland who'd helped utility engineers overcome repeated attacks. The hacker had a one-man business but had come forward and volunteered. He'd showed up uninvited and became the feel-good story of the day, in striking contrast to the dead guard, destroyed transformers, and a school bus crash in Tennessee that killed seven kids when a stoplight stopped working due to a cyberattack and an 18-wheeler broadsided the bus.

The guard's death disturbed me on several levels. I saw a war vet in the night in his pickup, trying to make ends meet, with his wife and son at home. I'd heard the facility engineer disparage him for falling asleep. We've made our military all volunteer, and the result is the middle and lower-middle classes have stepped up and carried our water. They've done tour after tour as the rest of us put the wars out of mind. How many of us know the longest war in the history of this country is Afghanistan?

Here's this vet, home trying to figure out a way to make it working two jobs, and his wife gets berated after he gets shot and killed. I can't live with that. I really can't. At a minimum, I owe them finding his killer.

23

Late that morning from the LA office I returned a call from Sheriff Callan in Butte County, where we'd met Gary Farue at Tower 36. Callan's office was in Oroville, an hour north of Sacramento. We'd become improbable phone buddies. He called sometimes just to talk about life. I took his calls because he didn't linger on the line, and like a lot of cops, it was his habit to communicate information orally. He'd also left a message that I saw was his but hadn't listened to yet.

This morning he was sick with a throat thing that he'd had for a month but now burned like hell. Last night he'd tried whiskey and warm water. His wife thinks it's strep, but her way of diagnosing is to type "sore throat" on Google.

"Did you listen to my message?" he asked.

"Talk me through it."

"This is coming from the same grow-field farmer who gave us the cell-tower shooter tip," he said. "He thinks the sniper is camping in a back canyon not more than a mile from him."

"How would he know?"

"He lives out of those woods. He's a marijuana grower, a dope guy with a field somewhere else and not in my county. He camps up there because a friend of his was killed one night sleeping near his grow field."

"You know an awful lot about him."

"That doesn't matter. What matters is he's pretty sure it's the same guy he saw come off Buckhorn Ridge. He's gotten a good look at the guy coming and going."

Callan coughed and held the phone away. I heard his chair squeak, heard him catch his breath, then continue.

"Are you hearing me?" he asked.

"You're saying he thinks the sniper who shot up Tower 36 camps in the area on and off."

"That's right, and I know you don't believe it, so here's the next piece, which you'll believe even less. He watched a man and a woman hike in yesterday late afternoon. There are only a few ways in and out of those canyons."

"Are you going to tell me she was blond?"

"Yes."

"You're late. We've had ten thousand tips already. We're on our way to identifying every blond woman in the state, so I'm just going to cut to it. You know this dope grower or you wouldn't be calling me. Why is he credible to you?"

"He's my sister's son. She died. I keep an eye on him. I've known him his whole life. I trust him."

"Your nephew is the anonymous caller?"

"Didn't I just say that?"

"And he's putting the Blond Bomber, her companion, and the Tower 36 sniper in the same woods. Is there a wooden sign with 'Terror Camp' and an arrow pointing toward the trail?"

"You're not listening. He's not putting them together. He hasn't seen them with the sniper. As far as he knows, they're not even in the same canyon, and the sniper is only there on and off. He's gone for days and then back. He must know he's safe there. He probably leaves his gear hidden. There's trailhead parking far enough back from the highway that the most likely thing to break into his vehicle would be a bear."

"Does your nephew know what he drives?"

"No."

Callan coughed hard again and said, "Hold a minute." He dropped his phone with a clack, and I heard him hacking as I texted Jace and Mark, Need to talk in the next ten minutes. I'll call.

"Sorry about that," Callan said. "I was about to say I grew up near there. I know the area very well. There are three canyons with streams running through them. My brother and I used to camp there all the time. If I send deputies in to look, they'll stick to the trails but tell me they climbed everywhere. You've got to get on the rock for a view into the canyons, and my deputies don't do rock. A couple of them can barely climb stairs, and FBI agents aren't much in the woods. No, they're worthless, so I don't think sending a posse of Bureau agents makes sense."

"You'd like me to come there."

"It's actually federal land, so I might need you. And a spotter plane if you can get one. Or just get me permission and I'll do it alone."

He would do it alone and have no problem with it. Jace labeled Callan a relic of a former age, but we all are at some point. My counterargument was that local law enforcement agencies that kept close tabs on their counties might be our best chance of stopping the physical attacks.

"Your card says you're a bomb tech," Callan said. "Did you get that limp mishandling a bomb? You were dragging a little when we were up on Buckhorn Ridge. I'm asking if your leg is all right walking across rock."

"I have bomb injuries but made it back to active duty."

"I'm not asking about your career. I'm asking if you can cross a steep slope and climb open rock, not just loose talus."

"I'll be fine."

"When is the last time you did that?"

"It's been a while."

"How'd you get hurt?"

"I was working as a bomb tech in Iraq. A motorcycle blew up in a market in Bagdad."

"You and I hike in and have a look, and we seal the exits with my deputies. The only road out goes through my county. We'll go in as tree surveyors checking on spring growth. Plan on a long day. Call me back today if you're one hundred percent on coming. I'm going either way. You decide. Yes or no."

Reacting without enough information is what I coach younger agents not to do. I'd have to drop everything, fly to Sacramento, and drive to Oroville or wherever Callan names as a rendezvous point. I guess he wasn't looking for an answer just yet. He hung up.

24

That afternoon Samantha Clark showed up at the office asking for me, which raised a protocol issue, since I'm not working the Signal Hill officer slayings. LA County Sheriff's detectives owned that investigation. Agents Sara Decca and Bruce Lorimar were assisting.

"Check with Decca and Lorimar, then go say hello to her," Fuentes said. "Let's find out why she's here."

I called Decca, who said, "I don't like it, but it's okay with us."

I shook hands with Clark. Fame and the subsequent notoriety hadn't done her any favors. But few deal well with either. She was about the same height as Julia and dressed a similar way. I took in more of her, lean in tight jeans, a body-hugging shirt, and sandals, with her toenails painted lime green.

"Call me Sam," she said. "Everyone else does."

"All right, Sam."

"I know the shooting of the Long Beach officers is not your investigation, and the Sheriff's Bureau detectives have told me not to talk to anyone else, but more came back to me last night. This will sound crazy, but I might be able to identify the gunman, but I don't want to do this with LA County detectives or the FBI agents I've been interviewed by one too many times."

"They're here, and at least one will need to be in the room."

"Can I be blunt?"

"Go ahead."

"Agent Decca is a bitch."

She said that with a vehemence I really didn't like.

"The other agent, her partner or whatever he is, is fine. I don't remember his name. He was like a lamp on a side table, but I'm not dealing with her again."

Sara Decca I've known twenty years. Lorimar the lamp I didn't know well, but he seemed like a capable guy.

"It's not my call," I said. "Have you let the county detectives know you remember more?"

"Not yet."

"I'll go talk to the agents. You okay waiting here?"

"I'm fine."

"She's the poster child for self-absorption," Decca said after I told her and Lorimar why Clark was here. "Bullshit, her memory has come back. More like your niece moved to Long Beach and Clark sees some reason to reach out to you. How do you read it? Don't tell me you believe her."

"Same as you, she's after something."

When Lorimar walked into the interview room, he said, "Ms. Clark, thank you for caring enough to come in. That takes real courage."

"It's not courage; I'm just remembering more."

Lorimar nodded. "It took my grandfather twenty years to remember how two good friends who were right next to him were killed during World War II. So I know it can happen."

She began to describe the man's face as lean but not thin, eyes a little hooded from the bone at the eyebrow, a straight nose. She watched Lorimar with glances at me. Lorimar held a kind, sympathetic smile as I opened the file on my laptop that held six headshots Decca had just sent me. Clark would see three across the top, three on the bottom.

One of them Decca had put in to make a point to me about what she thought of this interview.

I turned my laptop so Clark and Lorimar were looking at the screen. All six headshots showed. Only one was a mug shot. Two were from surveillance video and grainy black and white. Three were in color. Clark didn't react to the differences. She looked at Lorimar watching her, then back at the screen and at me.

"Click on any you want to enlarge," I said.

"Of course, we're not saying any of these are the man you saw," Lorimar said. "These six are based on your description and who the detectives have as possible shooters. We're getting closer to him. We have other evidence we're working." That wasn't true but Lorimar was right, we needed a little bump. "There are more headshots if you want to see more," he said.

She touched a face on the screen and tapped it with her finger as she thought it over.

"I think this is him. It's definitely not any of the others."

"Okay, let me get rid of them and enlarge him," I said and turned the laptop around as Lorimar asked, "You're ruling out the other five?"

"Yes, yes, I am ruling them out." Her voice lit up as she added, "I really think that's him. You can't know what this feels like. It's been so awful to not remember and feel like the detectives doubt my honesty. It's been very hard."

She bowed her head and wordlessly moved to a meek posture as if the thing was done, the burden lifted. She sighed. She exhaled. She was good. She almost had me believing she'd identified the shooter and felt redeemed.

"I know the light wasn't great," I said. "What spilled from the restaurant and the Chevron is all you had."

I said that, then checked myself and shut up. That was Lorimar's to say, not mine.

"Here's something I remember," she said. "His shoulders are really square. It's not like a big confirming thing, but I notice shoulders a lot. He's sort of 'military square posture.' Do you know what I mean?"

I turned the laptop for Lorimar and asked him, "What do you think?"

What Lorimar thought was what I thought: the military will do that to you.

The FBI agent she identified had been a naval officer for five years.

"The hoodie he was wearing was thin," she said. "I could tell when he ran toward them what his build was like. He's in good shape but not stiff, not a chunk of muscle like a weightlifter, more like fast, quick, and strong. Like I told you before. He closed the gap fast."

She gave me a shy smile and said, "I'm embarrassed and humiliated. I don't know why it all came back so slowly."

"We're just glad it did," Lorimar said.

The naval officer turned FBI agent worked out of the Las Vegas field office. He was a good guy and would be happy to hear about his shoulders, but nothing Clark had said would help solve the murders.

"There was much more light when he stood in front of me at the restaurant window. That's where my memory jumped around most. But I have him now, and really it's because of his eyes. He looked at me for a second before he turned and ran."

Lorimar shifted a little, and I willed him to stop. We weren't going to drop it on her that she had gotten the wrong man, but I could tell Lorimar wanted to. I also got a strong feeling she'd just mixed in something true, which was spooky.

The shooter had looked into her eyes. She said it with particular force, yet she had just picked an FBI agent as the shooter. Was she trying to communicate something else?

"He didn't look to see if they were dead. He turned away as the second cop was collapsing, looked at me, and then hurried down the right side of the lot. I couldn't tell anything about the car that picked him up. Nothing has changed there.

"His nose is right. I remembered a mole on his right cheek, but he doesn't have one. I thought he had a bigger mouth. I'm positive it's him." She smiled and added, "I'm the one with the big mouth."

I could almost hear Decca gag. Lorimar leaned in and said, "If you had to put a percentage on how certain you are it's him, what would that percentage be?"

"I'm actually one hundred percent sure."

25

That same afternoon, Mara called from the Vegas office and said, "I've got bad news. Your house was broken into and vandalized last night. A neighbor across the street heard banging and what she thought was gunfire. She called her son who's a Vegas police officer."

I knew her son but couldn't remember a burglary on the street as long as I'd lived there. With the power outages it made sense burglars would adapt fast, but burglars aren't vandals. In a quiet voice he continued.

"I sent two agents by half an hour ago. They say it's a mess. The back patio slider was pried out. Your kitchen cabinets are in the pool. Inside, it looks like someone walked through with a sword and fought a battle with your furnishings. The agents didn't see a burglar alarm. Do you have one?"

"No."

"You may want to rethink that," Mara said.

"Thanks, Ted. I'll do that."

"Do you know a handyman or someone who can put up some plywood? If you don't, I've got a guy. And you're cleared to come home. We're treating this as possibly work related."

"I can't come home," I said. "I'm flying to Sacramento tonight to meet up with the Butte County sheriff early tomorrow. Did you get my message about that?"

"I did. I'm just saying you can reschedule."

"Not really, not for this."

I'd left him a message as to where I was going but not the purpose, in part because I was still skeptical of the quality of Sheriff Callan's lead.

"Is anyone else staying at your house?"

"Julia moved to Long Beach, so no."

"What about your girlfriend?"

"She has a house. I've got an old carpenter friend. I'll give him a call," I said.

"Give him my number and call your insurance agent."

This was the Mara everyone liked. He could be selfless and generous and ever the problem solver.

"Has anything like this ever happened before?" Mara asked.

"No."

"Anyone ever threaten you?"

"Sure, but most of those have promised to come kill me, so they'd make sure I was home first."

"You can joke about this?"

"Not really."

"Who comes to mind, Grale?"

"Julia's ex-boyfriend, Nick Knowles, but he has a lot of reasons not to be within a thousand miles of there."

When our call ended I called a carpenter friend, Dan Jenkins, who had a one-man handyman business. Dan said he'd pick up plywood and deal with the slider today. I texted him Mara's number, and Mara went by in the afternoon and helped him carry plywood into the backyard. Then he videotaped the damage and sent it to me.

I watched the video on my laptop with Jace after I arrived at the Sacramento field office near twilight. The damage was systematic and depressing. In the living room, the leather couch I'd bought last year was slashed, as were the chairs and shades. So was a desert painting I'd bought from a woman known as Nora the Dawn Artist in Ocotillo

Wells. I don't know much about art, but that painting always moved me. It saddened me more than most of the other damage to see that canvas cut open.

Spray-painted graffiti was in symbols and signature marks unfamiliar to me. Mara said it smelled as if an acid was splattered on the hardwood floors and mattresses. Bedding and clothes jerked out of the closet were urinated on. When the kitchen cabinets were pried off the walls, glasses and dishes had slid onto the floor and shattered.

"Home, sweet home," I said and froze the video on a photo of my parents and me, the three of us along a lakeshore on one of the family summer trips.

"Could it be an old girlfriend?" Jace asked.

I smiled, but little was left untouched. *Systematic, unabashed, and unconcerned about noise, real anger,* I thought. Tile counters and the porcelain toilet tanks were shattered, holes punched in walls with a mallet or small sledgehammer. Something with a five-pound head that could be wielded fast and hard. Clothes in dresser drawers were coated in motor oil. Mara had videotaped it all.

"Mara is thorough as a videographer," Jace said. "Do you have any known enemies, anyone that's alluded to getting even?"

"No, everyone loves me. I'm going to give Mara a quick call before we get on with things here."

Mara answered right away and said, "Did you watch the video?"

"Just did. There's a photo with my parents and me that was shot at."

"Oh, that's what the photo was. It's damaged enough that I couldn't tell. The gunshots took out each head. There were .22 shell casings on the other side of the room. I'm surprised they left them there. I'm not saying they shot from there and hit three small heads in a photograph. If they did, that's one damn good shooter. I collected them to see if we can pull DNA, though from the smears it looks like the shooter wore gloves. I'm sorry, Grale."

"Let me know on the DNA."

I doubted there would be any. Heat usually burns DNA off a shell casing. But was it a statement? Was the shooting done from across the room and the casings left where they fell? It was just possible.

I had to compartmentalize it and put it aside. Jace and I ate a couple of dry sandwiches as we talked, then conferenced in with Manfred, the data tech at FBI headquarters I'd worked with the past nine months.

Last fall I was on the grid task force, and we'd started to see shooting attacks on cell towers that differed from typical vandalism. That's when I struck up a conversation with Manfred about how to map the attacks and the characteristics of them. Our task force focused on western states, and there the cell-tower shootings were very spread out. You could read them as two guys with their rifles and couple of six-packs of beer practicing for deer season, except they were hitting receivers and transceivers with surprising accuracy and purpose.

By March this year they'd intensified and were beginning to show more pattern, and Manfred was including more data. In March he'd done a run for us on California, Oregon, Nevada, and Arizona. He was the only person I knew who sounded excited when we talked about the electrical pathways, 66 and 15. He was three hours ahead of us into the night yet sounded ready to go at it. In California he'd modeled correlations between cell-tower attacks and nearby subsequent attacks on the electrical grid. He and I were on the same hunt for a pattern.

That night I sent Mara's videos to my insurance guy. He wouldn't like them. He was thirty-five and just hitting his stride. His haircut was that of a rock star. He drove a low-slung BMW and was a friendly and exuberant guy, but this was a messy claim.

I told myself most of what was in the house was just stuff and didn't matter. *Get the kitchen put back together. Get the house cleaned and operable. Redo the floors you were going to redo anyway, paint, put in new locks, and install two cameras.* That's the way I'd deal with it for now, all the while knowing I was ignoring the violation of privacy and the statement made by whoever did it.

Later that night in a small hotel in Oroville, darker thoughts seeped in. Call them visions of retribution. Well before dawn I made coffee. I checked messages and e-mail, and scanned the headlines before driving to meet Callan. At Palo Verde, the Army Corps had joined the fight to keep the cooling towers functional. "Exodus from Phoenix" was a *New York Times* headline. Accompanying the article was a photo of a long ribbon of headlights weaving through the desert. In an odd way it was rather beautiful.

26

Callan's throat was so bad he could barely talk as we crossed a scree field in the early cold air. When we rested he was still quiet but pointed out where we were headed, the base of a granite escarpment across the slope.

"From there we'll have a view into the first canyon," he said. "A little further on we'll be able to see into all three."

I nodded and asked, "Are you feeling any better?"

He didn't answer at first and stared at where we were headed next.

"I saw a doctor, well, two of them yesterday. It didn't go well. It's not good, Grale."

I dreaded what was coming. I've heard that anxiety-laden yet withdrawn tone enough in life to know what it often presages. I always feel sorrow at the shocked and quiet voices of those sharing this very personal sad news.

"It's advanced metastatic disease," he said. "That's what they called it. It's cancer. I told Mary last night."

"Mary is your wife?" I asked.

"For almost fifty years. She didn't understand me coming out here today. She broke down."

"What about kids?"

"A son and a daughter. My daughter lives in the East and only talks to me on holidays. I was a hard father. They want to do more tests the day after tomorrow."

"What are you doing out here, John?"

"I'm doing what I do. It's the best thing I can think of. They're going to try radiation and chemo, and if the tumors shrink enough they'll operate. Of course, you can hear as they talk they know I'm gone." He looked at me and said, "Let's start walking again." When we started he said, "I don't really know what else to do."

"No matter how it works out, be sure you make time to talk things through with your daughter."

"I should. I really should. She has said some hard things to me. I was young. I didn't know how to deal with the stress of being a cop and took it home."

"That was then," I said. "Talk to her."

"I haven't crossed this face in forty-one years," he said. "See that stand of pines sagging up there under that little rock overhang? That's where we'll get a view into all three canyons. They each have streams that feed the creek running through the valley."

"What do I tell the pilot?" I asked.

"Tell him an hour and a half because I have you slowing me down." He attempted a smile then said, "I will talk to her."

"Is she as stubborn as you?"

"Worse. Your spotter-plane pilot will need to fly by as slow as possible. When I was young I was up here all the time with my brother, Jeff. We did everything together. He got killed in Nam in the Mekong delta." After a beat he added, "Another wasted war."

"And you didn't come back here after that?" I asked.

"I tried, but it was different. It changed."

An hour and a half later we looked down into the canyons. I talked with the pilot, who was at horizon in a Cessna closing in. I could hear the faint thrum of the plane's engine, but it took me a moment to find him in the sky. Callan had binoculars up and was scouring the canyon from the shade of the pine stand. He spotted a bear bag hanging in a tree.

"It looks like somebody is camping in the first canyon, and it's a big bear bag," he said. "If a bear sees that, he won't stop thinking about it the rest of his life. I don't see anybody down there. Let's go check it out."

We walked and slid down scree to the tree line, then followed a small stream flowing into the canyon. Anyone looking up at the rock would have spotted us. Callan must have heard me think that because he said, "Don't worry about it. We're tree surveyors."

I untied the rope and lowered the bear bag. It was waterproof and tough as the hide of a rhino, but I could feel hard objects inside and should have known right there I wasn't feeling food bags. I opened it slowly with Callan watching.

He said, "Aw, shit," and lifted his binoculars as I pulled out rocks. He called out, "Camera," and I looked up and saw a black plastic camera with a short antenna mounted high in a fir tree. For a moment I toyed with the idea the bear bag full of rocks and the camera trained on it were a grad student's black-bear thesis project. But that didn't fit. Their camera would be a bulky, boxy, ancient unit that weighed ten pounds. It would record but not transmit. This camera looked cutting-edge.

No doubt it had recorded us. Callan, who'd been county sheriff for twentysome-odd years, wouldn't be hard to identify. Neither would I if they did much of an Internet search.

"What would you do right now if you were them?" Callan asked.

"Leave fast and never return."

"Me too. We'll follow this stream down to the creek, to the main trail. That's our best move. If they know we're here they aren't going to waste time."

"Where's your nephew?" I asked.

"I told him stay away today, though taking instruction isn't his strong suit."

The spotter-plane pilot checked in. "I've got a man and possibly a woman breaking camp two canyons over, a half mile from you. They're in a hurry. One checked us out with glasses. One more thing, they've got a big dog."

We radioed the officers out on the road, then picked up a trail leading down to the main creek. At the creek's edge, Callan said, "We wade up to those rocks and hide behind them. It's shallow here and quicker than picking our way through the trees."

I didn't see that but followed him into the water then out and behind the rock outcrop. It was no more than a hundred yards upstream. As we got out and behind the rocks, he was coughing. He fumbled for medicine in the small backpack he carried. When he caught his breath, he didn't give me a chance to ask how he was doing.

He said, "My brother and I all but lived out here. Dad was the meanest son of a bitch ever born. We ate the same berries as the bears. Home was the wild. Here was safer."

The dog came first. Rottweiler. Big and trotting, stiff-legged, tan and brown, supple in sunlight. Behind the dog fifty steps or so came a young man moving fast. He could be the alleged husband in LA but hard to say. Dark haired. Olive skinned. I zoomed and took photos and video before he passed out of view. Then Callan tapped my arm, meaning don't move, don't breathe.

The dog had paused. Rottweiler hearing was better than that of many breeds, making them popular with police. It looked across the water in our direction for what felt like a full minute, then moved on.

Ten minutes later, when no one else had appeared, Callan asked, "What do you want to do?"

"Wait a little longer."

Twenty minutes passed. Callan was restless but deferred to me, and soon a young woman appeared. She was without a pack and running though carrying a rifle. She wore a knit cap and moved quietly as I took photos.

"That's her," I said. "That's her, and she cut her hair short but not off. And she didn't dye it. I'll be damned. That's definitely her, and we need her alive. Make certain they know that out at the road. How long to reach the road if we go back out behind them?"

"An hour, maybe less," Callan said and, still watching her, added, "This is not her first time moving down a trail with a rifle."

We let her disappear, then Callan radioed a deputy as I listened.

"A man and a woman are hiking out with a dog. When they passed us, half a mile separated them. The male is leading with a dog, a big Rottweiler. We're going to follow the woman, and so you know, this is not her first time moving down a trail with a rifle."

"Copy that, chief."

"There's more. The woman is the suspect in the LA bombings, the Blond Bomber. She's wearing a dark-blue T-shirt, jeans, and a knit cap. He's in shorts, a gray T-shirt, and blue Nike running shoes. We do not want a gun battle. We want them alive. Repeat that."

The deputy did as I thought about our next best move. If she was bringing up the rear hanging that far back, she was watching for anyone following. We didn't want to walk into her gun sights, so I asked Callan if he knew another way to get us out.

"It'll be slower," Callan said, "but you're right. Let's go. We cross the creek, and I'll take us out another way."

Half an hour later we heard gunfire, then return fire, and we stopped walking. I marked the time: 12:32 p.m.

"They must have run all the way out," I said.

"I would too."

Before we got out, a deputy radioed that the male was dead of multiple gunshot wounds. The dog was also dead, shot after it flushed a deputy hiding along the trail. The blond woman never appeared, and we later learned she'd done a U-turn, rousted the dope-growing nephew, Vance Sidle, out of his tent, and marched him four miles to where he kept his van hidden.

Vance was found barefoot and hypothermic near Mount Lassen at four the next morning. He'd been caught in a late-spring snow and hailstorm. The van was left on the shoulder twenty miles farther north. My guess is she rendezvoused with a ride.

Sidle was taken to a medical clinic in Chico. His potassium levels were high. If he'd been out much longer he likely would have died of hypothermia. He got lucky and was in a hospital bed sleeping when I walked in and woke him the next morning.

◆ ◆ ◆

"Am I busted?" Sidle asked as he looked around trying to figure out how to escape.

They were able to get him back with heated intravenous fluids, and he was definitely back and didn't want to answer questions. He closed his eyes as I slid a chair over.

"I was with your uncle Callan yesterday. I'm working the grid attacks. Your uncle called me when you told him that the people camping near you looked like the Blond Bomber and her friend. You were right, and I want everything you can tell me about her and him. How are you feeling?"

"I'm ready to get out of here," he said.

"Your uncle also told me you've seen the cell-tower sniper more than once back in the area. Is that true?"

"Yeah, same dude."

"Ever see him with the Blond Bomber or her friend?"

"No, those two just got there. The cell shooter dude comes and goes."

We were another hour getting him checked out, and he was very agitated about the bills he signed for. He didn't have medical coverage. I let him talk through that then got to it.

She had opened the flap of his tent with a rifle barrel, then marched him out four miles to his van. She sat behind him with her gun pointed at him as he drove. He'd seen tears running down her cheeks when he looked in his rearview mirror.

"She wanted to know why I'm living the way I am and what I want for the future. She said the second war for independence has started. I didn't know what she meant by that."

"Didn't she explain?"

"Yeah, we talked. Some of it I get."

"Were you surprised when she drove off and left you?"

"It sucked."

The closest field office was Sacramento, but I took him to San Francisco, where Jace and I could question him together. On the drive he told me more of what Balco had said to him about the rebellion. "Rebellion" was her word. She'd told him people would join them once they understood what they were trying to do. It was as improbable as an ISIS soldier dreaming of a caliphate, but if Sidle's account was true, she believed people were ready.

Sidle was nervous when we reached the field office. At the security checkpoint, he emptied his pockets, handed over his wallet, and took off his shoes, belt, and a ring. This procedure was so unfamiliar to him I realized he hadn't flown anywhere in a long time, if ever. In the interview room I tried to calm him.

"You're not under arrest, and I brought you here."

He looked at photos that included a woman named Laura Balco who early this morning had been identified as the Blond Bomber. Without hesitation he pointed to her. Balco's companion who died on the trail was in a morgue and would get identified soon. We didn't really need him to ID that man, so I focused on the mysterious third man who was the Tower 36 shooter and camped on and off in the area.

I mixed Corti's photo in with five that looked a lot like Corti, then spread them on a table in front of Sidle. It took him about five seconds to pick out Corti.

"I'm deadass sure," he said. "That's the cell-tower dude. He's not around much, but he comes back there. I never saw him with whatshername Balco or the dude the deputies popped, but they weren't there for that long."

I tried to get my head around the three of them in the same area. Wasn't coincidence, that was for sure, but I didn't have a good explanation today. And yet, Corti connected with them somehow. I dropped Sidle at a bus stop and gave him money to buy a ticket home. That night I dreamed of a long-ago painting. In it, warriors are bringing down a huge bison with spears and arrows. No single wound will be enough, but eventually the bison would drop to its knees, and the fatal wound would come.

27

In Klamath Falls, Oregon, an ANFO bomb in a retired school bus and another built in the bed of a Ford 350 diesel pickup exploded outside the Captain Jack substation at 2:46 a.m. The blasts interrupted the California-Oregon Intertie and woke people forty miles away. An intertie connects two or more utilities, but an easier way to think about it is scale. Hydroelectric power generated at dams north of Captain Jack and flowing toward California just got interrupted.

I caught a flight to Portland, and an FBI pilot ferried me southeast to Bend, where I rented a car and drove farther south to Klamath Falls. Like a number of other key substations, this one had been hardened with perimeter upgrades, but what the bombers did was simple and effective.

They brought four vehicles—cameras captured this. An ancient dump truck rolled up to the gate, maneuvered back and forth and blocked it. The bomb vehicles—the old school bus and Ford pickup— drove in opposite directions along the perimeter. The pickup broke off to the right and parked close to a set of towers that fed the substation from the north, bringing electricity generated at the dam. The bomb bus struggled with a sandy patch as it worked its way to the south towers. I saw the deep sandy tracks left behind after the bus made it through and nosed between two high transmission towers outside the fence on the southeast side at the start of the run to California.

Along a dirt road heading northwest away from the substation, a nondescript white Land Cruiser waited. After the bombers and the dump-truck driver climbed into it, the Land Cruiser drove slowly away.

Four minutes, eleven seconds later, at 2:46 a.m., the bombs detonated, bringing down the towers and severely damaging each of the next towers in the chain in either direction.

At the substation there was chaos and a frantic call for help from a battery-powered radio. The lone operator panicked, fearing the dump truck held another bomb. Who could blame him for scaling the fence and running rather than following shutdown procedures?

When I arrived, the dump truck had been moved and emergency power restored to the control building. I watched what video there was, then talked with the FBI bomb squad from Portland. The blast wave appeared similar to the LA bombs. No investigation would occur until the high-tension lines were cleared out of the way. The Portland squad didn't need me working the bomb site, but it was good to talk and share information.

We watched the surveillance video together. The getaway vehicle, the Land Cruiser, had five occupants, not four. The three drivers got in the back. In the front seats the driver was male, the individual in the passenger seat was likely a female.

A BOLO—be on the lookout—went out on the Land Cruiser, now identified as a 2007 model, to all of Oregon and Northern California. Locally, a hard push was made to find anybody who at that hour might have been outside or driving.

That push resulted in a resident of Klamath Falls coming forward on the condition he remain anonymous. His wife was out of town. He was returning from a friend's house at 3:30 in the morning. That friend was a close female friend of his wife. He was promised anonymity.

He'd seen an older white Land Cruiser southbound on Highway 140 and remembered it because there was next to no traffic, and he was watching every vehicle for anyone who might recognize him and wonder why he was out so late. CNN had his name before noon. An affiliate TV station sent a cameraman and a reporter. They knocked, and he opened his front door with his wife standing nearby.

The blast cut the school bus in half. I stood near the sandy white crater torn in the soil. *Enough is enough,* I thought. *We should, as of today, limit the size of vehicles anywhere near a substation anywhere in America.* I considered that as I walked a wider perimeter and found the school bus steering wheel thrown two hundred yards from the blast site.

As FBI agents and more police officers arrived, there was talk, but it was quiet talk. It could have been the wind making it hard to communicate, but I didn't think so. The repeated attacks were taking their toll. We were realizing how much of what we have is built on trust and how difficult it would be to protect without that.

"Should I fly there?" Jace asked.

"No need. There are a dozen agents out of the Portland field office here, but let's talk. It's ANFO again. It's similar if not the same bomb design as LA. Add up the ammonium nitrate used between them, and it's enough volume to where it's got to be a legitimate buyer."

"Doesn't have to be."

I said, "Okay, it doesn't, but it's leaning that way. I'm not saying the legitimate buyer would be a suspect, but ammonium nitrate is funneling from somewhere."

"Our analysts have looked at farms and other businesses using ammonium nitrate. We've got that report. I thought you read it."

"I did. But maybe we take another look with different criteria."

"Such as?"

"What farms," I said, "with significant regular orders of ammonium nitrate have changed hands in the last three years. No, make it five years, and let's zero in on the opaque entities and changes in crops versus five years ago. I don't think those get tracked well. You buy a certain tonnage of ammonium nitrate, they look for you to buy more or less the same, but what if the crop is different so you don't need as much. Is that change reliably being tracked without self-reporting? DHS says yes, but I don't know."

"What about this Land Cruiser seen driving southbound at three thirty this morning?" Jace asked.

"They got too much of a head start, but we might catch them on a camera. Take a look at Highway 140. That's where the Land Cruiser got seen heading south toward California."

I heard her fingers clicking on a keyboard. She said something to herself and her fingers stopped, then the clicking started again.

"Some of the passes they may have crossed over have cameras. Caltrans might be able to help. I'll get on that," she said.

"Worth a try. If you find something—"

"I'll call you. There's something else to talk about too. The Sacramento office called my domestic terrorism supervisor. Oroville is their territory—"

"I thought it was all worked out."

"It is getting worked out. I'm just giving you a heads up," she said. "Sacramento may require an agent with us anytime we're in their area, or they'll put a timeframe on it or limit what we investigate."

"Tell them it's just Corti. We'll stay away from everything else."

"They got hot about you hiking in with the sheriff without letting them know."

"I did let them know."

"Then it got lost somewhere."

"Give up everything except Corti."

"I heard you the first time."

She called again after I'd left Klamath Falls and was across the California border, at least one hundred miles south with a long drive still ahead.

"Just maybe," she said. "The timing is right. It's a 2007 white Land Cruiser, a male at the wheel, a female riding shotgun, three people in back. I just sent you a photo, and a blow-up of the female."

"License plates?"

"Partial, but we found it, and I talked to the former owner. He sold it eighteen months ago to a guy named Nick, Rick, or Dick."

"No last name?" I asked.

"None. Sold it in a parking lot for cash."

"A 2007 Land Cruiser is going to suck gas. I don't think those things got more than fifteen miles per gallon."

"We're checking," she said, "but it's not going to be easy."

I looked at the time: 2:08 p.m. They probably crossed into California no later than 4:30 this morning, so more than nine and a half hours ago. They could be anywhere.

"Take a look at the blow-up of the female."

"Okay, pulling over now." I exited onto an overpass at the top of a long rise where the surrounding country was forested, then crossed over and sat off to the side of the onramp. I looked at the photo expecting our Blond Bomber. But I was wrong.

"It's not her," I said, "but you know who it could be. I see some resemblance . . . I don't know. Let's see if facial recognition gets us anywhere."

"I ran it. It gets us a list of low probabilities with known suspects."

"How low?"

"Nine percent chance it's the Blond Bomber."

"Run it with Samantha Clark," I said.

"Seriously?"

"Yeah."

"Okay, I'll do it right now. They're waiting for me to call anyway. Hey, Grale, are you still thinking we'll follow up with the tip in Tracy? That's a long drive for you."

"I'm good for it. I'm still game. I'll meet you there, but call me back before if you learn any more."

When she called back she said, "Nothing definitive, but it's interesting. The probability jumped to fifty-three percent when we ran it with Clark's face. You might be onto something. What if you are? This is your niece's friend. What would that mean, Paul?"

28

Julia called as I drove south toward Tracy and said, "I want to check a story Mom once told me."

"What's it about?"

"You."

"Why today?"

"I want to know if the story is true. Mom said you were fifteen and a half when you trashed a guy's car with a tire iron. Tell me what happened."

"I'll tell you the condensed version."

I told her Melissa and a friend got worried about an older guy—he was maybe twenty years older—who drove an old El Camino. They remembered the El Camino better than him because it had white stripes on the hood. He seemed to be following them.

"They'd seen him too often," I said. "One night your mom and a friend met at a theater. They drove there separately, and Melissa was pretty sure the guy with the El Camino followed her home. That was the night she told me. This was in July."

"And when did the thing at the river happen?"

"The following Saturday. There was a place where people would swim in the river at night. In some trees there was this area where everybody parked, and then you went down the trail with flashlights unless there was a good moon. But there were also other places people parked farther back and upstream."

"Was it mostly a boyfriend-girlfriend thing?"

"Definitely that, but others too. Groups would meet there."

"And party?"

"Sure. Your mother came up the trail one night planning to go home, and he was near her car and tried to keep her from closing the door as she got in. Your mom was quick, though, and got the car started and backed up so fast he had to dive out of the way. The police came out and looked around for a couple of days or so, and then about two weeks later Melissa was back out there with friends. But so was I."

"And you did what?"

"He was down along the water sitting on a rock. I got the keys from Melissa and got a tire iron then hiked up the river and found his car."

"He wasn't parked in the lot?"

"No."

"And he was just sitting on a rock by the river?"

"Yeah."

I didn't tell her about the rage inside as I broke every window of the El Camino as well as the headlights and taillights. Or that I knew he wouldn't call the police.

"Mom said you destroyed his car."

"Those El Caminos were more like a small-bed pickup, so I didn't destroy it. But I made it a problem to drive."

"Why didn't you call the police or go get them instead of attacking his car?"

"I probably should have."

"What did you do with the tire iron?"

"I broke the windows, headlights, and taillights, and other things that would send a message."

"What do you think now?"

"Melissa never saw him again."

"And that's all, that's enough for you?"

"I learned I have it in me."

"Do you regret it?"

"In some ways, but no, I don't regret it. Can I ask you a question?"

"Of course."

"When did you last see Sam Clark?"

"A few days ago. I've been thinking about Sam and Nick and a lot of stuff. I should stand on my own more. I've trusted too much."

Jo sees intense humiliation and a loss of self-esteem in Julia. She says we have to talk and keep talking to her, keep countering any comments she makes diminishing herself. Jo hasn't voiced it, but I'm sure the risk of suicide has crossed her mind. What I was hearing from Julia was a tracking back, a reexamining of the relationships in her life looking for what was true, if anything.

It may sound callous, but I knew the feeling from investigations where I'd made a wrong turn and then built on my mistake. Later, you go back. You try to figure it out. When you do, your confidence returns, you go forward again, and things get better.

I talked more with Julia, then got into a debate with Mara about whether to go public with Corti's name and face. I was against it, but Mara was all but telling me he was going to put Corti's face out there.

In Tracy, Jace and I met with a young PG&E systems manager named Drake Brown. Brown monitored substations along Path 66, among other duties. The paths are the routes high-voltage lines travel. They number from 1 to 81. I've seen my share of those 81.

Some of the paths I've looked at make me think someone took a pencil one morning and drew a line on a map, then said, "Clear me a space one hundred feet wide. Start here in Oregon and go to LA. Follow this line. If something is in your way cut it down or go over it. Do what you have to but get it done."

Hydroelectric dams were built and a way was needed to deliver the power to cities hundreds of miles away, so they cut pathways and put up high transmission lines that tracked through substations. Brown knew all about high-voltage paths. He'd called several times but was nonspecific in his messages, so we'd been slow getting to him.

"We live on the outskirts of Tracy," Brown said and pointed toward dry hills in the distance. "My wife quit her job when our son was born. If I got killed in a substation bombing, I don't know how she would make it. So I watch everything and everyone."

He showed us surveillance camera video he'd spliced together. When it finished I asked him to replay it. He replayed the video six times for us with numerous starts and stops. Sometimes you can sense someone watching you from across or down the street. You can't yet make their face out—you just know. In the same way, a driver casing a site can give off a vibe.

Whoever was driving the Chevy Tahoe couldn't know the employee inside monitoring surveillance cameras was hypervigilant. As we watched the spliced video a sixth time, Brown started talking about the 2013 Metcalf transmission station attack so authoritatively I had to ask, "Were you there that night?"

"No, I've studied it. I've—"

Jace touched his arm to quiet him. "Freeze, right there and see if you can enhance the license plate."

He enhanced the left rear bumper and part of the license plate. The bumper had a red decal on it that looked like something an employee might have for a company lot. I felt Jace watching me, then looked at her and nodded. Tehachapi, where the security guard was killed, and we had a surveillance camera record of a Chevy Tahoe on the access road twelve minutes after the shooting. That Tahoe had a faded, peeling decal and dents on the left rear panel.

"Drake, run that video once more," I said, then asked, "Why did you notice this vehicle?"

"This one slowed way down when it went by."

The Tahoe held a steady fifteen to twenty miles an hour. The passenger window behind the driver was down two or three inches throughout the video, but even freezing and enhancing we didn't see a lens or anything indicating they were shooting video.

"What else have you got?" I asked.

He had spliced together a record of hundreds of vehicles that had passed by, including two kids on bikes.

"What's up with the kids?" Jace asked.

He responded by asking her, "What were kids doing way out here? ISIS uses kids as bombers and human shields."

"Got it," Jace said.

"Do you want a copy?"

We got two copies of the videos he'd spliced, then thanked him and left. Overhead the wires hummed against a darkening blue sky. I walked to my car then turned when Jace called, "Hey, Grale!"

She was standing outside her car with the driver's door open to let the heat out. She waggled her phone at me as I walked back to her.

"We're cleared on Corti indefinitely, but Sacramento will handle any bombing. Anything we learn we brief the Sacramento domestic terrorism supervisor on. There's more, but let's head there and talk on the drive."

That night Jace and I ate at a brewery in midtown Sacramento and kicked back for a few hours. The next morning before dawn I drove north fast with a pair of evidence-recovery agents out of the Sacramento office tailing me all the way to a trailhead parking lot south of Mount Lassen.

The sun was still high up on the mountain when we got there. It had yet to work its way down, and it was chilly near the 2007 white Land Cruiser parked in the far corner of the lot. The evidence-recovery pair would make a preliminary swipe for DNA, then wait for the tow truck to carry it to our Sacramento yard.

It was probably needless paranoia, but I checked for any booby trap or bomb before they disabled the alarm and opened the driver's door. They were meticulous as they collected fibers and swiped. When the agents gave me the go-ahead, I unfolded a cotton flag lying on the passenger seat that had no doubt been left for us.

It had been folded in the triangular manner of an American flag. Its design was a green background with a map of the continental United States broken into three sections, as if three countries, one red, one white, one blue. The largest section was blue and included most of the American West. The red included all of the South and Texas on up through Kansas as well as up the Eastern Seaboard as high as, but not including, Virginia. The oblong mix of what was left of the lower forty-eight states was white.

"They're telling us who they are," I said to the agent nearest me.

"Can you draw that much from this?" he asked.

"I'm speculating, but I'll take it further. They're claiming the country. We're hunting homegrown terrorists for the infrastructure attacks. This is the flag of one group, or maybe they share it. Red, white, and blue pretty much sends a signal, don't you think? See you guys back in Sacramento. I'd like to get this flag examined as early as possible."

During the ride back, numbers and chemistry on the Captain Jack bombs were texted to me. Close to a ton of explosives for the big one. Three-quarters of a ton for the other. Ammonium nitrate nitromethane bombs similar to, if not the same as, the McVeigh–Oklahoma City bombing that killed 168 people.

Disabling the Captain Jack substation fit my "California as primary target" theory. If you add up all power usage in Alberta, British Columbia, and the western states, California consumes one-third of it. If you want a crippling blow to California's economy and way of doing business, hit the major pathways.

I was close to Sacramento when Julia called.

"I need to know if something is true about the FBI," she said.

"I hope I have the answer."

"I know how I sound, but I'm freaking out a little. Maybe I should already know this, but if the FBI is suspicious of someone, can they go into that person's friends' computers and phones and everything else?"

"What's everything else?" I asked.

"Let's say phones and any computers."

"Depends."

"Does that mean it could happen?"

"Yes."

She said, "Someone has been on my computer and in my phone."

"How do you know?"

"There's an app on my computer that warns if there's an intruder. A dot flashes red on the screen. That's happening."

"Can you send me a screenshot or photo?" I asked.

"I'll do it right now. But have you ever read someone's e-mails even if you didn't know if they'd done anything wrong?"

"If it's a terrorist investigation, the rules are different, but we're pretty careful."

"That's not what I asked," Julia said.

"In bomb investigations, yes, I've looked at friends of a suspect without having direct evidence."

"So if you were prowling around and found something, you could go after them."

"More likely we'd be looking at an associate of someone who is already a suspect," I said.

"So someone might look at me over the bullets because I was Nick Knowles' girlfriend?"

"That could happen."

"If they found something about bullets in my text messages or e-mails, could they charge me? People send me stuff. Not stuff that I believe in but what some people I know send in blast e-mails."

"Agents might question you, but they recognize that a large group e-mail can be indiscriminate. It would be easier if I knew what it is we're talking about," I said.

Instead of telling me, she asked me another question. "Could they hold or jail me, even if I didn't know anything?"

"Are we talking about terrorism?"

"I don't really know," Julia said. "I just know some people think what's happening right now is pretty cool. Taking down the grid, I mean. They think it might be the catalyst that lets us remake things and get off grid. That, and after I moved here I got sent some weird e-mails and stuff on Snapchat and Twitter."

"Did you respond to any of it?" I asked.

"I deleted them, but more came, and I noticed the e-mail addresses are sort of similar to some people I know but not the same. I saved two. I could forward them. They're the most recent."

My laptop was on the passenger seat. I reached for it after pulling over. I wasn't entirely sure I understood her. We kept talking as she found the two e-mails and sent them.

"There's also one other weird follow-up," she said. "I shouldn't have opened it, I guess. They're talking like we're friends, but I don't know who it is. It's like they know what's going on in my life. They know I moved here, but I don't recognize these e-mail addresses. People I know who are pretty smart say it could be the FBI. Could it?"

"I don't know the answer to that question. If someone thought you were affiliated with people trying to take the grid down, then sure, yes, it could happen you're approached," I said.

"That's like making up evidence."

"What is?"

"Sending me these e-mails and tweets and stuff."

I could tell her there was public outrage at first over the violation of privacy or that those most easily frightened give up their rights willingly and first. They said things such as "the FBI can look in my computer anytime they want. I don't have anything to hide." They don't see that they're giving up anything. What's the big deal, right? When it becomes habit to give up privacy it becomes normal. You can believe you're not really giving up anything. My answer to that is fifteen years ago it would have surprised me law enforcement was on her computer. Not anymore. Little surprises me anymore. Think about that.

My computer pinged twice, and Julia said, "Weird. One of these e-mails won't forward to you. It's the one that one of my roommates was copied on. It's the one thanking me. I'll just copy what's in it and send that."

"Do that."

While she did that, I read the one she'd forwarded.

> Hey J, thanks for the box delivery. B's will go to good things. Much change ahead. Stay strong! Ca

Ca was Carla, Julia had said. The next was direct and oddly troubling.

> You rock! Nice delivery. Nice job!

My computer pinged as the last came through. It read,

> Wish I could say more to thank you. Viva la . . .

"It's all bullshit, UG. Don't believe any of it. I'm totally confused. Who would do this?"

"No idea?"

"None. But, duh, it's somebody I know or somebody that knows somebody I know to have my e-mail. It doesn't feel like a joke. It feels like I'm being framed," she said.

It did feel that way.

"I'm scared," she said. "This is just too weird. It's like phishing. This is somebody who wants something from me and they're already in my computer. UG, no way this is the FBI, right?"

29

I gassed up at an Exxon in Sacramento and figured to call Jace from the car to let her know I'd pick her up at the Sacramento FBI Field Office in ten minutes. She beat me to it.

She called first and said, "Hey, a San Francisco realtor is on her way to the field office here, she's just minutes away. Her name is Francine Macomb, and this is about Corti."

"How do we know that?"

"We don't know it but she owns a string of vacation rentals up and down the state, including a cottage she rented along the American River to a guy she's worried about. Let's hear it in her words. I know you want to get going, but this won't delay us that long."

Francine Macomb and I arrived at the same time. I got her through the lobby and into an interview room. Jace questioned Macomb as I scanned her website promo on the place she'd rented to the guy in question.

> *Romantic 1930's river cottage. Two bedrooms, a cozy kitchen, a wood burning fireplace, garage, gravel driveway, and mature oaks. Perfect for a second honeymoon!*

"I've been a realtor a long time. It's hard to be too careful. I like to know who I'm renting to. He had a nice smile and a Portland basketball team cap that I kept asking him to take off so I could get a screenshot." She leaned forward and said quietly, "I didn't want him to know I wanted a screenshot."

"Trail Blazers," Jace said. "Did he take off the cap?"

"No, but he was cute about it. He said if he took it off, the Warriors would beat the Trail Blazers again in the playoffs."

She started to go on about her rental business, but Jace brought her back to the renter, an Eric Wright.

"He did a crazy thing," Francine said. "He was supposed to meet me at the house to give me a check. As I got there he called me and said he wasn't going to make our meeting due to work, but he'd hidden an envelope with the rent in cash." She paused and looked from Jace to me and back to Jace. "Who does that?"

"Did he say why he wanted to rent your place?" I asked.

"The river. He wanted to be along the river. Years ago, before I owned it, there was a dock, but that was back in the days when the river would flood. It got swept away."

"What else did you talk about with him?" I asked and wanted to move this along.

"I mentioned restaurants and somehow we got on pork. He loves pork burgers. He said he grew up with the best in the world. He has a southern accent, not strong, but there."

"If you had to pick a state, which state?"

"North Carolina, Virginia, Kentucky, but I would guess he hasn't lived there in a while."

Corti was born in Kentucky, but the family moved early. I nodded and said, "We have some photos for you to look at."

Francine failed several times to identify Corti, yet remained confident and returned to her original question.

"Who rents a house and doesn't use it?" she asked. "He's barely been there. The neighbors say lights are on at night but no more than half the week."

"We'll check him out," Jace said. "And we very much appreciate you coming forward."

"I'm sorry I identified the wrong man, but I've never done this before."

"Don't feel bad in any way," Jace said. "Thank you for reaching out, and let me know of anything you hear about in San Francisco."

We walked out with Francine and as we left her she called out, "I didn't pick him out of the photos you showed me, but I'm telling you there's something wrong about him. If you go by the house, you have my permission to go anywhere you want on the property."

I turned and said, "Thank you," and then we were gone.

"You rushed that," Jace said. "She's probably imagining things, but she came in to try to help us. It's not as though where we're headed now is more important."

For now, I left that alone. We drove north on 70 for an hour, exited onto Cottonwood Road, went west, crossed a creek, and there was the Table Mountain substation like a fort in the distance. To the south through pastureland, the line of the towers stretched as far as I could see. The sides of the substation were protected by concrete walls painted a pale brown. Near the gate were six National Guard members. We said hello to the Guard, toured briefly, then met with the manager who'd been on duty last September when the vehicles showed up. He showed us video he'd taken.

We watched it twice, then got in his Jeep and drove the perimeter of the substation with him as he talked us through it. He pointed at a line of electrical towers in pasture across the road.

"It was the strangest damn thing," he said. "Across the street and on this side they cut the cattle fencing. Across the road they drove the van up under that big tower right there. Over here it was an SUV driving no more than five miles an hour around the substation perimeter."

"Scouting the substation," I said.

"That's definitely what went through my head, and I reported it to Sacramento FBI."

"And we've read the file. We wanted to see the substation and talk to you."

"Cattle got out," he said. "It took a while to get anyone out here, and they were gone."

"Was that worth the trip?" Jace asked as we drove away. "We're running around everywhere. You've been driving all day. We could have called this guy from the office and heard the same stories."

"I wanted to see the substation and hear his version."

"Exactly. You wanted, but if you ask me it's a waste of time, and you rushed Francine Macomb in and out after she went out of her way to come talk to us. How many hours did you drive this morning to get that flag? There's only so much time in a day. Running around doesn't solve investigations."

"Let's get lunch and talk," I said. "There's a Thai place called Nori in Oroville. I'll buy."

I go dark and get quiet. When that happens it's like riding with a stone statue. Jace gets combative and petulant. That's how we roll when things aren't going well. Lunch always helps.

The unspoken rule is that if you're the cause of the friction, you buy lunch. Which is tricky if you both think you're in the right, but this is where Jace and I click and why we work well together as investigators. We're both willing to accept the possibility we're wrong. We're both strong willed, but neither of us is dogmatic, so I'm owning it today. And I like Nori's noodle soup.

I looked at Jace. She stared back at me still not giving an inch, and wiping her mouth with a paper napkin then eating more. When she looked up again, she said, "This is good food."

"It is."

"You think they were as bold as they were because they were playing at being terrorists," she said.

"That is what I'm thinking and why I needed to see the place. They were still growing into the idea of attacking the grid is what I think now. They hid their faces and took off the license plates, but at any moment a county deputy or CHP could have come along and stopped them due to the cattle in the road. Then what happens?"

"They go to jail and there's a record of them," Jace answered.

"Under ten minutes, the PG&E manager said, so efficient but still a kind of 'look at us, look what we're doing.' No, it was them saying 'we're telling you what we're going to do.'"

"And self-righteous about it," Jace said.

I nodded. "Yeah, carrying a banner for justice."

"Which means they weren't enemy sleepers," she said.

"No, this was bold and in your face. This was 'we want you to know.'"

"Like the flag this morning."

"Exactly."

We were both quiet, and Jace finished eating as I paid.

"Thank you for lunch," she said.

"My pleasure."

She laughed, then as we got in the car, said, "I agree. We're looking for our own. We're looking for Americans. We always were. But not with the cyberattacks."

"Right, the cyber is bigger than them."

"So a collection of small domestic cells with some common cause."

"Something like that," I said.

It was near dusk when we checked out Francine Macomb's American River cottage. It was farther up the river than the ad would lead you to believe.

We didn't see any vehicles, but there were multiple tracks in the gravel driveway.

"She gave us permission," I said. "Let's take a quick look."

No one answered, so I looked in windows but saw little and decided to follow the path down to the river. The trail for the most part was drying, but as I neared the junction with the public path there was dried mud with a boot print. Which brought me back to Idaho and asking Bill Mazarik, "How will we know him?"

"From his boots," Mazarik had said. "Kelley Zipper Tactical Boots. We all loved them."

I'd researched the boot and had a feel for its sole. This was similar enough to take a photo and send to Jace, who knew all the Internet tricks. She called a few seconds later.

"Do you remember what Mazarik said?" I asked.

"Oh, right, the boots."

"I'm on my way back."

I drove as Jace worked on the boot print. She wanted an answer before we got back to the field office, and I understood. We had so many tips we checked them off as fast as we could.

A few minutes later she looked over at me and said, "If you were targeting electrical pathways or rural telecom facilities, that cottage is a good location."

I agreed, but we didn't have anything to show for the day.

"Did you write down the exact boot?" she asked.

"Kelley Zipper Tactical."

"You're funny with what you store away. You don't remember half the computer things I teach you but then you remember all these random things," she said.

"It was the way Mazarik said how much they all liked the quality of that boot."

She got quiet then turned and said, "Grale."

"What?"

"You're awesome. I mean it. After Macomb couldn't pick out Corti's face, I wasn't for checking out the house, but so what. Remembering a boot print and recognizing it in dried mud, that's awesome. Look."

She turned her phone screen toward me.

"It's a match," she said.

"Okay, but we don't know whether other manufacturers use the same sole."

"No other manufacturer came up."

"It's the Internet. It doesn't prove anything."

She ignored me and said, "Now we have two things, her worry and a possible boot match. We want to find out who's staying here. The field office here is strapped. We'll have to watch it ourselves and brief them at the office."

"I'll watch until someone comes home or until one in the morning. At one I'll leave if there's nothing."

There was nothing. No one came home to the little cottage with a river view while I was there, but there were new bombings south of Sacramento that night, a small substation and an electrical tower. I was asked to assist Sacramento agents in collecting evidence, so I gathered up my gear at dawn. We'd take separate cars, and the domestic terrorism supervisor made it crystal clear these were Sacramento office investigations. That left it to Jace to figure out the next step with the river cottage.

"Don't forget to write," she called as I shouldered the gear and left.

30

Southeast of Sacramento in Amador County, a tiny substation sat in a field, surrounded by chain-link fencing, three-foot-high ryegrass, and the yellow and orange blooms of mustard and poppies. Two Amador County deputies, who'd answered the call five hours ago, toured the Sacramento bomb techs with me trailing behind.

As near as I could tell, explosive charges had detonated simultaneously, and the concussive force from six spots crushed the substation and flattened brush.

The shock wave also dropped an old oak. I skirted that and took my time walking wider and wider circles away from the blast as the Sacramento agents, Torrez and Liu, worked the core.

During all those widening circles I worried about Julia. My phone showed I'd missed three calls from her but no message.

I walked through grasses and weeds up to my thighs, scouring the ground as the day heated. I watched for bomb evidence as I thought about my brother-in-law and best friend, Jim Kern, the guy who, in the Air Force, earned the nickname "Cool Hand Kern" for the way he'd once landed a B-52 in wind shear during a thunderstorm. Jim died in the Alagara bombing along with my sister and nephew. I wasn't dwelling on the Alagara this morning.

I saw a morning eighteen years ago and the tears running down tough-as-nails Kern's cheeks as he told me that Melissa, my sister, had just given birth to a girl. The baby was breathing, crying, warm, alive, and named Julia. Now Julia and I were all that was left. I'd lived alone for so long after my wife, Carrie, had died, I'd lost something that I wanted back, and I needed to help Julia find her way. I was unsure how the two thoughts connected, but they did.

In the way she stood or sat tall on a chair, Julia reminded me of my sister and a quality in our family that didn't want to get lost. We weren't a family with wealth or rich stories of famous relatives, but we were there when it mattered. We were there in the wars. We were stand-up when things got tough at home. I saw a kind of courage in Julia that I remembered in Melissa; it's just "the way" in our family. It was in her and I knew if she could connect to it, it would help her.

But for burn marks in the grass I would have missed the cylindrical fragment that was likely part of one of the bombs. I bagged it and we assessed everything we'd gathered at the tiny substation before moving on to the high-voltage tower downed within minutes of the substation explosion. The electrical lines were no longer hot, though in my head I heard the hissing as power lines sliced air and slid along the falling tower. I pictured the steel frame crumpling. Fragments of the porcelain insulators were scattered in the weeds. Liu and Torrez had it covered and didn't need me. They agreed, and I shook hands with both, then left.

I tried Julia again as I drove away but still didn't reach her. I called Mara.

"Hey, my niece is getting random e-mails and social media messages that suggest she's part of an ongoing effort to topple the government. 'Rewrite the Rules' is a heading on several of them. The e-mail addresses are similar to, but not the same as, some of her friends'. Are those coming from us?"

"I can't talk about your niece. You know that."

"She says an app that detects intruders is lighting up, meaning someone is on her computer," I said. "Do you know anything about that?"

"What did I just say?"

After a silence I said, "I believe her."

"Where exactly are you?"

"South of Sacramento in Amador County. If we're phishing Julia, I want to know."

"I'm going to forget this conversation."

"Don't do that."

"You could jeopardize your active status pushing into investigations you could compromise just by being there," he said.

"I haven't stuck my nose anywhere. Julia called me. She may have screwed up with who she's chosen as friends, but no one is going to wrap her in by tricking her," I said.

"As in frame her? This conversation is over."

"Yeah, you're right."

I killed the call and texted Jace I was on my way back to Sacramento. She texted back she was down the street from the river cottage and to hurry. A few seconds later, she called.

31

"We're on," she said. "I just talked to SWAT. They've got a small drone they want to get up first. We're live. Corti is here."

"You saw him?" I asked.

"Drove up in a white Ford Taurus. Doesn't really seem like his kind of car." She laughed.

"Where are you watching from?"

"A neighbor gave us a spot down the street. It's nice. It's a rental over a garage. I'm very happy with it. Good view and a bathroom. He's here. We've got him, Grale."

I said, "Text me the address. I'm half an hour out."

"Hang on, I've got more. I talked to the gun-shop owner again in Pocatello, where Corti used to buy ammo when he was in the Brigade. He opened up a little."

"Sure, they're losing power in Idaho, and he's figuring out he needs electricity," I said.

"Corti's a regular who hasn't been in to buy ammo in almost three months," she said. "Or that's what he told me. He also said Corti is rock-solid American and one of the good guys. He thinks we're looking for the wrong man."

I'd talked to the gun-shop owner several days ago, and he'd done a riff on Waco and the FBI. He was condescending about my motives.

"Corti was careful not to show much of his face this morning," she said.

"So you looked at his boots."

"Of course," she said, "and he had them on, so maybe Mazarik's boot story is true. I saw more of his face when he moved something shaped like a bag of concrete or sand."

"That could fit. Sand is a way to help create a stable platform for shooting."

"What came next were a green duffel bag and a folding tripod that looked like prone-shooter gear. He transferred everything to a brown Yukon that pulled up a few minutes later. The man who got out was dressed and acted like he knew there could be surveillance. I couldn't get any kind of good look at him. Baggy clothes. Head hidden. He went straight into the house."

"Is he still in there?"

"As far as I know."

"Does our SWAT team have the river side covered?"

She replied, "They will, but not yet."

"And Corti switched into the Yukon?" I asked.

"Yes."

"So now he's got a vehicle he can take off-road, it's big enough to sleep in, and as far as we know both are in the house."

"Correct. Wherever the second man goes, undercover officers will go with him. We go with Corti. Or I go if you don't get here in time, in which case you catch up and I call the Sacramento field office and ask for backup."

Corti came out just as I got there. He was long-limbed and lean. He moved easily, even carrying a red metal ammunition locker that looked heavy as he lifted it onto the passenger seat and put the seatbelt around it, and then loaded a cooler and another gear bag. He laid a coat on a back seat and got in the driver's side.

"Go time," Jace said.

"Where's the other guy? He didn't help carry anything out."

Jace didn't answer because she was talking with the SWAT commander as we pulled away a block and a half behind Corti. It was a situation where we needed at least two more surveillance vehicles. After ID'ing Corti, Jace talked with SWAT as I drove. They were ready to move into the house as soon as they identified where the second man was inside.

When Jace ended the call she said, "Within five minutes they're inside."

Five minutes went by, then ten and twenty and we hadn't heard anything. Jace said, "Hey, you're old enough to know. Does that old Yukon Denali have hands-free phone capability?"

"I'm not sure, but I don't think so."

Jace's phone rang. It was the SWAT commander. No one was in the house, so the second man must have gone out a window to the river path much earlier. They had spread out and were looking for him.

Ahead, Corti got on the 50 eastbound, and we followed him past Folsom and into the foothills toward Placerville. Jace called for more backup, and two agents got on the road behind us. That led to the old debate: keep following and see who he leads us to, or apprehend now.

"What do you think?" Jace asked.

"I think we follow for now."

That led to a two-lane county road before Placerville. We kept him in sight and figured we had him cold. At some point he'd put it together that the car behind was following and so were others. Granted, he was a skilled sniper, but overwhelming odds tend to make suspects surrender. My way was to keep it peaceful. You can project body language with a car to let a suspect know it doesn't have to be a shootout.

Enough backup was almost to us when Corti braked hard and turned right onto a road that served a handful of houses and a ranch below. He drove through an open wooden gate and out onto a dirt track into a meadow and stopped. The meadow was bright with wildflowers. Corti got out and looked around.

"He's out of room," Jace said.

"We're missing something. He's not out here to picnic."

"Some sort of meeting," Jace guessed. "Out here where no one can overhear."

"Or he picked up on us following him driving, or before that, back at the house."

"But now he's parked in a meadow." I didn't have the answer either. I looked at Corti, then at a broken-down barn in the distance as Jace confirmed our backup didn't miss the turn onto this road. She talked them through it. East of the open field the hills were grown over with oak and pine, and farther back the hills became mountains and the slopes were forested. Where could he go from here? I didn't see any way out other than the way we came in.

I felt like a fool when I heard the sound and saw a Bell helicopter rise over a ridge. It came fast and we were too far away. It skimmed treetops and yet Corti, who'd gotten back in the Yukon, didn't get out yet. He was doing something inside, moving around. I took a dozen sequential photos of the helicopter's call numbers as its downdraft flattened the meadow grasses, and called an FAA emergency number on my phone.

Then I watched Corti get out of the Yukon and duck under the helicopter blades with a gear bag in his right hand. He got in, and the helicopter rose, its nose dipping as it raced away.

32

When the helicopter disappeared on a northwest heading, I asked the FAA for help tracing it. We asked for help from CHP, local law enforcement, everyone. Another thought struck me. We may have underestimated Corti's importance, may have misread his role. We had him as a disgruntled loner activated by opportunity and ties to a misguided militia leader. How does a helicopter escape fit into that?

I left Jace with the backup agents and went down to the meadow. Corti had fussed with something in the vehicle as the helicopter arrived, and I wanted to check it out alone first. When I looked in the windows nothing was obvious. The red ammo box wore a seatbelt on the passenger side. A small carry-on and clothes were left behind.

The Yukon's ground clearance was high enough for me to easily slide under, inhaling the warm sweet smell of spring meadow grasses as I did. Lying on my back I looked for unusual wiring or a tie-in to the SUV's battery. I took my time, then shimmied out and walked the windows again.

I stepped away and called Jace. "Give me another few minutes. The doors are unlocked, the keys in the ignition, let me have a look inside before you bring anyone down here. I'll call you."

"Okay, and what about going out with his name and face?"

"Give me a little longer on that," I said.

"We've got a short window where it might make a difference."

I doubted that. Corti wouldn't catch a helicopter ride then walk into a 7-Eleven. Was it an evacuation plan similar to what he might have had in the military as a remote sniper? Or was it a prelude to something new? My gut feeling was we needed to rethink him.

"Hey, I'm going to turn my phone off as a precaution when I get inside the Yukon," I said.

I focused binoculars on the inside of the driver's door. First the door, then the floor mat, then up and across to the red ammunition box. Would Corti leave behind armor-piercing bullets? Not likely, so what's up with the ammo box?

At the FBI we have the Bomb Data Center. From them I'd received a recent e-mail with info on new wireless detonators where two components are placed inside of a preset distance, let's say a meter apart. If either component moves more than the preset distance away from the other component, then bang! One component can be placed under a vehicle, the sister component inside with a bomb. Driver gets in, drives away, and doesn't get far.

Corti moved around in the front seats as the helicopter was landing. I had thought he was pulling out gear and ammunition. He wasn't. He'd gotten out, opened the left rear door, and pulled only the gear bag he took with him, which was heavy. I saw it sag. I still believed it held a long gun, a sniper rifle broken down. When he'd opened the driver's door, he didn't open it wide. He sort of slid out and shut it. It was an odd move. What did it mean?

I opened the driver door, though less than Corti had. It was enough that I could examine the contents of the pocket in the side door. Didn't see anything, and no wiring taped anywhere, nothing but an old Yukon interior with some gear in the back, a cooler, and a red ammo box. I turned and looked at the cooler. It was big enough. It worried me.

Only then did I realize it would be the passenger door not the driver's door that needed to be wide open to examine the ammunition box. From the driver's seat I leaned across the box to check the storage slot on the passenger door.

Nothing but a package of tissues. I pulled that out then felt something hard nestled in the Kleenex. It could be a coin that had somehow slipped in. Maybe a quarter, but no, it was too thick. More like a small round battery. I eased it out and was looking at a round stainless steel object similar to but not a battery.

I stared. I remembered the Bomb Data Center e-mail: "A cell phone will not detonate these."

I took a breath, then a photo, and sent the photo and a message marked high priority to Mara and the Bomb Data Center. A confident FBI tech on the other side of the country identified the detonator type. By then I'd backed away and was with Jace, and we weren't there when the Yukon was blown up. The Sacramento FBI bomb squad debated opening the ammo box, then took the more cautious course and blew up the vehicle with C-4.

A rancher outside Roseville heard an alert on the radio. He knew helicopters. He'd flown them. A Bell 505 Jet Ranger had passed over his fields and crossed the highway no more than two hundred feet off the deck. He matched five of the numbers given in the radio alert.

"It's black," the rancher told me. "There were two occupants. I may have seen where it landed."

"We're on our way," I said. "We'll be there soon. Tell me where you are."

He did, and I laid my phone down. Neither Jace nor I said anything for several minutes then Jace summed it up.

"We had him and we fucked up."

33

May was the anniversary month of Jace's fiancé's accident, so maybe that was why she started talking about it. But not before asking me more than she ever had about my bomb injuries and the months healing in a Frankfurt hospital.

"Yet you still work bombings," she said. "You got in that Yukon and held the detonator in your hand. After what you've been through I have to ask why."

"Back then, the Army was just looking for help clearing Bagdad of IEDs. It meant more after I got hurt, and more again when my sister, brother-in-law, and nephew died in the Alagara bombing. Bombings affect me. The cowardice and indiscriminate cruelty may not be any worse than other ways of killings, but I've figured out I don't want to be a witness to a bombing. I want to be the guy that stops it from happening."

"I get that," she said and was quiet for a while, then said, "This is the day of the accident. In my head, today is the day Gene died. We both had bikes. I had an old BMW. He had a Harley. He liked to cruise along, and sometimes I just wanted to roll harder. Gene was more peaceful than me. In many ways he was gentler."

Her voice broke then steadied, not unlike a suspect resolved to confess.

"He was catching up to me when he got hit. He was happily going along looking at the country, but I'd speeded up and pulled ahead. It was how we always rode, except that day we'd argued. It was a stupid argument, and we would have laughed about it later, but we never got the chance. I speeded up because I was angry. I didn't want to ride near him, and Gene being Gene was already over the fight. He was catching up to let me know that."

"You're not the one who was texting, drifted over the line, and hit him."

"It wouldn't have happened if I hadn't pulled ahead. I'll never get over that."

"Maybe not, but it's in your voice that you loved him. You didn't get him killed, Jace. A driver texting crossed the line and hit him. You didn't cause that," I said.

"I speeded up because I was angry."

"We all get angry."

"I know we're flawed and all that, but it shouldn't have happened."

"But it did and you loved him. Maybe it's time to forgive yourself."

"If we hadn't argued . . . or if I'd had a chance to say I was sorry."

"You loved him. He loved you."

Tears ran down her cheeks. "I loved him so much."

"That will always be, but you've got to move on," I said.

"I don't know how to."

"You got shot once and had trouble with your right arm, didn't you?"

"How does everybody know about that?" she asked.

"I don't remember who told me, but like me, you had to fight to get back to active duty."

"It hurt. That's all. It doesn't compare."

"But it could have gone either way, right? I was told there was a lot of pain involved," I said.

"There was pain."

"And every day you worked through it. You made yourself do it. I think it's a little like that."

She didn't answer, so maybe she'd just suffered more advice from yet another person who doesn't really know. But I lost my wife. I do know some things. She turned back to the view. Twenty minutes later we were standing with a rancher named Ned Geist on a dirt road running through pasture. He pointed toward the mountains.

"See that V notch there?" he asked.

"Give us a little more," I said. "I see five or six V notches."

"With the black rock face on the left."

"Okay, I see that."

"There's a road that runs out there, but you have to know where to turn off to catch it. Nothing is marked. That's where I think he may have landed. There's a flat area big enough. I saw a copter come down fast like he knew where he was going."

"How far is that from here?" I asked.

"Three and a half, maybe four miles out. I could take you there."

I glanced at Jace and then said, "Take us, but we'll drive."

Geist was in his late sixties, maybe older. He was big, lanky in worn jeans and boots, with a sweat-stained hat lodged on his left knee as he sat in the back seat giving directions and talking about the long years of drought and the forgiving year of heavy rain.

We turned down a dirt track where the weeds were already high in the middle hump. It's unlikely Jace and I would have found it on our own. It ended near a small meadow bordered by oaks. Before we parked, Jace was on her phone calling for backup. We could see the helicopter and someone sitting in the trees near it.

As Jace made calls to say we'd found the helicopter, the man stood and started toward us, raising his right palm to say hello as if expecting us. We walked to the helicopter. I could read the call numbers and smelled fuel. Then I saw other damage.

"Your helicopter?" I asked him.

"Yeah."

"Where's your passenger?"

"Gone with the guy who was waiting here. Who are you?"

"FBI," I said, then showed him my creds.

"The guy waiting here threatened to find me later if I talked to you," he said.

"I'd worry more about us than him if I were you."

"Look, I'm just an air taxi. You can check me out. I'm not flying drugs. I don't do illegal. You can check me out."

"Start with your passenger, how you met him, how he hired you, and a very clean description of him and the other man. What name did he use?"

"Jacob, and he paid cash."

That Corti hadn't used an alias disturbed me in some way. To rent the American River cottage he was Eric Wright. I saw Jace react as well. It could mean he was moving into a different space with new goals, possibly an endgame where he was going to stand and fight us. I've seen it before.

"I'll do whatever you need, just don't trash my business because I carried the wrong client. I don't know diddly about who he was."

"Tell us how you got the job."

"It was all short notice and cash. I don't usually take those. Check out my copter. They trashed it."

"Did you get paid?"

He shook his head. We were there until dark. A hound picked up Corti's scent and followed it to close to where we'd parked. We found tire tracks but not deep enough to cast. We received some varying tip calls, but no real leads. The helicopter pilot identified Corti's photo, but the pilot knew we'd seen him pick up Corti. He was squirrely on the other description to the point where Jace challenged him and said, "That's who hired you, right? The other guy, not Corti."

We were much closer to the Sacramento office but took him to San Francisco, where Jace's domestic terrorism supervisor was waiting for us. Before the pilot passed through the scanner, he had to empty his pockets. In his wallet was a thick wad of cash with a rubber band around it. I called him on it.

"You told us you didn't get paid."

His forehead broke into a sweat and his story changed, though not enough to get us any closer today. Tracking Corti and losing him took me away from worrying about Julia but that all flooded back in the late night. There was no word from her, and the Verizon recording said, *"The caller you're trying to reach is out of the area."*

I checked into a hotel and talked a long time with Jo.

"You sound down," Jo said.

"We missed a chance with a suspect today and I'm worried about Julia. I'm going to go find her."

"Are you worried about her or worried she's getting in deeper?"

"Both. How about you? How are you doing with the outages?"

"I'll call Julia," she said. "Here they keep tinkering with the hospital backup power. One of the diesel generators has a problem, and a charge nurse here was badly hurt in a car accident where the stoplight was out. There's no fresh food in the stores. I don't like coming home to no lights. It's wearing. I'm more and more on edge, but I guess that's the story with everyone. Have you watched any news tonight?"

"No."

"Lights are out in Miami and New York again. They're flickering in DC. Check out the National Mall. They say LA is barely sustaining rolling blackouts."

"I know about LA."

"And Palo Verde is getting scarier. The cooling towers are heating up again. How can this be happening so quickly? I feel like somebody was asleep at the wheel. I thought we were the ones with all the cyberprowess."

Neither of us said anything for a moment, then Jo asked, "Do you know what would make the dark much better?"

"What?" I asked.

"Holding you."

"And me you. I'll look forward to that. See you soon."

But I didn't know when that would be. In dreams that night I heard sounds from other places in other centuries. I heard the creaking of wood and the singeing burn of lines pulled taut as the canvas sails of a ghost ship filled with air. I called to my sister, Melissa, as I followed her down into a cave filled with thousands of bats with human faces. They watched me descend along slick limestone onto rocks grown over with mold. When I turned back, the limestone was too slippery to climb. I heard the chirr of wings and felt a stinging bite and another and another and woke drenched in sweat.

34

Near dawn, Samantha Clark called and said, "You wrote your cell number on the card you gave me. I hope it's not too early."

"What's up, Sam?"

"Julia freaked out two nights ago. I just want to make sure someone told you. She cooked her phone and laptop in the fire pit in the backyard of the house, then told her roommates there were bugs in them that she had to kill. They didn't know if she meant computer bugs or bugs from the garden. Her face was shiny with sweat and her eyes crazy when she left."

"Were you there?"

"No, they called me. They know I know you and you've helped me with the Signal Hill thing," she said.

"How have I helped you?" I asked.

"Your advice was good."

"I don't remember giving any. Where's Julia?"

"They don't know. They thought she was high on something. Does she have addiction problems? Or maybe you don't know. Does she take any prescription drugs?"

"Who called you?" I asked.

"Her friend from Las Vegas, the mousy girl who wants to be famous. I always forget her name. That's embarrassing, but not, you know what I mean? Dora, Dorothy, something like that, but it doesn't matter. I was at the house twenty minutes ago. I just left there. Mousy found her. She heard sounds outside and went to check. Julia was holding herself and rocking back and forth. They think she snapped."

She paused. She waited. She wanted a reaction, but I wasn't going to give her one. I'd be back to LA later this morning. I'd change my flight to Long Beach and go by the house. I didn't have any of the phone numbers of her roommates, but I might catch someone there. I'd lean hard on Mara and Fuentes for names and phone numbers. I was out of the loop but had learned enough to believe those in the house had become persons of interest.

"What can I do to help?" she asked.

"Give me phone numbers you have for the roommates."

"I'll do that, but I've got a question for you first, and kind of a problem. I've been getting calls from an FBI agent out of your Los Angeles office. He wants to interview me, but he's not saying about what. I told him I'm not going to be reinterviewed about the shootings. I mean, no more. I'm done. So what's he calling me about?"

"If it was something new on the officer shootings," I said, "it would be the LA County Sheriff's Department calling."

But she knew that.

"Let's do this," she said. "I'll try to find Julia, and you find out what's up with the FBI and call me. I realize I'll have to get interviewed, but I want to know what it's about first. Tell whoever it is if they just show up and arrest me they won't get a word out of me."

"Why would they arrest you?"

"You tell me. I have no idea. I like Julia. A lot. I'll help find her. I hate to think of her crying herself to sleep in her car out on some empty road just because her ex-boyfriend thinks she's a slut."

"Do you mean Nicolas Knowles, the guy with a fugitive warrant out on him?" I asked. "Or maybe you know him by a different name."

"There we go. That's more like it. I knew you had your doubts. I knew you had it in you. Talk to you later, Agent Grale."

I flew into Long Beach and caught the roommate, Dora, at the house. Her version of what happened was similar to Clark's. Then, without me asking or saying anything about it, she brought up the video Knowles had posted.

"It's no big deal," she said. "No one is going to watch it. It's grainy and dark and you can't tell it's Julia. She should watch it. She'd feel better. I'm moving out of here. It's gotten strange. I'm sorry I got Julia into this, really sorry." She touched a grocery bag on a kitchen counter that was folded shut. "Her laptop and phone are in here. Do you want to take them?"

"Yes."

I looked at the fire pit and in her room. Her bed was unmade. Her mother's silver talisman that Julia never went anywhere without lay on the small table. Dora watched me slide it into my palm.

In the LA field office, Fuentes was waiting.

"Mara is on his way. He'll be here in half an hour. We're going to meet with you about your niece, so stay in the office and stay available. If she's gone somewhere it's in her interest to return here. But we'll get to that when your supervisor arrives."

"Has something happened I don't know about?" I asked.

"I have to make a call, Grale. Make sure you're in the bullpen where I can find you. Don't go anywhere."

35

Mara is lean and hawkeyed with black hair cut short. He uses the gym at the field office religiously and has little fat. Some believe he lives on coffee and gingerbread. No one cares about the gingerbread. It's the coffee that's a problem.

On the DT squad, domestic terrorism, there's a code for it. Before lunch, there's five-cup Mara and three-cup Mara, but rarely four-cup. If there's something you need that is also a budget consideration, you want three-cup Mara. Five-cup never approves spending or any changes to an agreed-upon plan.

The coffee codes are real enough but pale next to the drive of a late-thirties supervisor with the ambition to go up the ladder all the way to headquarters in DC. That's the real fire in him. He wants to make a difference and leave a mark. That's a good thing, but a source of tension when things don't go as planned. I like Mara. I like him personally and like working with him. That said, he shares with other supervisors I've known the illusion that because he oversees so many investigations, he knows more. That's just not how it works.

Put two supervisors together and you get yet another mix. That's what I had when I walked into the conference room, Mara and Fuentes, the Las Vegas and LA domestic terrorism squad supervisors. I met their confident stares with a hard look and sat down.

"We aren't going to waste time here," Mara said. "So let's just get to it. Here's what we know, Paul. There's an offshoot to Witness1 that Samantha Clark is part of. We believe Nick Knowles is as well. There are others, and they may be sheltering him."

"And you've known this how long?"

"We'll get to that," Mara said.

"Is this coming from multiple undercover agents?"

"From one," Fuentes said. "A very good one."

"Any proof on Knowles' participation?" I asked.

"Yes."

"I'd like to see that too."

"You will," Fuentes said. "Two of your niece's current roommates appear to be members of the offshoot."

"What is this offshoot called?"

"They've left it unnamed. Cathy Ruiz and Jill Hogue are the roommates suspected of being part of it. Your niece wrote a check to Jill Hogue for $15,000 recently. Did she say anything to you about that?"

"No. Do you know why she wrote it?"

Fuentes contemplated that a moment, then gestured to Mara to take it from there.

"We're having this conversation because we believe Julia delivered stolen ammunition from the Colorado hijacking to Samantha Clark in Needles, California, on March 12 of this year," Mara said. "I'm sorry, Paul, but that's how it looks."

"Are you certain it was ammunition?"

"We have video we're going to show you."

"Who took it?" I asked.

"An undercover agent tailing Clark."

"Before we watch the video," I said, "let me tell you what Julia told me after the Knowles box in her car turned out to be stolen bullets. She said she'd delivered—as a favor to Knowles—a box for Clark that was similar but marked 'books and clothing.' He showed her a couple of books before he taped the box shut and loaded it in her car."

"How do you know she didn't know what she was delivering?"

"I take her at her word," I said.

Mara looked away and Fuentes flinched. I didn't blame either. What kind of answer was that from an agent?

"Why did Clark become a person of interest?" I asked.

Fuentes stepped in and fielded that one. That was a lazy fly ball for him. He was fluid and confident.

"It stemmed from her contradictory and hostile witness account of the Signal Hill shootings. A decision was made to investigate whether she'd been tipped to be there in that booth just before closing. There's more, but that's where it started. Where it's leading may be very bad for her."

"Are you going to tell me where it's leading?"

"Not yet," Fuentes said, "and as you well know, showing you this video is something we really shouldn't do. We're justifying it by saying you may see something we don't. You know your niece. You're a career FBI agent. The expectation is you won't forget who you are."

"Let's see the video," I said.

Neither Fuentes nor Mara was adept at getting the video loaded and playing. I wanted to think about what Julia had told me so I didn't step in and help them. They fumbled around until they got it.

"We can't say Julia knew the ammunition was stolen when she delivered it," Mara said. It seemed to be his job to coach me since I was one of his. "In the March 12 video we're about to watch, there's a cardboard box similar to the more recent one. You'll see in the video she was standing alongside Clark as the box is opened."

"Why don't you run it and I'll tell you what I see. Where was the agent who videotaped this?" I asked.

"Across the lot."

"With an angle to see into the box?"

Mara said, "No."

"Let's play it."

Mara started the video. Julia and Samantha walked toward Julia's car. Julia pointed her keys at the car. The rear taillights flashed as the door released. She lifted the hatchback. When she did, a brown cardboard box was visible. "Books and clothing" in black magic marker was fairly easy to read. Julia leaned in and pulled it toward her, first one side then the other. From how her legs tensed and muscles rose on her arms the box was heavy. That was reinforced when Clark reached in to help. They carried it about thirty feet to Clark's car.

When they got there, Clark tried to balance her end of the box on her left knee as she unlocked the trunk. She tried twice, and both were laughing as they put the box down so she could manage the keys. Clark rested the box on her sneaker so she could get her fingers easily under to lift it again. When they inadvertently tipped the top of the box toward the camera, the video caught gray duct tape crosshatched across the top.

"Stop it there," I said. "I want a good look at the duct tape before they lower it into the trunk."

Mara froze it, and I got a look. Julia straightened and laughed after they lowered it. I read that as Julia laughing about how hard it had been. She wiped her brow as Clark looked around before leaning in and picking up what looked like a knife. She kept her hand low so all we could see was part of the blade.

"Aware that someone might be watching," Fuentes said.

I looked at him and nodded. That's what I saw too, but that someone might be Julia. Clark turned and smiled at Julia, then turned to the box, and I saw her right arm moving back and forth as if sawing through the tape.

"Verifying the contents," Fuentes said. "But who knows why she didn't just peel the tape off."

Clark straightened and looked down into the trunk, with Julia alongside her looking also. Julia shrugged in a familiar way, and Clark leaned over the box. She was working at it again. I saw her arm moving. Julia was no longer looking in the trunk and had turned and walked out of the video.

Clark turned and glanced at her, then returned to the box. As Julia came back into view Clark straightened and shut the trunk hard. I asked Mara for the controller and started the video over, then fast-forwarded to Julia and Clark lowering the box into the trunk.

I turned to Fuentes. "Has Julia been wiretapped?"

"Others have, and she's been on some of those calls."

"How do you mean 'on them'?"

Fuentes said, "Speakerphone."

This was awkward for Mara, and he cut in. "There hasn't been a wiretap request on Julia."

"Why didn't you wiretap her if you had this video?"

"We needed more proof of what was in the box. The box in her car after the accident corroborated that." Mara continued, "That Detective Allred has a witness who saw her help Knowles carry the box to her car doesn't prove anything but is another aspect."

"He doesn't have a witness."

"He told me he did. It was part of his narrative in getting a search warrant for your house."

"He was fed a story by someone who promised to give their name later but hasn't come forward. Probably someone Knowles got to make a phone call to Detective Allred. But keep going," I said.

"There was a surveillance app on your niece's laptop," Mara said. "It was erased last night, and her phone is down. Have you heard from her today?"

"No, but how did that app get there? Did you run some sort of phishing campaign targeting her that got approved in the name of antiterrorism?"

I realized no one thing yet was enough to justify a warrant on Julia, and whoever was surveilling the Long Beach house didn't know what had gone down last night. Unless I was fed a story by Clark and Dora, but I didn't see that. Clark wanted something from me, and Dora I read as genuine. It struck me that agents under Fuentes intended to get a FISA warrant, and Julia would get swept up in it. Mara and Fuentes didn't know how I'd react, and another thought occurred to me, a darker one. They lost their phishing app when Julia's computer got baked along with her phone. Showing me this video would cause me to look for her. Agents could tail me. But like I said, just a thought.

"Even if Julia wasn't my niece I'd say you're moving too fast with too little evidence."

"No actions have been taken yet," Mara said. "It's part of why we're having this conversation."

"Her laptop and phone are down because she laid them in a fire pit and melted them. I saw them today. Someone Julia and the others in her circle know has created software that picks up on surveillance apps. She knew her computer had an intruder. She had talked to me about it."

"Where is she now?"

I said, "That's why I was there. I'm trying to find her. At the house, one of her roommates gave me a grocery bag with her laptop and cell phone. I can show you. I can't confirm they're hers, but they're destroyed. Both are Apple devices, which is what she had. She's closed her Verizon account. Her roommates say she was distraught when she left."

"Do you have any idea why she wrote a $15,000 check or where she got that kind of money?" Mara asked.

"She got it from the sale of the family house, from the savings my sister and her husband had, and from a modest life insurance policy. The car in the video belonged to my sister, Melissa. They had a living trust, and I was named as executor and guardian of the children. I gave

Julia control when she became an adult in Nevada at age eighteen. It's looking like a mistake."

Mara cut in. "I'm sorry we have to do this. I'm sorry it's so uncomfortable."

"I'm fine with it, and if Julia hasn't committed any crimes I don't know what there is to be sorry about."

"You just watched the videotape," Mara said.

"If you're saying she saw what was in the box, I'm not seeing that. If that's what you think makes it so compelling, pass me the controller. I want to run that section in slo-mo."

Mara slid it across to me and once I got located in the video I found Julia and Samantha looking down at the box in the trunk of Clark's car. Clark was smiling.

"She's happy about the guns and ammo," Mara said.

"Watch Julia, she's going to shrug. I know that shrug."

I rewound it and played it again. "That was her teen attitude shrug. I know it very well. Okay, this next bit is a big deal, and you've got to watch Clark's right hand."

I froze the video where the knife blade showed best. Clark involuntarily raised her hand as she turned to watch Julia walk away before leaning forward and sawing furiously.

"Two things here," I said. "The blade is very dull, and she's hurrying so she can see inside before Julia returns."

"If that's true, why didn't she open it somewhere else or after Julia left?"

"I don't know. She'd have to answer that."

Mara said, "What I see is Clark closing the box up."

"If she did that she'd put the knife down. Clark is trying to hide how hard she's sawing, but you can see her right elbow moving. She's cutting. The knife is dull and the tape sticky. It's the same motion as before. She was joking earlier about the dull blade when she was smiling at Julia, and Julia didn't care. Julia gave a shrug and walked away.

"She didn't wait around to see the clothes and books. She wanted to deliver the box and go. She told me she called Knowles at work to let him know she'd gotten to Needles and was just about to meet up with Clark. She'd spotted Clark's car. Turns out Knowles wasn't at work. She was told he hadn't come in that day. That after asking her to make the delivery for him," I said.

"That box held ammunition from the hijacked truck. We know that now," Mara said but looked perplexed. "Play that again."

"Hold on," I said. "What do you mean you know? If you knew, we wouldn't be having this meeting. You don't know and you're trying to sell me on your assumptions."

I replayed the video and Fuentes said, "Grale, you might be right, but I still don't see why Clark's opening it with Julia there if she wants to hide what's in it."

"Okay, I'll throw down an idea. Julia had told Clark earlier that Nick showed her a few of the books in the box. Maybe Clark just wanted to be sure. Maybe she's got questions about Knowles. She wouldn't be the first person with those."

"All right, we can debate all day," Fuentes said, "and we don't have all day. We're worried about the $15,000 check she wrote. That would buy a lot of ammonium nitrate. The agents working this are confident that money made its way to the offshoot group. That raises the specter that your niece is part of what you're trying to solve, even if she doesn't know it."

That was my fear too.

I said, "Here's what I see. My niece, reeling from the breakup with Knowles and the revelation he wasn't who he said he was, was left distraught and humiliated. She got an offer to move into the Long Beach house at a time when she was trying to figure out what comes next. One of the roommates was a high school friend who vouched for the house and the people sharing it. She'd been talking about moving out for months and made an impulsive move driven by a video Knowles posted.

"For six months Julia had talked about moving out. The breakup and what may have been a date rape made her get away from Las Vegas and go somewhere no one knows her to start again. If she wrote a check for $15,000, she thinks she's supporting something worthwhile and probably expects to get something back in return. This is a tough young woman and nobody's fool. She inherited money when her family was killed, and they must know that. She'll figure out that she's getting used and stop writing checks."

"Would you agree she's susceptible?" Fuentes asked.

"She calls herself a pacifist and is against all violence. Within a year of losing her family she embraced pacifism and has stayed with it. And when I say she's tough, I'm not just talking. Julia is not naïve. I'd say she's with this group because of their aspirations for how to live. She'll figure it out and leave them."

Fuentes didn't respond. Neither did Mara. They thought the pacifism talk was all smoke. They were going to fall back and conference with each other, but I wasn't quite finished here.

"Show me proof," I said. "You haven't." Then I demanded, "Do either of you know where she is, or do the agents who've worked the surveillance?"

Neither knew, which disturbed me more than anything said earlier.

"You lost her?" I asked.

It was Mara who nodded. Fuentes had already figured the meeting was going nowhere, and he had other things to do.

36

Mission Hills, LA Basin

After I left Fuentes and Mara, I called Jace. She was laughing at something as she answered the phone. Coming off the serious meeting I'd been in, hearing her contagious laugh was like warm sunlight on a cold morning.

"Drake Brown, the manager at the Tracy substation, left me a message," I said. "He went through more video and found the same Chevy Tahoe as three weeks before."

"Same decal, same dents?" she asked.

"Same everything and a readable license plate. I ran it and got an address in Mission Hills, west of San Bernardino. Hofter and I are about to go there. I'll let you know what we find."

At the Mission Hills address, a middle-aged man opened the door and immediately read us as law enforcement. He was balding and genial, dressed in baggy shorts, sandals, and a T-shirt.

"Who are you?" he asked.

"FBI. We're looking for Evan Gavotte."

"That's me."

"We'd like a look at an SUV registered to you," I said.

"It's not mine anymore. I sold it to my son a year ago. He may not have completed the registration change. He's still a kid in a lot of ways."

"How old is he?"

"Twenty-three. He lives in a large warehouse along the Sylmar–San Fernando line that they call the 'Colony.' Jody's an artist, or wants to be. Another artist owns the building and carved it up into living spaces. I'll show you the Tahoe. It's in the garage. He can't always park where he lives so brings it here. Tell me why you need to see it."

"It showed up on a surveillance camera, and we need to talk to Jody."

"He's just a stupid kid who thinks he's Hertz or Budget. I couldn't count how many times I've argued with him about it. I'll guarantee you it wasn't Jody driving."

He pointed at a car at the curb. "The garage door opener is in my car, or I can hit the button inside the garage if you want to follow me."

We followed him through the house to the garage. When he hit the button, the garage door creaked, shuddered, then rose. Sunlight bathed the rear of the old Tahoe. Its paint was fading, its tires worn. I verified the plate numbers, and we compared the blown-up images of the left rear panel dents to the real deal. Mark took several careful photos, then walked out to the edge of the driveway and called for a tow truck.

"Jody has strong opinions and he's caught up in politics, but he's a good kid," his dad said. "I'm hoping he'll get over the artist thing. He's not making any money selling his paintings."

The tow truck and Jody Gavotte arrived at the same time. Jody got out of the car agitated. The older sister I'd seen in the house probably texted him, and he'd gotten a ride here. He was wiry and energetic with a mane of black hair cut so it crested in a narrow band along the top of his head then flowed down between his shoulder blades. His neck and his arms down to just above his elbows were tattooed, the half sleeves colored with red, black, and blue ink.

For our benefit, he asked his dad in a loud voice, "What's up with the suits?" Then he confronted me, demanding, "What's up?"

"Let's see some ID," I said.

"Dude, I'm not playing the game. I don't carry ID. I don't do wallets. You've got my dad and sister right here. What the fuck else do you need for ID?"

"Dial it down, Jody," I said. "Your vehicle has showed up on video in two locations we're investigating."

"I rent it out."

"Where are your rental records?"

"I don't keep any. I look at the drivers' licenses and make sure they're current. I don't run credit cards. These are cash deals."

I looked at him. "You don't keep track of who you've rented your vehicle to?"

"This is like a B movie, dude. It's not a V-E-H-I-C-L-E. It's a Chevy four-wheel SUV. I'm saying I get a read on the people before I hand over the keys, and I don't put out a vibe saying I'm worried about where they're going or what they're going to do. Positive energy attracts positive energy."

"We're attracted to you, Jody. You're coming with us to the FBI office. Your four-wheel-drive SUV is going for a ride too."

"Man, that's such bullshit," Jody said.

"Do you want to be handcuffed and arrested?"

"No."

"Then ease back."

Dad backed the Tahoe out and the impound driver loaded it. We let Gavotte Junior absorb watching it slide up onto a platform and leave.

"Nice," Jody said sarcastically as he got into the back seat of our car. Dad and the daughter, Kris, followed us to the office. In an interview room, the attitude and bravado left him when we played the PG&E video of the Tahoe pulling up alongside the Tracy substation and returning an hour later for several slow cruises. While we questioned him, an analyst completed a comparison of video footage.

I went out in the corridor and returned a call from the FBI tech who'd run the new software program. Artificial intelligence was getting very good at comparing images. The video we got from Drake Brown in Tracy had been compared with video taken in Southern California. We didn't want to let Jody know about it yet. Both were looking at the left side of the Tahoe as it passed by.

When I came back into the room, Gavotte was explaining to Mark, "This woman rented the Tahoe for a week. She paid me five hundred bucks cash. That was before any of the resistance bombings happened."

No one blinked at the word "resistance." It was out there now anyway. We'd all seen it.

"What did the woman say about where she was going?" I asked.

"Coastline camping. I told her to fill the gas tank and wash the salt off before bringing it back."

"How do you advertise the rental?"

He said, "An artist's thing, a monthly magazine some people I know started."

"Here's another video," Mark said and ran it. "Is that you driving? It looks like you." Hofter was losing patience.

"It's not me."

"How old are you, Jody?" Hofter asked.

"Twenty-three."

"You ought to think about what's going on in your country."

"Excuse me? My country? I'm not the one with the money. You're working for them. Why don't you talk to them?"

I stepped back in. "How many times has it rented in the last two weeks, Jody?"

"Four times."

"Where have you driven in that time?"

"Nowhere. Errands and stuff."

"Not to the beach or mountains?"

"No."

I reminded him, "Don't forget we're videotaping this interview, and I'll say again, you have the right to have a lawyer present. We need your help. We need you to tell us everything you can remember about the four people you rented the Tahoe to in the past two weeks."

As he started on that, I heard something in his voice that I thought was worry. He did his best to describe two couples, one in their forties but trying to look younger, a solo dude, two gangbangers who promised no violence and brought it back a couple hours later, and a "chick about his age."

"Could you sketch the young woman's face?"

"I don't do line drawings. That's not where it's at, but white girl with black hair parted in the middle with blond roots. Sort of average height and decent looking . . . that's about it."

"The next video we're going to show you wasn't taken in Tracy," I said. "It was taken at night by a camera no one figured on. If you were driving, we're going to advise you to be very clear and straightforward. The cameras have gotten a lot better, but what's really changed are the computer programs that can read a dent in a car in the same way facial-recognition software works. That left rear panel of the Tahoe is a distinctive set of dents. It's been matched to an image a surveillance camera caught."

"You're not going to frame me."

I asked, "Are you clear you're on record?"

"Yep."

"Do you want an attorney present during questioning?"

"Your whole way, man, it's gone. It's not happening anymore."

"The young woman with the black hair parted in the middle, was she the last person to use the Tahoe?"

"Yes," he said.

"Did she rent it or borrow it?"

That caught him. He couldn't hide it but didn't know how to answer that without screwing up something else. Or that was my guess. He shook his head and got a quizzical smile going, then said, "Dude, what's up with you?"

"Why won't you answer whether she paid or not?"

"What's it to you? Why do you care?"

"It's about you, Jody, not us. What are you hiding?"

Gavotte shook his head, and Mark ran the five-second clip, and then again in slo-mo. The left rear panel dent was visible, as was the faded bumper sticker and the license plate as the Tahoe slowly passed by.

"That's my rig."

He smiled and Hofter asked, "What about this is funny to you?"

"All of it."

"Do you know where this was taken?" I asked.

"Nope."

I said, "Okay, now we're going to show you a clip from a utility company camera taken twelve minutes before the clip where you identified your vehicle. I have to warn you there's a shooting."

"Show me whatever, let's get this over."

"Here goes," I said. "See the man walking up? There's a guy in the truck who was hired by the utility as additional security."

Gavotte recoiled at the muzzle flash. His reaction looked genuine.

"It was a second job, a night job," I said. "He was making ends meet. He had a young family. Those muzzle flashes are him getting killed sitting in his truck up at an electrical substation in the Tehachapis. The video we watched just before this one was your vehicle leaving there a few minutes later."

He thought about that a few seconds, started to say something, then stopped himself. He looked at me and said, "Fuck. That's bad."

"Is that you shooting the guard?"

"What? No, kill somebody? Never. Okay, she and I did a deal, not a big thing just trading the Tahoe rental for dope and some beer. I know her but I don't know her, okay? She's been around a couple of times, and I've seen her at this coffee place and another converted warehouse. There's like a whole group of warehouses run by a trucking company. A lot of empty spaces they lease out in Sylmar, but mostly San Fernando and Burbank or along the freeway north of there."

"I want to be very clear with you, Jody. The shooter appears to have a build very similar to yours. You—"

"No way, that's crazy. I would never shoot anyone."

"Figure out who you rented to."

"Okay, I can, and I didn't shoot anybody," he said. "That guy wasted a dude in the truck? That's raw. Oh, yeah, I heard about that, the security cop. All right, I'll figure her out or where that place is they rent. The owner where I am probably knows. Are you serious about the software that matches the dents?"

"We are. Your license plates are there too."

"I get it."

I wasn't sure he did.

"Just give me a few hours."

37

JULIA

The Farm, Tulare County, California, May 4th

Julia walked the rows of tomato plants. In the sun their smell was pungent. She inhaled it as she bent over and pulled a weed.

They'd said, "Check out the vegetables. Walk around. You bought in, girl. You own part of the farm." She pulled another weed, this time letting her knee sink into the soil, then stood and walked out to the gravel road that ran from the outbuildings and the house to the property gate. The gate had an electric release and a code that, when she tried it, didn't work.

On either side of the gate was barbed-wire fencing that followed the roll of the grassy hills. In the distance to the right were mountains. The high peaks were snow covered. She rattled the gate again. Easy to climb over and walk out to the road, then down past the big olive and avocado orchards. She was in California, in Tulare County.

For a year she'd heard about the farm as a kind of mystical place. She closed her eyes with her hands resting on the top of the gate and the sun on her face and stood there several minutes. Then she turned back to the farmhouse with the big deck out front and shade surrounding it.

Rule one was you couldn't stay more than three days unless you worked. Last night she was given her jobs. She was down with that but wanted her car. Danny, the tall guy, the quiet one who was always watching her, had said, "I hear that. I wouldn't be here without wheels either. If you want, I can take you down to pick up your car the day after tomorrow, or there are some things we need here that could be brought in if you're okay with someone else driving it. The guy who would drive it is the slowest, most careful driver you've ever met."

"Bring what things?" she'd asked.

"I do all the equipment repairs. It's just some parts and wiring I need, nothing oily. It would all fit in a small trunk."

She'd agreed to that but now kind of wished she hadn't. Today she'd gotten a free day to explore. Tomorrow she would start working. Tonight, with Paula's phone, she would call UG or Jo, probably Jo since the last times she'd called UG she couldn't reach him. *You can leave anytime you want,* she thought. *With or without the code. With or without your stuff, just hop over and go.*

A creek fed by snowmelt ran just inside the east side of the property to a pond that in the summer they said sometimes dried up to almost nothing. Brush and trees lined the creek She guessed it was two miles to the highway, though it might be longer. Trucks glinted in the sun when they drove by, but cars were harder to see. When she had her car back, she could buy a new cell phone. She turned and walked back to the other buildings.

One they called the tractor barn, where Danny worked. He was weird but maybe just shy. Tom did deliveries, the farmers' markets, and a lot of other things to keep the farm running. He and Paula chose what to plant. Paula did the books and the marketing.

Last night, Paula said the farm doesn't make any real money. She said it straightforward and matter-of-fact as if no one would dispute that, although when Julia bought in, no one had informed her of this. She still didn't have any papers proving her share of ownership, and she couldn't even get into the tractor barn. It was almost as big as the farmhouse and was locked. She walked to it and tried the door again. She knocked hard and then called, "Dan!" Supposedly, he ran the machinery and boxed the vegetables in there.

"Go to the farm," Sam had said. "Put in a year and learn to work with your hands. Grow real food. Work, get tired, sleep, and get up early. It's basic but it's chill there. You'll love it. Go get whole. I'll let your uncle know you're okay."

She walked back to the fence and followed it east until she reached the creek, where she squatted and put her hands in the water. The water was cool not warm. Earth has the same amount of water as it had billions of years ago. No matter what they say, nobody owns the water. She remembered them at the fire pit talking and saying that. Some of the dudes saw wars over water coming soon. They all talked like somehow they knew, even though they were just getting it from things they read or heard.

Here they had a well with a pump. She checked it out, then walked back to the farmhouse. As she went up the steps, she heard Paula and one of the guys talking inside. The farmhouse had an old-style screen door with a wood frame that slapped shut behind her as she went in.

"What do you think in daylight?" Paula asked.

"Pretty cool."

"Did you check everything out?"

"What wasn't locked, and also I need the code to the gate."

"Want some iced tea?"

"Sure, would love some. Can I borrow your phone later, Paula? I need to tell my family where I am. Also, I'd like to get into the tractor barn. I want to see what I invested in."

Danny heard that. He was standing in the kitchen. She said it for him, and they stared at each other. Then he half smiled like he'd heard something funny. He was tall with broad shoulders and hard, sharp cheekbones. His eyes were the bright color of bluebottle flies.

"What's up with you?" Julia asked him.

"Nothing."

"Why did you look like you were about to laugh?"

"I don't know."

Paula cut in, saying, "Back to work, Danny. See you at supper."

He left, and Julia poured some of the iced tea and sat down. This was nuts. Paula had said "See you at supper" like she was in charge of the house and his job was outside. He obeyed her like a boy doing what his mother tells him to do.

"I used to counsel people," Paula said. "I know you're hurting. I know you need time to heal. It's a very simple life here, but it's what you need. Let it be what it is. Two pairs of clothes, wear one, wash one, bathe every day because we have the water, and forget everything else except brushing your teeth. And birth control if you think you might want one of these guys."

"I won't."

"You're young. Sometimes things just happen. But only stay if you want to. Do not bring bad energy here."

Only that last bit reached her. She had to stop thinking so many negative things.

"Are you there, Julia?"

"Right here. I need to get a phone in the next day or so. How do I do that?"

"I'll ask Tom to pick you up one, but you need to limit your calls to one per day. Those are the rules we all agreed on."

"I still need to use your phone today to let my family know I'm okay."

"You're with your family. You just don't realize it yet. I'll hold the phone and you talk. We agree before the call how long the conversation will last and what will be said."

"If it gets me a call today, okay, but that's not going to work for long."

"We'll do the call at the end of the day. We'll take one day at a time."

Paula reached out, took Julia's hands in hers, and squeezed them. "I channel energies. I have that gift. We will heal you. Do you want that? I need to hear you say you want to heal."

Julia nodded, then asked, "Can I use your phone at nine?"

"Say it, Julia."

"I want to heal."

"Good. So let's not think about phones or time. Let's get dinner prepared without thinking about anything else. Can you do that?"

"Sure," Julia said, and then followed her to the kitchen.

38

From a broken asphalt lot outside the warehouse called the Colony, I talked with Sheriff Callan.

"I'm stepping down as sheriff. I signed a stack of forms today that releases everybody from liability after they put an artificial esophagus in my throat. Do you know anyone walking around with one of those? I don't either."

"Where's the surgery?"

"San Francisco."

"When?"

I wrote it down and said, "You'll make it through."

"I'd better. Mary wants to go to Europe."

"Book it before your surgery and it'll give you both something to look forward to. Make her promise to go anyway if you can't."

"I like that, Grale."

He hung up a moment later.

The warehouse was not the first I'd seen with this name. Living communally may make the difficult task of surviving as an artist in America easier, but it's still a tough road. I waited for Hofter to arrive then left him outside on his cell phone and went in and found Gavotte. He gave me a short tour, pointing out different artists' spaces and referencing their art as if the names of pieces were common knowledge. Some spaces were no more than pitched tents made from blankets strung with ropes within the cavernous two-story space. Above us, an ancient wood floor creaked with footsteps.

"Let's go do it, Jody," I said. "Show me where you park the Tahoe when it's not in your dad's garage."

Outside, I put on sunglasses, and Mark, tie flopping, walked with us as I talked.

"Your sister says you wanted your dad's Tahoe because it's big enough to sleep in."

"My sister talks too much."

"Was she right about sleeping in the Tahoe with your girlfriend in this warehouse space?"

"Yeah, I've got a spot, but it sucks. It's got chemical spills. It's down there at the end of that building. We did sleep in there in the Tahoe for like a month. There's a rolling door I can leave a little bit open at night so air comes in, but it's a big space and they stored something in the back that leaked and is friggin' serious. I mean, it's nasty, dude."

When we reached the rolling metal door, Gavotte punched numbers into a keypad. As the door went up, an eye-watering chemical smell washed out.

"I can't do this. I got sick sleeping in here. I got this rash on my body and my nose was running all the time. Take a look, then I'll shut the door. The smell is bad, isn't it?"

"Let's walk through," I said.

"You sure? What for?"

Gavotte flicked the light switches up and nothing happened. "Guess we're not walking," he said.

"Yeah, we are," Hofter said and handed me one of two small LED flashlights he'd brought. We passed piles of debris, Sheetrock and 2 × 4s, the remains of interior walls when this must have been an office space. I saw tire tracks from something like a Bobcat, and more recently cars. Deeper in were larger debris piles, and the chemical smell worsened. Our light beams swept across tire tracks up ahead turning left.

Near the back wall the chemical smell was too much. It came into your throat, and no matter how shallow you breathed, it burned in the lungs.

"This is bullshit, I want out of here," Gavotte said and coughed.

We turned, but I slowed and fell back when I reached the tire tracks that had looked recent. The tracks led to what looked like a large debris pile but wasn't. It was debris spread over a tarp covering something. I started pulling off boards that held the tarp in place and saw the rear end of a blue Nissan. I swept the light across, and there were no license plates. I needed my phone to look at a photo of the car Julia had bought, so I pulled it out and jerked more of the tarp off. I shined the light inside the car and saw red sunglasses I recognized as hers.

The car was empty and locked. I couldn't open the trunk without prying it. I called Hofter over and showed him a photo Julia had sent me. "This is Julia's new car."

39

Julia's car hidden in a garbage dump of a warehouse took things to a different place. I popped the trunk with a pry bar and stared into the empty space with relief, despite Julia having talked with Jo at nine last night. I questioned Gavotte with a whole different tone, and he admitted parking the car there. When he did, Hofter stepped away and called Fuentes and asked for two more agents.

Before they arrived, we questioned the Colony owner, a late-middle-aged guy named Max Tona, who out of earshot of Gavotte confessed, "I'm not actually the owner. I inherited the building but had debts. The Hazen Group LA Beautification LLC is the owner. I'm a partial owner of this building and not at all of the warehouse where the car was found."

"Are you saying you're not responsible?"

"I manage both," he said.

"Gavotte thinks you own this building."

"So do the rest of the artists."

"Did you give Jody Gavotte a key to the warehouse where the car is?"

"Yes."

"Then you're in. You want to be truthful with us."

Tona wore his hair in a graying ponytail. He had a kind, sun-damaged face and had expressed shock, disbelief, and concern, yet said,

"It's probably just what Jody told you. He was trying to make a buck and didn't think it through, same way as he rents his Chevy."

Gavotte had claimed to us that he got $200 for storing the car. The same woman who'd traded dope for using his Tahoe had made the deal with him. He didn't know or care whose car it was—which was probably the truest thing he'd said. Some of the rest was a lie or he wouldn't have buried the car under a tarp and trash. But the car didn't matter. What I needed from him was everything he remembered from the night the car was dropped off and where to find the woman he'd made the deal with.

Tona rounded out his version of events and thought he was done. We turned Tona over to the two agents arriving and took Gavotte back to the space and stood outside the roll-up door as he walked back through the sequence of events that night.

"There were two cars," he said. "The car parked inside was driven by the woman I dealt with. The other had people in it and was parked over near that light pole."

He pointed across the lot.

"That light is burned out, so I couldn't see them."

"Who paid you?" I asked.

"Her, the one I made the deal with. She gave me two hundred bucks. The reason I covered the car was so the friggin' owner here wouldn't freak out if he went in there. He, like, prowls around checking out his properties and sometimes goes in with this county dude figuring out how to clean up the chemicals."

He showed a solid, earnest look he'd probably learned over years facing his frustrated dad. After another hour of questioning, he admitted walking across the lot and checking out the other people in the waiting car. Including the woman he'd made the deal with, there were four people, three women and a man. The only description he gave us was the young woman he'd made the deal with. He was devoid of any concern for Julia. Jody Gavotte was all about himself, but from his very rough descriptions, one of the women sitting in back could have been Julia.

We got the car to an FBI lot, and then drove back to the FBI office. I'd only been there a few minutes when Jo called and said she'd just talked to Julia.

"It was a much more detailed conversation," Jo said. "The farm is in Tulare County and it's beautiful. It's not far from the town of Three Rivers and Lake Kaweah. She still doesn't have the address but will get it to us very soon."

"Very soon? How can she not have an address?"

"Let me tell you what else she said. They want her to stay for a year to get her spiritual health back. She said she might stay a couple of weeks at the most and that she'll be working on the farm while she's there. They grow vegetables they sell at farmers' markets and to smaller grocery stores. When I asked her what the living situation was like she said, 'Communal.' There are three others there with her, two men and a woman. One of the guys she said is a freak, and the other is on the road all the time delivering or selling. She said the woman, Paula, told her they'll bring her car to her, and then she'll get a new phone. She otherwise sounded normal or close to it. Whatever else is going on there, I don't think she's frightened, and in some ways she sounds calmer than last week. She said to tell you she loves you and that she's fine. I wouldn't call it a normal conversation, but she sounded intact."

After I hung up with Jo, I called Mara and had a heart-to-heart.

"Ahead of your sworn oath and in the middle of a terror assault on our electrical grid and cellular network, you'll walk away?" Mara asked.

"Give me a break, Ted."

"If you're not saying that, what are you saying?"

"I'm saying I'm worried and I'm not going to sit back and wait. Give me room to find Julia. You and Fuentes still have her marked as possibly involved, and I'm afraid of her unwittingly getting drawn in deeper. That's why—"

Mara interrupted. "At least speaking for myself, that's not true."

"You were plenty clear when I looked at that video with you and Fuentes."

"You changed my mind. I'm back to neutral. Look at it this way: if Julia is away from the Long Beach house, where at least two people are under surveillance, that's a good thing. Hang in there. Don't rabbit on me. If she's calling, she's not in danger. I don't want a phone call from you in Tulare County."

"I want the flexibility to move quickly if I learn more and need to go," I said.

"I can't make that guarantee in this environment."

"Then don't."

I was ready to end the call when he asked, "Are you angry we sandbagged you with the Needles surveillance video?"

"I'm over it."

"We need you working. We need everybody," he said.

I left the LA office soon after and drove back to the Colony, knowing I should just go to the hotel and get some sleep. But I couldn't, not yet. I would soon, but I wanted another look at the whole warehouse complex, not just the Colony.

From Max Tona I'd gotten a map that was mostly marketing but did show the locations of various warehouses and commercial buildings from Burbank up to Sylmar that the Hazen Group owned. Tona had told us the woman managing the warehouses for Hazen also managed a trucking distribution business. Odd but believable, as more and more people took multiple jobs trying to make ends meet.

I called the number he gave me for that manager, a Deborah Inze.

First thing she said was, "Don't call me Deborah, I hate it. Call me Deb." I'd go see her tomorrow. I don't know what I expected to learn, but I was missing something I should be seeing. I couldn't tell you what it was, but I could feel it.

40

May 6th

"You never call or text anymore," Jace said. "Are you seeing another agent?"

"Yeah, a guy named Mark Hofter and all the time. It's busy here. The rolling blackouts are doing a number. Sorry I haven't been in touch. My niece disappeared and seems to be at a farm in Tulare County. Her car was hidden in a warehouse and I've been very worried. I'll tell you about it later today."

"Where are you this morning?" she asked.

"At a warehouse about to meet a manager who oversees a string of warehouses and office buildings between Burbank and Sylmar."

"We've got some things to talk about. Call me when you've got more time."

I parked the car and walked into a huge open warehouse that smelled like idling 18-wheelers and diesel-powered forklifts. Deb Inze was in her office. She was diminutive but tough, small but fierce, as Shakespeare had said. It wasn't enough for Inze to see my creds. She called the LA office to verify.

When she hung up she asked, "Why aren't you out there stopping this mess? What are you doing here?"

"I'm checking out a lead. I'd like to tour your buildings with you."

"It would take us all day, and I don't have one to waste. If you want a list of addresses, I'll give you one. If you want to ride around here with me and visit a few, I'll do that, but not for long. We can talk on the ride, but give me a few minutes first."

She went off, and I made calls. When she came back, she said, "At this hub, meaning where we're standing, we redistribute cargo. We need storage capacity so we can hold, recombine, or reload freight. The large spaces here are for that. The other warehouses are a variety of businesses. Many are empty. Some are rat nests of temporary renters."

"Rat nests?"

"That's my opinion, not the owners'. The Hazen Group LA Beautification LLC owns all of this. Ready to go? I've got an electric cart we can ride around in."

The electric cart was a golf cart she drove through the lots and on the street. Once away from the din of forklifts and diesel trucks I could hear her more easily.

"There are seventeen businesses," she said. "Most are along this stretch. We're coming up on one the FBI has had an interest in before. The guy who runs it is named Bill Stuckey, like stuck in the mud. You'll see him through the window. He's a salesman dealing in used vehicles but mostly specialty trucks. That's why agents were here before questioning both me and Stuckey, which I'm gathering you don't know about."

She looked over at me. "That's okay, you don't have to embarrass yourself if you didn't know."

"I know he was questioned about the sale of used Edison trucks."

"Okay, so you do know. Do you know about the prison time Stuckey did?"

"No."

"Ask him about it." Through the window I saw a balding, middle-aged guy sit down at a desk. Deb added, "We dated for a while, but honestly, now I wish he'd take a long one-way swim in the ocean some night. I'll wait for you here. Don't buy anything."

In the warehouse was Stuckey's spare, elegant desk, and behind it maybe twenty large vehicles parked with space between each on the stained and polished concrete floor. Stuckey took off his glasses. He looked like the curator of a museum. If he'd told me I needed to buy a ticket to walk the floor, it wouldn't have surprised me.

"The FBI has already been here about the Edison trucks used in the bombings. We handle auctions and/or buy from a number of large corporations, but primarily utilities. How can I help you, and why is she here? Did she bad-mouth me?" Stuckey asked.

"She did." I gave it a beat. "But I'm not here about that. I want to talk with you about people who shopped for used Edison trucks."

"FBI agents have already looked at the record of every single sale," Stuckey said. "They checked everything we sold at auction. I don't know what else to show you. Is this something she put you up to?"

He stood, stretched out a long arm, and pointed at Deb. She couldn't miss it.

"I did prison time for embezzlement twenty-five years ago. I was an accountant and had debts that got out of control. I made the mistake of a lifetime. Look at her looking in here."

I didn't turn to look, and some aspect of this felt phony.

"One night she's at my place and we're half undressed and I tell her about prison. I feel like I have to at some point, you know? She stands up, puts her clothes on, walks out, and the next day tells me she never wants to see or talk to me again. She said go find another job or I'll ruin your life here. Well, I'm going on sixty and it doesn't work that way in sales. I don't just go find another job. I'm lucky to have this one."

"Let's get back on track, Bill. I'm going to show you some photos, but these aren't used Edison rigs. These are people, male and female. They're random. I want to know if you recognize anyone."

He sat down again. He'd stood, I'd thought, to be more convincing and now wanted it all over and done.

"Look at photos. Sure, why not? I've got to get last month's numbers to my boss, but that's fine. Let's look at pictures together."

I didn't spread the photos out on his desk or make any kind of show of it, and instead handed him a dozen photos.

"If you're not sure but might recognize the face, lay the photo faceup on the desk. If you're certain it's not them, lay it facedown."

He looked at me and muttered something about sorting them however he wanted to. I left it alone and he went through them at about one every two seconds, twelve photos in less than thirty seconds. Then he went back through them slowly. He laid one facedown on his desk, a second faceup, and handed me the remaining, with the comment, "I'm good at this. Everybody who comes through that door is a potential buyer. I study their faces. Been doing it for years."

The faceup photo was Jody Gavotte, about which he explained. "I don't know that he's been in here. There's a start-up coffee roaster among these buildings. Sometimes I'll walk down there. I feel like that's where I've seen him. I don't remember him in here." He handed Jody's photo to me and said, "Now this other photo, the one I have facedown, she was in here in February with a lot of questions, buyer questions, a lot of interest, and then I never saw her again. She was serious enough that I figured she'd bought from a competitor. There are three others in Southern Cal that deal in used utility vehicles. She must have gone somewhere else. She was a buyer. I'm sure of that. Her name was Dalia. We had fun talking and I expected her to come back."

He had trouble flipping the photo over and finally got a nail under it, but I already knew who it was. I'd been thinking about Gavotte and Julia's car and the blue Tahoe caught on the Tehachapi security camera. It was too many things coming back to one location. Here was another. He handed the photo to me. I was looking at Samantha Clark.

"How sure are you?" I asked.

"Dead certain. Like I said, I remember faces."

41

Deb shook her head. "Why did he point at me?"

"Ask him. Let's see the rest of what you're willing to show me, then stop by the coffee roaster and I'll buy."

"It'll have to be to-go."

When we stopped there, they didn't ask for her order. They made a small Americano with two shots, held the coffee down an inch from the rim, and handed it to her. We toured the rest of the businesses in the half block of warehouses before she dropped me at my car.

I drove back to the LA FBI office and sent Hofter the list of businesses I had gotten from Inze, then met for twenty minutes with Fuentes and told him, "I've just come from the warehouse complex where Jody Gavotte lives and where agents from here interviewed a used utility vehicle salesman named Bill Stuckey. The firm he works for refurbishes and sells used specialty vehicles."

"I know who he is. His sales records checked out. Why were you there?"

I slipped the photo of Samantha Clark out of a notebook and across to Fuentes.

"Out of a dozen photos he picked her. She came in last February with a different name and asked about used Edison trucks."

Fuentes picked up the photo. "You talked with him today?"

"I just came from there."

Fuentes nodded. "You're wondering if we knew this and you've been left out of the loop. We didn't know." He waved the photo. "This is new. What you haven't been told is that Clark connects to Laura Balco, the Blond Bomber, and the unidentified dead accomplice. We'd heard whispers about a secret militant edge of Witness1. An anonymous tip gave us a way in. Agent Hofter has been briefed all the way along. You've been left out as we've tried to resolve your niece's role. The night Julia disappeared they managed to lose us. We had no idea her car was where you found it." He handed the photo back saying, "That warehouse complex is coming up way too much, isn't it?"

"Yeah."

At the door, I paused for two reasons. One, I didn't quite understand the exchange we'd just had, and two, to say, "I think wherever Julia is, they talked her into it."

"I hope it's all just as you say, Grale. I really do. Find her and we'll take it from there."

42

Fuentes will let Mara deal with me. Good decision for both of us because I still didn't accept how easily Julia had become a person of interest. Nor did I accept the decision to keep me in the dark about what had been learned through wiretaps of those suspected of being part of a Long Beach cell. Fuentes was unsurprised Clark had shopped for used Edison trucks. I saw that standing in front of his desk looking at him. No matter how I turned all the pieces, keeping me in the dark came down to suspecting Julia was involved.

Fuentes, the agents here, Mara, the rest, probably all were concerned for me. Worried how hard it would be when Julia was busted on terror charges. I knew myself. I knew I'd pull back and work more on my own.

Late in the afternoon I left the LA office and drove back to the storefront Stuckey worked out of. He'd told me he likes to lock the door at 5:30 in the afternoon. I'd wait for that and follow him, but only up to a point. If he locked up and went to his favorite watering hole or picked up to-go food or sat down in a diner or went straight home, I'd leave him be.

At 6:45 he locked up, got in his car, and drove slowly away then started turning down one street, up another, driving fast, driving slow like a spy in a TV movie. He did this for ten minutes in an area between San Fernando and the south edge of Sylmar, then followed Polk east until the road dead-ended in hills. There, he turned into a steep drive-way with an awkward ornamental iron fence and gate at the bottom, as if the house above was a hacienda rather than a stucco ranch notched into the dry, steep slope.

I changed streets for a better view and saw Stuckey's car and another side by side. When Deb Inze and Bill Stuckey walked out and Stuckey had a hand around her shoulders, I called Fuentes and told him I might need backup.

He listened then said, "Okay, but kind of walk me through this. You think they played you?"

"I do, and now after the drama show I think they're worried, so they're having a little meet-up. Stuckey just got in his car. I'm going to let him go and stick with Inze."

"I'll get two agents headed your way in separate vehicles. They'll call you. You coordinate with them. You can fill me in later on how you happened to be there."

Fuentes hung up, and Deb stood in the dusk at the edge of the parking slab looking out as if she was unsure about what came next. It had darkened, but I could still see her silhouette.

What are you thinking about, Deb? Waiting for dark and feeling unsure about whatever it is you got into? Nothing feels well planned any-more, does it?

Her headlights came on. She drove slowly down the steep drive-way and started south, then reversed. She tracked north of Sylmar up a frontage road and then crossed I-5 north along the west side of the converter station, past Water and Power, then left and back into Sylmar, and left again. She pulled over on a wide street, killed her lights, and sat for a while before driving the whole loop once more.

The two agents Fuentes sent took over after Inze drove to the Burbank address on her driver's license. Jo called as I left them and said, "Photos of the farmhouse, pond, crops, and outbuildings were sent to my phone along with a text that said, 'Super tired. Weeded today. Love you both.'"

"That was all?" I asked.

"Yes, and from the same phone as before. It doesn't sound like she's in danger, but it's weird." After a beat she added, "I don't hear fear."

"But she's still dodging giving an address and she didn't call. Or they didn't let her."

"It worries me," Jo said. "It doesn't really sound like her."

"They know we'll get the address at some point but they're slowing it down."

Jo didn't say anything, but one way to read it was that something was about to go down. Not next week, not sometime later, but very soon, and they were trying to keep everything stable. If something was going down, did Julia know? I chose to believe she didn't. If I didn't believe that, I didn't believe in Julia. I kept the faith.

43

JULIA

The door to the farmhouse swung open. Julia was expecting Tom. He'd called Paula earlier in the day and said he'd get in around ten tonight. But it wasn't Tom who walked in, though. It was Nick.

Julia froze, then picked up a long knife from the kitchen counter. "Leave."

"What happened to the pacifism?"

"Get out of here, Nick. Fuck off. Go."

"We're going to talk and then I'll go," he said. "And you're not calling the shots here."

"I'm going to testify against you. You're wanted on a hit-and-run, multiple false IDs, credit-card fraud, possession of stolen military-grade ammunition, and I don't know what else. I can't remember it all. Plus whatever else you've got back there, all the people you've screwed."

"You know what, Julia? I've been thinking the same thing. They really need your testimony, and sooner or later they will find me. That's exactly what's been going through my head."

Julia took in the changes in him. No more scrabbly-ass beard, no man bun, no quasi-hipster look, just short black hair cut and clean around the edges. He wore fading black jeans and a gray T-shirt. The thin-soled sneakers got traded out for light boots, and he was standing straighter. Way straighter, a totally different look, but another costume well put together for the guy who had nothing inside. He'd just told her he was here because of her. That frightened her.

Earlier, Paula had acted like she was worried. She said something about calling Jo but then put three suitcases in her car and left.

She'd said, "I'll see you in a few days, and I'll be back with some chicks so we can raise hens and stop buying eggs."

She didn't sound like she believed it, and Julia thought, *Don't bother. I'm gone. Over the gate tonight and out of here after Tom returns and knocks back a few beers, and Danny is out in the tractor barn doing whatever he does at night in there.*

"I'm here to do some banking with you," Nick said, then smiled like it was funny. Asshole. "You won't believe this, Julia, but I'm kind of your last best hope."

"Then it's over for me."

"Could be."

"Why are you here?"

"What I just said."

"We're not doing any banking."

"Yeah, we are, and get the fuck over yourself. You weren't happy and I was bored."

"You drugged me, Joel raped me, you posted a video. You think it's over?"

"This is where you're at, Julia. Think of it as a chess game. You've lost Sam. Bad move. Everyone is in deep at this point, and Sam is the one who recruited you, but you never went the distance. You didn't join in when things started to go down."

"Join with what?" she asked.

"Exactly. You're making my point for me. You either played stupid or didn't want any part of it. So that makes you a kind of spy, given your uncle's occupation. To put it more simply, as things get tense, you look like a liability, which has led to all kinds of other talk. You can imagine. I mean, shit happens."

"You've got warrants out on you. Shouldn't you be hiding in a hole somewhere?"

"Remember those medals I showed you?"

"You didn't let me look at them," she said.

"Those were all for target shooting. If it comes to it, I can take care of myself."

"So you'll shoot people? Great."

He looked at her for the longest time, then walked over and sat down on the table with his feet on a chair. Being around him made her gut churn.

Nick said, "You're a liability, Julia. There are five who make the big decisions. I argued with them for a different way than dealing with you as an extreme liability. They're open to it, but you need to make a significant contribution that proves you're all in. That's why I brought my laptop. You log in to your Schwab accounts, and off we go."

"You're here for my inheritance?"

"It's a trade."

"Like my money or my life," she said.

His eyes were flat and unreadable.

"Okay . . ." she said, trying to get her head around it. She knew there was a fringe offshoot of Witness1, and she did get asked about joining people who were going to make change happen. She'd known it was a more serious thing but had ignored it. She gripped the knife harder.

"I'm going to walk you to the door," she said.

Nick was between her and the front door, but the door off the kitchen was behind her. She could go out the back and stay away from the road. Go over the barbed wire and then down through the grass and hide in the night.

"If you willingly contribute money, Julia, it might just work out for the pacifist. But otherwise you're a problem that's getting worse. Look, I didn't drive here because I wanted to take the risk. I don't want to see you die."

"You're here to protect me?"

"Not really. If you didn't have the Schwab accounts, I wouldn't have done anything. If I heard you'd disappeared, I'd think, 'Kind of cute girl, decent fuck, some goofy ideas, but so what, she's gone.'"

It was hard to believe that stung her, but it did, and at the same time what he was saying felt real.

"It's you and me and Danny here," Nick said. "Mother Goose got redeployed and Tom went to plan B after two of your former roommates were brought in separately today to the LA FBI office for questioning. They're there right now. If they follow their training they won't say anything. You're kind of the problem. That's how I got the inspiration for you to transfer all of your inheritance as a gesture of loyalty."

"It sounds just like you," Julia said.

"Even if we get right on it, it's going to take a few days to sell the stocks and bonds and let them settle. That's not counting your broker's resistance so, say, five to six days before it's cash you can transfer. During that time you'll be staying here with Danny. Oh, and speak of the devil."

Julia heard footsteps, turned, and there was Danny at the back door. She started to turn with the knife, but he was fast. He threw his weight into her, forced her arm down on the counter, and wrenched the knife away.

"Put her on the couch," Nick said, then opened his laptop and started talking.

"The FBI grilled that doofus artist at the Colony after nosey Uncle Grale found your car, and their storm troopers crashed the Long Beach house. But they were coming anyway."

Nick said that without looking at her, but turned now.

"I just logged in for you. I'm sort of proud of remembering your log-in. I only saw you log in once. It looks like everything had been doing well, but the market is starting to roll over, so that's what you tell your broker. Everybody is selling, Julia. There'll be nothing weird about it. But it's your call, what do you think, live or die?"

She closed her eyes and thought, *Good on UG for finding my car. UG doesn't quit. I'm going to be like him. I'll never quit.*

"Time to call your broker and leave him a message that you want to sell everything. You say you've thought it through. You say you're out of town and not to call you. You'll call him during working hours tomorrow. Let him know that you know he needs to confirm. The last thing is you thank him for everything he's done. You wouldn't be selling but you need the money for something else." Nick pulled his phone out. "You ready?"

"Okay, call him," Julia said.

He did, then handed her the phone, saying, "Be cheerful."

She left a message that was almost word for word what Nick had said. When she hung up, Nick said, "Good job, and it's a good trade, right? It's not like it's money you earned."

Julia got up from the couch and walked into the kitchen. She casually opened a couple cabinet doors with both watching her, wondering what she was doing.

"So what about food?" she said. "If I'm going to be here with Danny, we need more food. Paula was going to go shopping, but you're saying Paula isn't coming back."

She squatted and opened a cabinet with Nick's phone still in her hand. She reached into the cabinet with that hand and typed the number UG had made her memorize when she moved to his house. She heard him answer, then hung up and brought the phone to her side as Nick came around fast and knocked it out of her hand. He checked right away.

"You little bitch. Danny, take her to her new home."

243

She fought Danny and poked one of his eyes. He pulled her outside, threw her down on the gravel, and kicked her head. She heard Nick but didn't remember much else until she was inside the tractor barn.

Now she was standing in the cool damp, her nose running, and gravel ground into her cheek. She smelled ammonia. The smell was strong. In a corner was a little folding cot. They dragged her toward it as she fought them. Danny kicked her legs out and slammed her facedown on the cot. Nick sat on her, and Julia heard a snicking sound like a chain, and something cold and metal clacked shut around her ankle.

Nick stood and stepped back, saying, "That comes off when the transfer is done." He waited for Dan to walk away, then said, "I'll check in every day. Dan has to deliver something, so it'll just be you and me for the last few days unless something goes wrong. You have to hope it doesn't."

Julia felt along her ankle to the stainless hoop.

"Stand up, Julia."

"Take this off me!"

"After the transfers settle. Until then you wear it. There's food in the bag right there and a package of clean rags you can use to wash. Behind the black drums is a sink. In the bag is a bar of soap and a roll of toilet paper. Toilet's over there. That's what you've got. This is home for now. Better hope your broker doesn't fuck up. Oh, and Danny says there are rats in here, so be careful where you store your food. Those two gallon jugs are your water. There's a cup, plate, and plastic utensils in your bag." He pointed up. "The lights will stay on so you won't be in darkness."

"Take this fucking thing off my leg," she said. "He can lock me in here. It doesn't need to be on my leg."

"Danny makes the rules. Whatever he says goes, and he doesn't want you anywhere near his workbench."

She turned to Danny. "Why are you doing this? Why are you helping him?"

Neither answered. They walked away, and the lights went out as the door shut. In the dark it was colder. She reached down and ran her fingers around the steel hoop on her ankle. Her heart pounded as she sat down on the cot. She heard UG's voice saying, "Assess your situation and think." An hour later she heard scuttling. She heard one rat, then more. She felt around for the garbage bag with the food, then stood and moved around in the dark, feeling her way along some steel shelves. She found a short piece of pipe under the bottom shelf.

When she got back to the cot, something was moving inside the bag. In darkness, she swung the pipe down on it. She hit over and over until there was no noise but the wind blowing through holes, and her panting from beating a rat to death. She wished there was at least one light so if more rats came she'd see them. Nick said the lights would be left on, but of course, another lie. Another Nick lie.

44

At 2:30 that night, Jo called as she left the hospital.

"Where are you?" she asked.

"At a run-down motel close to Sylmar and a surveillance we have underway."

"I didn't hear from Julia tonight," she said. "I also realized the prior time she and I talked she said she hoped to have a new phone tomorrow, not that she would for sure."

"That still doesn't feel right."

"I agree," she said. "But she hasn't sounded anxious or scared. What do you think?"

My phone vibrated with another call coming in. "Jo, I've got someone trying to reach me."

"Call me tomorrow," she said. "I've got to get some sleep. I'm sure Julia is all right."

The agent calling was named Wayne Wu. In the LA office they call him Double W. I'd been around him enough to know he was concise and careful with facts, so I was glad he was one of the two staking out Stuckey.

"Something is happening, we're not sure what," Wu said. "Can you hear the sirens where you are?"

"I hear sirens."

"There's a big fire that came out of nowhere along a commercial strip near the Sylmar–San Fernando line. It all went up at once, and there's something happening on I-5 north right now not far from Sylmar."

"Where's Stuckey?" I asked.

"At home. Lights off."

"Hold on, we're getting more on the freeway deal. There's a white van that started weaving with someone throwing lighted flares out the windows. Hang on, another call is coming in."

"I'm headed for my car," I said, and walked out of the motel room in time to see a bright flash of light and feel the concussion. Bomb.

Wu came back on and asked, "Did you feel that? A helicopter pilot is saying the van throwing flares stopped in the middle of the freeway, and two guys got out and ran. Forty-five seconds later it blew up. There's debris everywhere and blocking the freeway."

"Where on the freeway?"

"Adjacent to the southeast corner of the Van Norman Reservoir."

I drove north back to Sylmar and made a hard left toward I-5, thinking there was some chance I might spot the pair who'd been in the van. Then something clicked inside and I slowed but didn't stop. I didn't turn around yet. But a large fire in a commercial strip in San Fernando and a van detonating and leaving enough debris to block I-5 happening so close together, what were the odds? I called Hofter as I braked hard and turned around.

Mark heard my tires squealing and said, "Careful, Grale, where are you? What's going on?"

"We're not sure, but here's what's happened so far. Sylmar and San Fernando fire departments are fighting fires in a string of commercial buildings, and a bomb has exploded on I-5 north after two men in the van threw flares to stop traffic, then parked in the middle of the freeway and ran."

"Just blew up the van on the freeway?"

"Yeah."

"That's bizarre."

"Can you do this while I check out the Sylmar Converter Station? See if you can get a Bureau helicopter in the air over the converter station. If not ours, CHP or anybody available, then call me."

I called the number I had for the head security guy at the station. Not our first conversation.

He said, "Agent Grale, we're watching, man. We're nervous. We heard the explosion."

"Park something on that paved access on the east side we've talked about. Make sure it's heavy and get it out there right now," I said.

"What's happening? What are you telling me?"

"That I'm worried," I said.

"I'm on it."

"Call you back if I learn anything."

When I turned onto Telfair a large truck blocked the street up ahead. I called in where I was, parked, got out, and took a follow-up call from Bob Thor, security manager at the converter station.

"We got a big-ass truck out there, Agent Grale. But there is a big white commercial van that came down A Street, so they must have gotten the gate open and knocked out the concrete barriers.

"Can the van get around the vehicle your guy parked?" I asked.

"No way, that van is already tippy. It almost fell on its side trying to go around."

"Good job. Now keep everybody a long way away."

The steel poles holding the gates were stout, but the gates were chain link and the barriers weren't enough. A Street was an obvious route in. I called Hofter.

"Telfair is blocked, the gate to A Street is down, and concrete barriers are pushed out of the way. There's a large white commercial van in there, but it can't get around the utility truck blocking the road."

"Grale, you've got to stay back. Snipers are on their way. They'll take positions where they can sight through the windshield."

"Make sure they talk to me first. I'm going to get closer. I'm moving up through cars in a business lot along the right."

"Don't do that," Hofter said. "You're walking into a line of fire, and what if the bomb goes off?"

Telfair Avenue rose and curved, and I stayed to the right where it was darkest until I felt it was safe to cross the street. Now I was looking down A Street. The van that Bob had described was there but no longer trying to maneuver around the rig they'd parked to block it. I walked down A Street on the left side so the driver of the van could see me approach. There wasn't a lot of light, but there was enough. As I got within two hundred yards, my heart rate picked up. The LA FBI SWAT team leader checked in with me by phone and let me know the sniper wouldn't be talking to me directly.

"He's setting up and will have a good angle on the van cab. He sees a lone female with her hands on the wheel."

"I'm going to try to get her to surrender," I said.

"No, you're not. We have operational command here, and I'm telling you no. Turn around."

"I'm doing it. We need her alive, and she won't be alive long sitting there."

"Don't do it. She'll take you out with her, and if not I'll make you answer for it later," he said.

"I'm going to try. Tell the sniper to sit tight. Let me try to talk her out before we take her out. Here I go."

45

The SWAT commander called and ordered me to turn around before telling me that the female terrorist had both hands on the wheel. They could see a plunger-type trigger in her right hand and tape around her wrist holding a detonator wire tight. A second sniper was in place, and the commander said, "You tell her to lay the trigger down or we'll put a bullet through her forehead. I take it you don't have any children or family, Grayly."

"It's Grale, not Grayly. Paul Grale. I'm an SABT."

"You're a bomb tech? Then you of all people should know better. That's the Blond Bomber you're approaching. We have confirmation."

"Her name is Laura Balco."

"She's a bomber to us, Grale."

"Do *not* shoot her. I want to talk her out then disarm the bomb. What do I tell her?"

"You tell her that if she lowers her hands below where we can see them, meaning the wheel or top of the dash, we shoot." After waiting for my reaction he added, "You're showboating here, Grale."

I got closer and was aware she was watching me in her side mirror. I held my hands near my chest palms out and kept them there as I slowly approached the driver's window, saying, "Laura, don't do anything yet. Let's talk. I want to talk."

When I reached the window I saw her thumb covering the trigger. I kept reassuring her in a loud-enough clear voice. I pressed my palms against the window and talked through the few inches she had lowered it.

"If I press down, the bomb goes off," she said.

"I get it."

"So leave. There's nothing to say."

"I'm not leaving. That red dot on your chest is a sniper sighting on you. You've got another on your forehead. I don't want you to die. Nothing has happened yet. You don't need to die. No one died in the Hollywood bombing. You'll do time, but you'll get out. If you lower your trigger hand out of view, they'll kill you," I said. "They just told me that, and I'm telling you."

"Leave while you can," she said.

"I'm not a negotiator. I'm a bomb tech named Paul Grale. Let me arrest you, Laura. You can't get the van close enough to damage the converter station. You don't have to take yourself out."

"So I surrender and the Blond Bomber gets a sensational trial, then gets shipped off to a supermax in Colorado where prisoners live in darkness. I'd be there the rest of my life. No, thanks. Let's just say I screwed up and checked out. Let's leave it that at least I tried to break the stranglehold the morally corrupt have on this country."

"How did you get to this seat in this van? You're twenty-eight with a PhD in philosophy. I'm guessing it was your dad who taught you how to run down a trail holding a rifle. Was he the one who taught you to fight?"

"How do you know all that?" she asked. "How do you know about running with a rifle or my dad? He died when I was nineteen."

"I saw you run a trail in Butte County. What would your dad think of New America?"

"He was a Constitutionalist. He would get it."

"Why help take down the power grid or ally with a foreign enemy?"

"We're not allying with any foreign enemy," she said. "It's temporary, and we don't even know who they are. I wasn't part of that. I heard it happened something like five years ago and they don't matter. This isn't about them."

"It's Russia. What do you think they want?"

"Who cares what they want. It's our country and it has to change. We never knew who bought the land or where the guy who wanted to teach us bomb making came from. People thought he was FBI, so we told him no."

"Why take down the electrical grid?"

"The only way we see is to disrupt the ways they control our lives, the ways we're dependent," she said. "We want to live off grid and produce our own power. We don't want our kids taught cell phones are critically important and be told they need to be chipped or the police won't search for them if they disappear. We don't want a military-industrial complex that tells Congress every six years the weapons are getting obsolete and we have to buy new ones. There has to be a rebirth of America."

"I have a niece who says some of the same things."

"You're that Grale?"

"You know Julia?"

"Yeah, she's legit. The pacifism is a fantasy, but Julia's legit. She got an offer to join the next inner circle and rejected it. She was never told anything explicit. Did she go to you?"

"No."

Laura said, "That doesn't surprise me."

"She says she's at a farm in Tulare County. Ever been there, and do you know who bought it?"

"We had help buying it. Whoever they were, they thought they'd bought into us, but no way they were doing that. For us, it started along the fork of a river flowing with snowmelt in Wyoming just after the president opened up thousands more acres of wilderness to gas and oil exploration. There are three hundred years of gas reserves, but that doesn't matter, right? Take care of the donors and politicians and screw the country. Screw 'government of the people by the people for the people.' Waste the land. Waste anything and everything if it helps you stay in power. It happened for us that morning. That's when we said enough is enough."

I knew it was strange to her for me to be talking about Julia, but I saw something of Julia in her. I felt the moment passing, the seconds ticking down. She almost turned and looked at me. Then she did.

"You want life to work out for her," she said. "You want her to be happy."

"I do."

We looked at each other, and she gave me a nod I would think about for a long time.

"Laura, let me call the SWAT commander and tell him you're getting out of the truck and walking back with me."

"You know how that'll go down. You've seen it before. We were picturing sun, water, sustainable energy, and some farming. We saw new tech but not like the companies we have now. Have you ever driven Billionaires' Row in Palo Alto?"

"No."

She said, "Do it sometime. Same old, same old. Enormous houses, new money, nothing changed."

"You'll do time, but you haven't killed anyone. You'll get out."

"In a country afraid of closing Guantanamo? You've got to be kidding. The land of the brave is bottoms up. The Congress of cowards only looks out for themselves. You need to really hustle, Agent Grale. I don't want to push this button with you anywhere close."

"Lay the trigger on the dash and walk out with me. You're not going to blow up a converter station, but you'll have your life."

"I know you understand why I can't do that. The countdown starts now."

After forty seconds I was still standing there. She looked again and said, "You're a stand-up dude. Meet you in another life, Grale. Remember the river in Wyoming. I walked there with Sam Clark and a couple of others. I'm not saying Sam's involved in anything, but she's tough. Tell her that and she'll believe you."

She dropped her trigger hand below the dash, and before I could move or yell, the windshield spider-webbed and her head burst. That's the only way I can describe it. What came next were sirens and the SWAT team. Their commander held them back from the bomb, and I was alone as I disarmed it.

46

Breaking News
FBI Marksman Kills Blond Bomber

The media knew Laura Balco's name, yet that's how they ran their banner. I saw that after being debriefed at the LA FBI office. The headline was one more reminder that news is a business, first and always. Challenge them on it and they'll tell you the public knows Balco as the Blond Bomber. Of course, they had given her the name.

It was still early morning when a bomb threat was called in for the Los Banos substation north of LA. A fence was cut. Two vehicles moved onsite. I headed there as soon as the debrief was over. From my car I talked to Mara, who was adamant I shouldn't have approached Balco last night.

"It was the one chance to talk her out of the van," I said.

"Get over yourself, Grale. You make her sound like a victim. She made choices just like the rest of us do. Her choices put her in the driver's seat of a bomb vehicle. You ignored a SWAT team leader and should get written up. Neither Fuentes or I are going to do that, but do not tell me she was a noble patriot resurrecting America and the SWAT sniper is a killer. If you want to do that then switch squads."

"I'll talk to you later."

"Don't go yet. You had a conversation with your niece that got recorded. Fuentes called me. They're looking for clarification."

"Tell Fuentes to call me."

"He thinks it should go through me. I can play it so you hear it over the phone. It's about days of darkness."

"I remember it. It's a waste of time to play it."

"Maybe you don't remember it. Give me ten seconds."

I didn't say anything to that. I remembered Julia saying she was calling from a roommate's phone. The recording started.

"Some of the guys here are into what happens after the days of darkness," Julia said.

"The power outages?" I'd asked, and she'd laughed.

"UG, it's much more than that. It's about when the spirit portals merge and days of free will and higher consciousness begin. Do you know about the Age of Aquarius?"

"I know an old song."

"Read about how the Age of Aquarius starts."

"Okay, but it won't be this morning."

"Do you believe in history cycles and the Fifth World?" she asked.

"I don't know what that means."

"It means the start of the new history cycle."

"Okay."

"UG, tell Jo I love her. We have to get ready for the days of darkness. Peace in your heart, UG."

"Julia?"

Mara came back on and asked, "How do you explain her saying 'Get ready for the days of darkness'?"

"Google 'days of darkness.' You've forgotten what it's like to be young. She's experimenting with ideas, and they're different than what you think. Check it out. Let's talk about the Long Beach cell. I'm aware there aren't arrest warrants yet, and charges aren't resolved, but I also know an example will get made of these young women. I've heard arrests are coming in the next few days. Is that true?"

"I can't comment."

"You can't tell me?"

"I can't comment yet."

I gave a half laugh tinged with bitterness. "I have a problem with that," I said.

"You're worried about your niece, but you need to get a grip. What you did with Balco was a bad idea," Mara said.

"Let me finish on 'days of darkness' and Long Beach, and then I'll say more about Laura Balco. In Long Beach, they'll all get charged. Some long-faced prosecutor will insist that, although there'll be no clear evidence, it's likely Julia is guilty of aiding them, and let's not forget she's related to an active FBI agent. The prosecutor will argue there cannot be any hint of any preferential treatment or the whole case could be compromised. Therefore, charge her either way."

"I don't agree with that."

"That's how it'll go down," I said. "From what I hear, we're close to shutting down the Long Beach cell. Then we'll find the bomb factory and make more arrests, but not everyone who goes to prison will be guilty. To wrap in Julia, they'll offer lighter sentences to those who testify against her. Maybe Julia was around for discussions that could be interpreted a certain way. One or two will have said something stupid while sitting around the backyard fire pit drinking wine, smoking dope, and talking and questioning life, the way young people have probably done forever. But they'll be charged too."

"You're forgetting what your job is."

I continued. "She—and it will be a she in Long Beach who, in the energy of the moment, will have said something stupid yet was never part of any planning or action, or ever really aware of the core terror group—will get a long prison sentence. When she's released, she'll be beyond childbearing and career-building years. So will all the others who were swept up in this secret fringe they weren't part of. They'll never get jobs with any meaning. They'll forever be terrorists. I asked Balco about Julia. She said what Clark has said, that with her pacifism, Julia was unreachable. They figured reality would bring her around eventually."

"You're an FBI agent first, Grale. Do not forget it. You talk like you need to understand where they're coming from. You don't. That's not your job. Your job is investigating."

"For a while, when I was talking to Balco, she wouldn't look at me. I don't think she wanted to acknowledge me as a human being, knowing I was an FBI agent. She might have detonated the bomb if she hadn't turned and looked at me. Most of what she told me came after that. She made it very clear this idea has roots that go back years."

Mara didn't respond. He wanted this conversation over with. Working as a bomb tech I often think of the young men recruited by ISIS who give up their lives once converted. We have a great capacity to absorb and embrace ideas, but is that gift also our vulnerability?

I can easily picture Balco's lithe, quick movements as she ran down the trail. This told me a lot about her, told me good things, and yet Mara was right: she chose her path. She brought herself to that moment. She brought it on herself.

But her blown-out skull will always haunt me. What I'd thought at first was one bullet was in fact two, one through her right eye and the other striking just below the hairline on her forehead. The bullets crossed paths as they tore apart her brain. You can shrug and say that's the choice she made, or it's just the way it is, but I don't believe that.

"Grale, where are you?" Mara asked.

"I'm two hours from the substation in Los Banos. A fence was cut and two vehicles driven across a field to transmission towers. I don't know what it means for LA if a bombing shuts down the substation, but already gas station lines go for blocks. Traffic-light outages have created gridlock. Except for gun stores, nothing is open. LAPD is still working twelve hours on, twelve off, A shift, B shift, everyone is in uniform. It's getting rough."

"That's what I hear," Mara said.

"So where are we at, you, me, and Fuentes? Does he want me out of LA? Is this too complicated with Julia in the mix?"

"It's headed that way," Mara said. "We'll resolve it in the next few days. I don't know how I'd handle it if I was in your shoes, but you've got to stand back and let the investigation take its course in Long Beach."

Less than an hour later, the two bomb trucks outside the Los Banos substation exploded. The bombs didn't just shear the tower legs. They blew the towers apart. Two people were killed. I got a call from Hofter minutes after I heard the bombs had detonated.

Hofter said, "A CHP officer, a local cop here, and the guard in the Tehachapis. That's it for me. The line has been crossed. I think we turn all the firepower we have on these terrorists. Last night I got home at 11:15 and my neighbor was in his backyard using a lantern for light with his wife yelling at him as he target shot with a gun he'd just bought. I asked him if he'd ever owned a gun before. He said no. Did you get that, Grale? He's never owned a gun and he's in his backyard at night shooting. He said all the shooting ranges are booked solid for months. Things are unraveling here. Where are you going from Los Banos?"

"To the Bay Area. Jace has something on Corti."

47

In Los Banos there was visible sadness in the officers manning a road-block. One of them wore a bloodstained uniform shirt. He said he was standing next to the CHP officer killed. He reached out and touched my shoulder.

"I was no farther from him than I am from you. We thought we were safely back, but this piece of steel about eighteen inches long and this wide"—he spread his hands to show me how wide—"fell out of the sky. I heard his collarbone snap and the air go out of him. It sliced down through the right side of his neck. Blood was everywhere, just pumping out of his neck. I just couldn't stop it. I tried everything. I've known him since we were kids . . ."

He was quite shaken, and we talked a while longer. The bombs had detonated and they crouched down. They'd stood again and the piece of steel struck. The blast scene looked a lot like Captain Jack in Klamath Falls except the bombs were closer to each other and brought down more towers.

Either the San Francisco field office or Sacramento would investigate this bombing. If it had been San Francisco, Jace would have come here along with an evidence-recovery team, but that's not how it worked out, so I didn't collect any evidence. Sacramento wanted everything left as is and were on their way here. I called Hofter after looking again at the dark patch of earth where the CHP officer bled out.

The death of the local officer was harder to understand. He was too close to the southernmost bomb despite the phoned-in warning of a 12:30 p.m. detonation. No one could explain it. A yellow flag in the grass marked the location of his right leg. Most of the rest of his body was close to there. A TV crew tried to zoom in on his decapitated head, so they moved the media back a quarter mile.

"Two ANFO bombs," I told Hofter as I drove away. "We've crunched data on farming orders for ammonium nitrate looking for the anomalies, but we've focused on large routine orders. We can't wait any longer. Let's go straight to the manufacturers."

"They're going to say they report to Homeland Security."

"They can copy us. We can ask for all medium to small farm orders in California, all anticipated refills, a list of criteria. I'll make the calls on the drive north."

Two and a half hours later, I got into the Bay Area, checked into the Emeryville Marriott again and found a place to eat before calling Jo.

"We've had more trouble with the backup generators at the hospital," she said. "The phone system there needs electrical power to work and that's a problem. That's how Julia calls."

"No new word from her?" I asked.

"She may have tried and not gotten through."

"She should be calling on a new cell phone by now. I'm getting to a place where I'll need to go find her. That may get me in trouble with the Bureau, but if I can't get it cleared I'm going anyway. I may be in Vegas tomorrow night, Jo, but I could be working a good part of the night."

"Me too. I'll be at the hospital tomorrow night until late. Good times."

"Soon, Jo," I said.

"Yes, soon."

The next morning near sunrise Jace and I crossed the Richmond–San Rafael Bridge, heading north into Marin County. We'd meet Farue at a shot-up cell tower just like old times. He was the real reason for the trip, but on the drive we talked Corti.

Corti was shooting less but still taking out towers, and now he was close to a major metropolitan area. The first and the second cell towers we looked at today were likely his. At the second tower we'd meet Farue. We were early, and as we waited I took in the rich green color of the hills, the smell of bay leaves and new grass, and saw a brimming reservoir and ravines with dark bands of oaks. I looked at the summit of Mount Tamalpais then back at the access road as Farue arrived.

He parked, pushed open the driver's door, and we heard him talking on the phone though we couldn't make out the words. As he walked toward us, Jace asked, "Farue's motives for messing with us?"

I answered, "Thrill. Money. Risk. Getting to talk regularly with the stunning Kristen Blujace. And he's got some feel for the endgame."

"What's that last bit mean?"

I didn't get a chance to answer before Farue arrived and said, "A Northern Brigade source says Jake is headed to San Francisco." Farue looked hard at me. "Don't arrest me. A Brigade soldier called me. I didn't call them. They got my new cell number from Corti. That's the only explanation I can come up with."

He nodded toward Jace.

"Jace and I have been talking," he said. "I told your partner here there might be a reason Jake is only killing inanimate objects. He met a pacifist in a chat room called the War Room. She's younger, but he connects with her. He's talked online with her for more than a year, but right now can't reach her, which is bad since she calms him down. He comes from a place of violence, so without her or something else to slow him down, he could take a turn."

"Sounds like you've known for a while he's been talking to her."

"I have but didn't put it together."

"How do you know it's a young woman?" I asked.

"That's what he told me."

"Give us something more. How does he know?"

Farue gave me a shit-eating grin. "Ask him," he said. "And take a look at this. It's a text from him."

He turned his phone and showed us a text that read, I'm freaking, dude. These people are pushing me. Peace Girl is gone. Think I scared her when I said I wanted to meet up. She's not answering. It's been days. I'm spinning and bad shit could happen. They put a big ask out there. They want a lot from me. They've got all these reasons why it's right. I need her.

"What's he saying to you?" I asked.

"I can't tell. He's been different ever since he partnered up with the woods crackers, but what he's saying is they're asking him to do something. Those dudes see a civil war. They think they're fighting a deep state. Whoever this Peace Girl chica is, she moved him away from that. She's helped him, and now someone is pulling him back."

"We're going to take your phone," Jace said.

"You'd need a warrant. Okay, hang on, I have something else. Here, Jace, I'll text it to you. It's how he signs in or signs off in that chat room. I told him I was interested in pacifism, and he gave me this so I would recognize him if I went to that chat room."

He texted L-Z-9-9-O&O to Jace, who then sent it to me.

"I'm still going to take your phone," she said. "It's a terrorist investigation and you've been protecting your friend. I'm tired of you with a new phone number each time we meet. You want to cooperate. You really do. Hand it to me and you're coming with us. I want to do this interview where I can tape it."

I stepped away for a moment. Peace Girl. Younger. Pacifist. Not online lately. I could hear Julia telling me, *There are more people against all war than you think. I go to these chat rooms . . .* " Was it possible it was Julia?

48

Later as I left Jace and headed to Oakland Airport to return to Vegas, I turned more pieces of our puzzles in my head. Stuckey and Inze had gamed me and did it fairly well. If they had met up without me watching, it might have worked. Inze had confessed to leasing a moldering warehouse space to people she knew were up to no good and lately suspected could be part of the bombings. She claimed to never have really known, but that's probably a lie. Their meeting up that night was only so they could be together, she'd said. They were seeing each other. Fuentes had left me a message about Stuckey. I called him back before getting on the plane to Vegas.

"I want your take, Grale. Stuckey is hiding out in San Diego, but there are agents following him. If we arrest and throw the possibility of terror charges at him then jail him, given his prison experience, could being in a cell again be enough to get him talking, or will he freak out and shut down entirely?"

"I'd be guessing just like you. But I've been thinking about Stuckey and Inze. She's confessed to trying to make side money leasing a space. It's gotten her fired, and she's facing possible terror charges. She may or may not have seen the three used Edison trucks parked in there. We don't know, and even if she did, it wouldn't prove she knew they were being turned into bomb vehicles."

"She knew."

"Okay, but not until those first three bombings is what I'm saying. Stuckey had the vehicles and sold them for cash as he's probably done for years with other vehicles. She came up with the space to lease. They both made money. Neither saw bombs getting built. We need the bomb maker or whoever bought the trucks, then we've got Stuckey cornered."

"We don't have those individuals yet, and he's trying to get to Mexico. I'm just asking what you think about Stuckey and the pressure of being in a jail cell. I know you barely know him, but what's your feel?"

I didn't have a feel for Stuckey, and I didn't feel anything for him either, or for Deborah Inze. They chose their paths. In the same way Fuentes and Mara felt nothing for Laura Balco, to me Inze and Stuckey earned what they had coming. Inze made a half-hearted run at putting it all on Stuckey, and then through her lawyer offered full restitution with penalties. Although the owners had fired her and a spokesman had conveyed their deepest sorrow that any employee of theirs aided terrorists, they were apparently interested in the offer and were negotiating with her attorney.

"Pick him up now as a flight risk, but focus on Inze," I said.

"Why?"

"I'm guessing he had the truck deal in hand then talked to her about finding a space for the buyers."

"Could the buyer or front man for the truck deal have been Jody Gavotte?"

"He fits, but I don't think it was him," I said. "The reason is Stuckey picked him out of the photos I showed him. Why would he do that?"

"Okay, keep thinking about it. We'll talk more."

My thoughts returned to Julia, who in so many ways reminded me of Melissa. When Julia stood defiantly in front of me arguing, I thought of her. Growing up, Melissa was nicknamed "Joan of Arc" by the neighbors. Julia had that same thing inside that allowed one hundred percent commitment to a moral cause. Passion is admirable, but passion is not truth. Somehow I had to teach that to Julia.

I should have called Mara earlier but waited until I'd landed in Vegas. I wouldn't be here long, and my guess was he would have said don't come at all. I heard a click as he picked up the phone and said, "Grale?"

"I'm in Vegas."

"Good, take a breather and we'll talk in the morning unless you've got something pressing."

"I do."

"Before you tell me, let me say you might be onto something with the smaller ammonium nitrate fertilizer shipments. Homeland reran the small farm sales with consistent to above yearly average orders. They ran it nationwide, but I'll break out California and send it to you."

Homeland Security was responsible for monitoring ammonium nitrate sales, but it was just one of many things dropped on them after 9/11. Sales of ammonium nitrate had declined but were still near a million tons a year, with a price that floated around $500 a ton.

"I'm at the point of needing to go look for Julia. I hear Samantha Clark is here in Vegas and we have a surveillance team on her. I want to talk to her."

"Tell me how that would work. Is there some referee we go to and say we want a timeout so an agent who's not on the surveillance team can have a side chat with Samantha Clark?"

"It could be a chance encounter. She'll call me out on it, but if she hasn't spotted the surveillance, it could work. We met Farue today at a shot-up cell tower, and he gave us a new angle on Corti that I want to talk with Clark about. It involves a chat room she might be familiar with. Farue is a big question mark for us, so it's important. He showed us texts from Corti on a phone with a different number than the one we have for him. I think there's a way I could talk to Clark without hurting the surveillance. It might even help. Clark doesn't know I was the agent with Balco before she was killed. If what Balco told me was true, she and Clark shared an understanding that led to the formation of their group."

"I'll call you back," Mara said.

When he did, I was out of the airport and had just about given up on him. He said, "Head to the Mandarin Hotel and the twenty-third floor."

"The bar?"

"Yes."

Mara and two agents were in a white SUV down the street from the Mandarin. One agent went up with me to the bar, the others waited on the ground floor for a call from us. I sat down at a table behind her and back from the bar. Clark was alone on the left side of the room, looking out the floor-to-ceiling windows, but every so often she glanced back at the elevators. When she picked up on me, she waved and came over with her drink.

"I don't know where Julia is," she said as she sat down. "And I don't know any bomb makers, so what can I do for you?"

"I just want to talk."

"About life?"

"You could say that," I said. "This isn't about Julia."

"Everything about you is about finding her."

"I'm the unidentified agent who was talking with Laura Balco before she committed suicide. I wish she hadn't."

"Committed suicide?" she said. "Don't you own a TV? An FBI sniper shot her. How can you say you're sorry if it's one of your own who took her out? I don't get that."

"It was sad. It didn't have to happen. Laura had the trigger in her right hand. She knew not to drop her hands below the dash. Or she could have detonated the bomb and taken me with her, but she didn't. She talked about the same dream of living a mix of agrarian and tech that Julia talks about. She couldn't see herself in a supermax prison for decades. I can understand that, but she shouldn't have died."

"How is it you were in Sylmar?" she asked.

I paused, then went for it.

"You made it happen."

"What are you saying?"

"Bill Stuckey looked at photos, picked you out, and then talked about you coming in last February shopping for trucks using the name Dalia. You made a big impression on him. I think he was attracted."

That got a rueful smile, then quiet sadness.

I continued. "That started me turning around different ideas. I was working grid infrastructure attacks for eighteen months before Seattle City Light went down. I saw practice runs. I saw the botched attempts, the bombs that fizzled, the small ones that worked, and then domestic cells activating after Seattle went dark. We counted the cells and differentiated between them within the first week via their different styles, methods, and locations. They were all waiting for a signal, and they all activated when they got it."

"Sorry to interrupt your recap," she said, "but let's be real. If I made a visit to this Stuckey person, the FBI would have moved on it. You of all people know I wouldn't be sitting here with a drink."

"Sam, we're entering the endgame. I guess that's what I'm trying to say. It's really why I'm here tonight. No one else should die the way Laura died."

"You almost sound like you care about the evil Blond Bomber."

"I talked to a young intelligent woman who took the wrong road."

She nodded. She didn't say anything, and I changed subjects to let her think about it.

"I was north of San Francisco today with another agent looking at a snipered cell tower and talking to a Gary Farue. Do you know him?"

"You really know how to jump it around. Does the Bureau teach that, or is it a brain issue, and why do I get the feeling this is all going to lead back to Julia?"

"Julia is where you and Laura once were," I said. "Or that's what I see."

"Are you wearing a wire?"

"I wanted to, but we couldn't get it together quick enough."

That caught her by surprise, and I continued. "I'm being straight with you, and yes I am worried about Julia."

Clark tried a pitying smile, but the smile failed. She took a good pull on her drink and was close to leaving the table. I had only a few seconds before she ended the conversation.

"This is no bullshit," I said. "Laura asked me to remind you that in the beginning you were going to do it all without violence. She wanted me to tell you that. She said when the others came, they came with money, and the money was seductive. You knew the money was foreign money, but it didn't really matter, you thought, because you had no loyalties to any foreign state and never would. Those were her words."

"I don't have any way of knowing you're telling the truth."

"She saw that coming too. She said there was a river in Wyoming running with snowmelt that I needed to remember. I think she wanted me to pass the message that everything that ever really mattered was said the day you walked the fork of a river together. She said to say this to you and you would know that she and I did talk. 'Otherwise,' she said, 'Sam will never believe you. She's the hardest of us all.'"

That broke through. Clark sat up and ran a hand through her hair.

"You of all people know idealism isn't enough," she said. "People need to know a revolution can succeed. If the fire-pit talk of resistance becomes grassroots revolution, that's a whole different thing. Even the hippies changed America. It can happen. We were as naïve then as Julia is now with her pacifism."

"Or maybe you, like me, took the easier well-worn path of violence," I said.

"Listen to you, I didn't know you had it in you."

"The cyberattacks are ending, and retribution is gearing up. Do you think it's coincidence the two biggest Russian oil refineries shut down today and one is on fire? The price of oil spiked. Frackers here are benefiting. Look for more like that. And still, it's going to wind down and end. Talks are underway. Without the cyberattacks, the ANFO bombings and the rest will just be loosely organized destruction that causes suffering for the wrong people. It's not worth it, Sam. I'm telling you something that isn't public yet."

"I don't control anything."

"I'm going to ask you once more to spare Julia."

"Spare her?" she said. "Who am I to spare her? You have a crazily inflated idea of my reach."

"If she didn't have an inheritance and an FBI uncle, you would have kept her at a distance. Or maybe you saw part of yourself in her and you wanted that feeling again. When did you lose it? Did it go away when you walked out of the Black Bear on Signal Hill, or was it before? I'm guessing Signal Hill is where it happened. Was it there you decided the end justifies the means?"

I expected a quick answer, but nothing came. Just a stare at something beyond me.

"Julia suffered grief and knows loss, so she prizes life," I said. "Leave her out of the ending."

"What a nice thought." She looked down at her hands. "I have to go."

"I'm not against your dream of a better world, Sam. I believe in it, but you and I are part of the old one. I have bomb injuries. I know how to make and defuse bombs. I've shot and killed people. You have blood on your hands same as me. Julia doesn't yet. Let her go. She could make a difference."

She reached out and put her hand on mine, then got up and walked to the elevators without looking back.

I texted Mara, No luck. She's on her way down. I checked the time, and Mara called.

"Get some sleep, Grale."

"I can't."

"That's an order. Stay where you are, get the government rate, and I'll sign off on it. Get four hours. You can't sleep at your house anyway,

273

though it is looking better. Your carpenter friend got the Sheetrock finished, and they're ready to go on the floors. There's no warrant out for Julia. She's going to be okay. Get some rest."

"Give me your word."

He didn't. He couldn't, and the call ended.

I did check into a room at the Mandarin and called Jo, then showered and fell backward in my head to a quiet space. Later I woke to a soft knock. When I opened the door, it was Jo, straight from the hospital. She started stripping her clothes as the door shut.

"I need to hold you," she said.

In the darkness, she slid through the cool sheets to me, her skin pressed against mine, our foreheads touching. I kissed her. I traced the curved lines of her. Her hips moved, her nipples tightened, and she said, "No. Sleep, Paul."

I fell backward again. When I woke it was 4:30 and Jo was touching me. We made love slowly, then lay looking out across Las Vegas. She rested a hand on my chest, then slid it down to my belly and pushed her face against me. Skin on skin.

We're here and then we're gone. It's inescapable. But things matter beyond us.

Laura Balco knew what she was going to do. Her mind was made up, yet she told me, "Find Sam, and say this to her." We care about things beyond us.

Jo and I eased away the sheet and blanket and lay in the cool air next to each other, just being together a few more moments as the sky lightened.

"Do what you have to," Jo said. "I'm with you. If they fire you, we'll just go from there."

"I have to go find Julia."

"I know."

49

JULIA

The Farm, May 8th

The same week she died, her mom had told Julia that her uncle Grale was once on a multistate FBI team that solved a string of kidnappings of teenage girls. They found three girls alive, four dead. Two of the girls had been held from age fifteen to eighteen. Julia remembered trying to get her head around something so horrible. Her mom meant it as a warning, the way moms do.

UG talked about some cases but never that one until she asked last fall because Nick was curious. All he would say is that the girls were chained up and held alone in remote places. The ones who had survived never gave up. She remembered Nick smirking at that and the way UG had looked at him. It was a hard look, one she'd never seen from him before.

Now she was chained to a steel ring in a concrete floor. Dan—Danny John, that was his full name—wasn't just the reserved, weird, "leave him alone let him work all night in the tractor barn" guy they made him out to be. He was seriously bright and seriously messed up.

Danny brought his laptop and a folding steel chair over but didn't sit in the chair; rather he sat down close to her on the cot, his thigh pressed against hers. He pulled up the website where he had bought the nine-meter stainless chain with the ankle hoop and the locking ring on the other end. He showed her where he'd drilled into the concrete and epoxied an eyebolt to attach the ring on the chain.

"Why are you showing me this?"

"I've seen you trying to get loose. I have cameras in here. I've watched you. You won't be able to get loose. You should quit fighting it."

She nodded.

"They should never have brought you here," he said.

"So take the chain off and let me go."

"I can't."

"Why not?"

"I'll show you, I'll explain everything," he said.

She sat on the cot in the weak light and watched him work, building what he said later was a detonator. The ammonia stink in here had made her throat raw and her nose burn. It stung her eyes. It came from the fertilizer in huge stainless bins.

"This was a larger farm once," he told her. "The olive groves down below were part of it. They stored the fertilizer up here. The same order of fertilizer comes every three months. I use it to build the bombs. You're going to help me. I'll teach you."

"Nick promised I would go free after the money transferred."

Dan looked like he knew that was true and was having trouble with it. He walked over to her. He was at least five inches taller and fifty pounds heavier than she was.

"You'll work in here and live in the house. I'll order a longer chain for working here and one for the house. Some of the chains are very light but strong. I'll get ones that are light so you don't really notice."

"Why do you have to chain me?"

"I don't want you to leave. You would leave."

He said that matter-of-factly, and she'd learned even in just a few days that he simply said what he believed. But it still took her several moments to realize he was serious. When she did, she couldn't talk.

"With the bomb I'm working on now, you'll pack the ammonium nitrate. I'll show you how, and over time I'm going to teach you how to make the detonators. It could be a long time. Wars of revolution often last a long time. It would be better for you not to think ahead so much. I know you like to talk, but I don't like to argue. I'd like you to tell me you'll do what I say."

"Just say I'll obey you?"

"Yes."

"Danny, you can't do that to people."

"Otherwise, I'll train you."

"You'll train me?"

"Yes," he said, "I know I can train you."

Train me?

"Stop this, Danny, stop it now."

She shook from the cold or nervousness as she looked at him. They said he was on the spectrum and very bright.

"The work has to be done," he said. "I can't do it alone. I can't do everything fast enough."

"I can't help build a bomb. I can't do it." She paused. "What do you know about me?"

"Not much. Your dad is an FBI agent. He's an SABT. You're from Las Vegas. You know two of the girls living in the house in Long Beach."

"My dad? No, he's not my dad. Do you remember the bombing at the bar in Las Vegas that killed drone pilots and other people?"

"I know about it," he said.

"Do you know there was one survivor?"

"There was a girl."

"I'm the girl that survived the Alagara bombing. My family died, and I moved in with my uncle, who's an FBI agent. I can't build bombs."

Somehow that got through. She pushed on. "Even if I could, and I can't, there are huge rats out here. They came for the food last night and weren't afraid. Move me inside. Even if the chain isn't bolted you can secure it. Nail something down. Wrap it around that post in the kitchen. It's not that hard. Don't leave me out here. Don't leave me near materials to make a bomb."

He was quiet, then said, "The one who survived had injuries near the spine. Show me."

Julia stood and pulled her shirt off. That startled him. He stepped back. She turned around so he could see her back. The bra strap couldn't hide the scars, and she felt his fingers probing a scar.

"Okay," he said. "I'll try to make it work in the house if you promise you'll stay."

"Screw something in. There's a way. You know there's a way."

He didn't answer and went back to the bench. When he finished his work, he carried it over and showed her. Then as if they'd never had the earlier conversation, he turned the lights off and left. She heard the lock click shut and his footsteps on the gravel, then bowed her head and wept.

50

JULIA

Hours later, the door creaked open. She heard footsteps and waited for the lights.

Maybe Dan was coming for her to move her inside. The light above the workbench came on. He stood in front of it only for moments and picked up something. A tool, she thought. He started her way and was quickly to her. A flashlight swept her face, blinded her.

"Sit on the cot. If you move at all, this stops."

Julia asked, "Are you—"

"Don't talk."

As he used two tools to work the ring on the chain where it tied to the eyebolt, her fear turned to anger. *Where did he get the right to hold me captive and control me?* She touched the pipe where she had hidden it, between her breasts under her bra and running under the loose T-shirt down along her abdomen, and under the first inches of her pants. *Slide it up, slide it out,* she thought as the ring clicked and came free. He stood and turned toward her.

"Do exactly what I say. We're going to walk out of here and across to the house. You're going to walk in front of me. I want to feel pull on the chain. Understand?"

"Like you're walking a dog," Julia said and knew she shouldn't have.

"Before we go, turn around."

"No, no, please don't touch me. Please don't do that."

She moved away from the bed toward the light and the door, keeping her voice fearful and anxious.

"I need to know you're not carrying anything," he said.

"I'm not! Check me inside the house, not here."

He didn't say anything but seemed to like her words. She pulled the chain taut, doing as he said, leading the way out the door. Her plan couldn't work if he was behind her. He was too careful. She didn't expect that. He was so much bigger and stronger than her.

"Walk right down the middle of the road," he said. Her shoes crunched on the gravel, and the idea gelled. She walked fast on the road and pulled the chain tighter. That held her leg with the ring back just enough so that it didn't seem faked when she started to trip. She went to one knee and got up fast, stinging from the gravel.

"Sorry," she said.

He said nothing. They were close to the stairs and the open door of the house, with the door open and yellow light falling in a line on the deck. She speeded up again nearing the stairs as if the house drew her, as if it was safety. She slid her right hand under her T-shirt, tightened the chain and tripped, stumbled, and then fell hard on her side at the base of the stairs. So hard it hurt. So hard it was believable. So hard he wasn't worried and just walked right up as she moaned and said, "I'm hurt."

She held out her left hand for him to help her up. He planted his right foot and held out his hand, still keeping some distance, but with ease pulled her up. With her right foot pushing off the stairs, she added momentum and force to her swing. The iron pipe hit his temple with a loud thump.

He let go. He staggered back. She swung again, and he went down to his knees and raised his left arm to block the next hit. But he was stunned and slow, and she was around the back of him and bringing the swing from higher up, like in volleyball when she was off her feet and the ball was there and the spike was clean. The pipe hit the back of his head and he slumped over.

She pulled and dragged and got the thin chain loose and out from under him. She bundled and wrapped it around her right wrist, picked his phone off the gravel with that hand, and ran down the road to the gate and climbed over it. She was all the way down to the olive orchards when she heard the engine and saw his headlights coming.

She was well into the orchard when his pickup roared past. He went a long way, a lot farther than she could have gotten. *You should have hit him more,* she thought. *He's going to search and search for you.* But she didn't feel so afraid anymore. She was fast. She was strong and cut across the orchard, and with each row of trees was farther from the road.

From beneath a tree she saw his headlights turn around, then go out, but still heard the pickup's engine. It came slowly back along the orchard, then stopped. She listened and waited, and the moon rose over the hills. Moonlight fell between rows of trees and the grasses there, gray in the light, and the tracks left by harvesting equipment.

If she'd hit him harder, he'd be dead, but she'd hit him hard. She'd heard the sound. She saw the blood. He was hurt. How long could he look for her? What would he do if he found her? Kill her? Take her back there and wait for Nick and the money transfer, then get Nick to leave her with him?

When she saw him in the moonlight in an open space between trees she almost cried out. He went row to row in a pattern, zigzagging and turning to look, all the time turning to look. With the moon nearly full, if she moved he'd see her, and the chain, even though thin, jingled. If she ran, he would hear her.

She thought of UG saying, "The ones who made it watched and waited. They kept their heads." He said he didn't know how but they did. As a species we'd learned to survive. *You cannot let him catch you. If you do, you'll die here.*

"Think," she whispered. *He's using the moonlight, but he'll have a really strong flashlight because he's that way. He won't use it until he's sure.* If she went back to the farm, he wouldn't look there, but she couldn't go there. What about the trees on the other side of the road? Big, but were there enough of them?

She moved slowly up a row, over three rows, and stopped near a larger tree. In the early morning she needed to be able to run out in the main road and flag down a car.

You have the darkness. You're faster than him. You're quick. You were always a great runner. Find a really good place to hide and wait all night. He'll get worried about the bomb. It's almost built. He's supposed to be finished with it, but he's not. There's some deadline. He'll go back there and work on it.

No, he won't. Not until he finds me. His phone vibrated in her pocket. Omigod. She hid the light from the phone screen and read the text. All going down faster. Lose her. Get on the road this morning.

51

Tulare County, California, May 9th

At the Vegas FBI office in the predawn, agents gathered around a TV to watch a jury-rigged line of pumps circulating water in the cooling towers at Palo Verde. A cheer went up as if we were watching a playoff game. The engineers had gotten it done just in time. Water started circulating at 78 percent of standard, enough of a margin to prevent a meltdown.

If there's a characteristically American attitude, it's "We'll figure it out. We may make mistakes first, but we'll get it done."

At dawn, I drove into California. Across the freeway, the traffic was thick with vehicles leaving LA. Loaded SUVs, pickups piled high with belongings, mattresses tied onto car roofs, trailers, campers, boats hitched to cars, all at a crawl. Going where, who knows? And yet I could understand. Power in the LA Basin might be down for months.

When I turned north toward Tulare County, there was little traffic in the quiet early morning. I was headed for the highway that tracked east along the shoreline of Lake Kaweah and then rose toward Three Rivers. This wasn't a blind exploratory expedition, worry expressed as action. I was guilty of that as a younger agent, driving city streets in the small hours as if it would lead me to a killer.

But not here, here I had a sense of where to look. I had the snapshot descriptions of landscape Julia had given Jo. Homeland came up with a list of properties in Tulare County that might fit, and I had Julia's description. I bought gas and coffee at a Chevron in Three Rivers, then continued all the way up to the Sequoia National Park gate before turning around and going slowly back over the river bridge down through country that was rocky and steep with brown grass drying toward summer.

She wasn't up here. The farms were all lower in the valley. I passed the Chevron again, reacting to gut instinct and the clues Julia had given me. I pulled over several times to let cars pass. I turned around again and in Three Rivers looked for the places where locals might eat. I wanted the right mix of cars out front. Inside would be someone who kept tabs on real estate sales. There was always someone. I found a café that looked likely, took a seat, and though it was noon ordered two eggs scrambled, toast burned at the edges, and coffee. After enough back-and-forth and another refill, I asked the waitress, "Who here could tell me about real estate?"

"What are you looking for?"

"A fifty-acre farm that traded hands three to five years ago that might not be doing very well now."

A middle-aged fellow came over and introduced himself as Larry Crane. He slid onto the seat across from me. Sometimes good fortune comes unexpectedly in the door, so he was interested, though I made it clear I wasn't looking to buy. I amended that to "I'm looking for people not farmland" and showed my FBI creds.

"Can I buy you breakfast?" I asked.

"Ate already but more coffee, sure. I can think of a couple that fit the description, but there are records for all that, so I'm confused."

"We've been looking at records and no luck."

"How urgent is this?"

"Very."

He said, "You caught me on the right day. If you drive, I'll take you to the ones I know of that have changed hands."

"Cost may not have mattered."

"It always matters."

We drove down below the reservoir, then north five miles and looked at one, then came back to the west and looked at another that was a citrus orchard but no pond or outbuildings. The third was closer in fit but no gravel road running to it and no fence or gate.

"There's one I didn't think about," Larry said. "I didn't because it was part of a large sale, and for reasons no one understood, they broke off a parcel of it later. There was a little buzz for a few months as bigger growers tried to figure if there was a loophole they were missing. Turned out no, and I think it's an organic vegetable farm now. The name will come to me. I've seen their stand at a farmers' market. What I hear is it's young people who don't know much about making a living."

He gave me directions, then added, "They're not like the hippies. It's not a back-to-the-earth thing in the same way. Their generation just wants something different."

I nodded, and he talked as we followed a creek in the canyon, crossed a small bridge and more meadowland. Then on our left we passed a gravel road with a "No Trespassing" sign on a metal gate. On the right side of the road were trees and brush and then a short open stretch with a view over hills falling to orchards in the valley below.

"This isn't it, but from here we can look down on it and the bigger piece it was cut from."

"Let's get out and take a look," I said.

I saw a two-story farmhouse and a deck out front, and then counted four outbuildings and a pond. Cattle fencing encircled the acreage running up, over, and around the hills. I saw rows of plants and a gravel road. The road fell maybe one hundred fifty feet in height to the flat valley and a large orchard of olive trees that looked blue-gray from here.

"This could be it," I said. "I think it is, Larry. If it is, I owe you."

"You don't owe me. If I can help the FBI keep the lights on, that's good enough for me."

I drove him back to Three Rivers and dropped him off, then drove hard back to the valley floor. I passed the olive orchard and turned left. I drove up the hill to a locked gate but didn't get any response on the intercom. I tried several times, then turned and drove back down, planning to call the Tulare County Sheriff's Department for help. I drove past most of the orchard, then stopped when I saw a young woman running through the trees then out onto the road.

"Julia!" I yelled and got out as she ran toward me.

52

Her hand trembled, and she pulled a cell phone from her back pocket and handed it to me.

"His phone," Julia said. "There's a text on it you can read without unlocking it. He searched for me a lot of the night."

I read the text then reread it, thinking about what it meant.

"I hit him on the head three times with a piece of metal pipe. It was how I got away. It's how I got down to the olive orchard. I climbed up in a tree and hid."

I put an arm around her again and held her close.

"He left an hour ago driving one of those white vans with doors on the side that slide open. It's got a bomb in it. He had the license plate taped over. His name is Danny John."

"Okay. Danny John."

"It's a Ford and it's wider and taller than most vans. It was in the tractor barn. That's the largest outbuilding. I'll show you. He's making bombs in there. No one except us is here. Sorry, UG. I'm really sorry for everything."

"Let's get you food and water."

"No one is there now, but Nick might be coming today. He was here. He's trying to get the money Mom and Dad left me. They forced me to call the broker and say I want to sell everything."

"He and Danny?"

"Yes, and Nick is coming back today or tomorrow. There were two others here, but supposedly they're gone."

We drove up to the gate, and Julia climbed over and hit a button several hundred yards up outside near a door on the main house. I drove in and up to the farmhouse while talking to Mara on my cell. I took in the outbuildings and saw what had to be the tractor barn where Julia said she was held captive. I gave Mara the address, then called a dispatcher at the Tulare County Sheriff's Department and asked for backup.

Julia came out on the deck drinking water. She pointed at a bloody length of pipe near the foot of the stairs. I saw a larger puddle of dark blood where this Danny John had lain unconscious and bled. I tried to picture Julia swinging the piece of pipe, then stepped away to talk quietly to Mara.

"Julia thinks he was unconscious when she ran. He recovered enough to hunt for her, but I'm looking at a pool of blood, all of it from his head injuries. He's running on adrenaline. This guy is seriously hurt."

I got out of the car, and Julia and I walked the fifty yards to the tractor barn.

"There's a door in the back of the tractor barn that might be a better way to get in," she said. "I heard Nick and Danny talking about a booby trap."

"Show it to me."

She showed me then said, "There's stuff up against it from the inside."

I left her sitting against an oak tree and went back to the car for a pry bar, then peeled off the exterior trim and worked the doorjamb loose. I ripped the door out of its opening and started pulling out the boxes that blocked the way in. Then I was looking into darkness and didn't want to flip any light switches before looking for booby traps. I went back and got a flashlight thinking it was probably needless worry since this Danny was walking wounded.

But I was wrong. It turned out the main door was booby-trapped. He'd driven out through a tall, power-operated door. I saw the button to open it, but didn't do that until I was certain it was safe. I saw the cot Julia had talked about and a steel eyebolt epoxied into the concrete slab floor.

I called Mara again, and he conferenced in Fuentes and Hofter.

"I'm in what they call the tractor barn looking at a bomb maker's setup and large, twin sheet-metal bins half full of ammonium nitrate fertilizer. But all that's being grown here are tomatoes, beans, and some herbs. Each of these bins can hold a couple of tons. On the workbench are scraps of wire and tape, what might be left over after building a detonator. There's evidence here. Who's sending ERT?"

"I will," Fuentes said.

"Get them rolling, and I need a locksmith to get this thing off her ankle. After Tulare deputies get here I'm going to defuse a booby-trapped door. I'll search for anything I can find on the van. You've got the address here. He's out there on the move with a bomb, and we don't know where he's headed. He didn't tell her, but Nick Knowles may know, and according to Julia he's coming back here today or tomorrow. I gave the deputies here a photo of Nick. I hope he's coming. I can't wait to see him again."

When I walked back outside, Julia had her eyes closed, with tears leaking out as she pressed the back of her head against the tree. I sat down near her and said, "You are one tough woman. How did you do it?"

"I knew I would never leave here alive if I didn't do something. Do you remember the story you told Nick and me about the two girls that survived years of captivity?"

"Sure."

"That story really helped me," she said. "And I was lucky. I was very scared, but I tried to think."

"There's luck, and then there's what you do with it. You made it happen."

Tears flowed and she shook, but I heard her say, "Instead of letting it happen to me."

Julia got up from the tree as the first deputies arrived, and I got her on my phone talking to a sketch artist. I showed the deputies the booby-trapped door I needed to disarm and sketched out the possible situation with Nick Knowles. I told them FBI teams were en route, then got my gear and disabled the bomb, which was designed to blow off your hand and maybe your lower arm as you opened the door.

With the lights on inside and sunlight flooding through the open door, I looked over the bomb maker's workshop. Like all I'd ever seen, it had a personal feel. A surprising number of bomb makers take pride in their work. Some even carry the fantasy they're doing God's work. I saw enough in that barn to believe this was likely the builder of the LA substation bombs.

Later, from my car I pulled out two pairs of booties and gloves and handed one set to Julia. We put them on and went into the house. We wouldn't touch much of anything, but I wanted her account while we were here. She described Paula and talked about a man named Tom. She showed me where she slept, and I couldn't say why, but I knew it was important for her to do this. We touched nothing except the few belongings she had, then left it for the evidence-recovery team.

When we walked back outside, a Tulare County sheriff's car was coming up the gravel road fast.

The officer said, "We've apprehended an individual who might be Nick Knowles. He spun his car around and tried to make a run for it but lost control and hit a tree. His nose is broken. He lost teeth and a fair amount of blood from a gash on his face. We need to run him to a hospital. Do you want to talk to him first?"

"I do."

After looking through the window, I got in the back seat with Nick. His nose was broken and swollen and off to one side. A slash from high on his right cheek reached down to his upper lip but had stopped bleeding and looked stable. His pupils were fine. I doubted there were any concussion issues.

"How's it going today, Nick?"

"Fuck you. I demand a doctor. I'll sue all of you, and I'll have your job as well as that shitty little house that got trashed."

"Not many people know about the vandalizing of my house."

"How's that crap painting of the sunrise looking? Julia told me how much you like it. Excuse me, liked it."

I took a longer look at him as a few other things clicked into place.

"I wish you hadn't slit it," I said. "I really did like it. I liked it a lot."

"Go to any flea market and someone will sell you another one."

"I've got to say the shooting impressed me. Julia tells me you have a box of medals for competitive target shooting."

"I never showed her any medals."

Nick waited. Even with all his injuries, I could feel him waiting. It was almost eerie.

"She said the same thing. She wanted to see them, and you didn't even tell her what they were for. You said, 'Another time.' When we got the search warrant and went through your apartment and didn't find any medals, I started thinking about you and that one photo I had of my mom, dad, and me."

"Aw, too bad their little heads are gone."

"We didn't find a box of medals in your apartment. You got rid of it."

"You never found any because I never had any. I lied to Julia."

"You lied to her about a lot of things, so why not that too?"

"It's what happened."

"I don't think so, Nick." I gave him a minute to think about that, then said, "Other things have happened in the last twenty-four hours.

Some negotiating with prosecutors is underway. That includes some cooperative horse trading between suspects and prosecutors."

"I need a doctor."

"You may want to hear the rest of this first. You'll have to tell me what you were thinking. Only you really know, but I think you bragged about the medals to Julia, then later decided that wasn't smart. But either way it was good to get them out of your apartment, so you threw a few books that Clark had left behind on top of them. You waved a couple in front of Julia, taped the box shut, then asked Julia to meet Clark in Needles."

"I've got to breathe through my mouth," he said. "My nose is broken, and there's blood running down my throat, so I can't do this shit. Why don't you ask Sam if she ever met Julia in Needles?"

"We've been talking to her but not about whether she was in Needles. The undercover FBI agent who followed her there videotaped the handoff from Julia to Clark. We've showed Clark the video, and when her place in Long Beach was searched, there were the medals. Can you see where this is going?"

He knew where it was going.

"With all the other charges, Clark wants to do some trading. Or Clark's lawyer does. One of the confounding things about the Signal Hill officer slayings is how good the shooter was. Clark has answered that. She'll testify at your trial."

I saw I'd hit home.

"It was her idea," he said. "Have them take me to an FBI office after the hospital and I'll make a statement today."

"All right, I'll set it up, and if that's true it'll matter. There's another way you could help yourself. Danny John dropped his phone and Julia found it, so she got to read your message."

I pulled the bagged phone out, and he could see through the plastic that it was Dan's.

"Tell us where he's headed with the bomb. What's the target?"

"I really don't know."

He leaned over and spit blood and mucus on the floor mat. I pushed my door open and said, "I would testify that you helped when it mattered. Anything you have will help. It could save a lot of lives. He told Julia it's his most powerful bomb yet."

When he didn't say anything, I got out of the car.

Then Nick spoke. "He's not Danny John. He's John Daniels. He flipped his name around for whatever the reason. He's from Phoenix, so if his name didn't come up, that's why. I have no idea where he's going."

"Keep thinking about the target while I pass on the name change."

I called Fuentes. I left it to him to resolve and relay the name difference. Then I leaned back into the car and was quiet and serious with Nick.

"Your friends aren't your friends anymore. None of them, but I'm sure you know that. They view themselves as idealistic and you as a criminal they needed temporarily. They're going to put it all on you. They already know you're going down on credit-card fraud, so the stolen bullets and anything else they can dump on you they will. Their attorneys will huddle without your attorney present and guess who'll get the full life term without parole?"

I gave him a couple of seconds. He didn't need many. He was quick.

"Or you give them up first," I said. "You think about it. Do you want to sit in prison and fifteen years from now watch Sam get released and write a tell-all book? I'd cut your losses if I were you. Preventing a bombing could be very big. Mull that while I talk to the deputy."

The deputy asked me, "What do you think? Pretty soon? It's going to take an hour to get to a clinic. He is hurt."

"I want another minute with him," I said. "Then take him."

I leaned into the car and looked at Nick. "What do you know?"

"Just that he's going to Northern California. He'll have someone there he's supposed to contact."

"What's he driving?"

"A white Ford commercial van. It's new and was leased in Vegas. I don't know what name it was leased under, and I have nothing to do with the bombs." Just before I shut the door he added, "I'm pretty sure it's San Francisco."

53

Later, as Julia and I drove toward Las Vegas, I brought up Jacob Corti.

"We haven't caught up to this sniper yet," I said. "Have you ever heard anybody talk about a sniper shooting at cell towers?"

"In my circles of anarchists and saboteurs?"

"Yes. Corti was a US Army sniper who, after his discharge, joined a local militia in Idaho. Something may have happened there that he participated in and caused him to rethink and question violence. Or maybe it was a combination of everything."

"But he's still shooting," Julia said.

"He is, but not killing. He's shot up cell towers. If our source is correct, Corti wants to overthrow the government through disassembly. Have you ever used that word to talk about changing our society?"

"Sure, it gets tossed around. That's fire-pit talk in Long Beach. They talked about the grid getting taken apart as disassembly."

"Nothing disassembles better or faster than a big bomb."

"UG, I wasn't ever in on any of that. I would never be. I might be the crazy pacifist, but that seems even stupider."

"What comes after the grid?" I asked.

"Living off grid and self-sufficiency. People got caught up."

"What do you mean when you say that?"

"They did stuff they wouldn't otherwise do. They talked themselves into believing it was the only way change would happen. Is it okay if I sleep? All of a sudden I need to. I'll sleep a little and then talk more."

Julia slept, and I drove. In the Bureau there was a debate about how the cell towers tied in. What Julia threw out was part of that mix. The foreign nation-state that attacked us may have cultivated for years a whole range of disenfranchised and disgruntled groups. Corti and the Northern Brigade could fit right into that. The Brigade believes the government is moving in progressive steps to track and control us from birth to death. Life expectancy will become a function of usefulness. Your job will be chosen for you. You'll be tracked and monitored by AI robots your entire life. Your choice of spouse will require the approval of a government clerk. It goes on and on.

Julia slept for an hour and a half. When she woke, we were back in desert country. I returned to Corti and the nagging unanswered question.

"According to our source—someone who knows Jacob Corti—there's a young female pacifist he met in a chat room called the War Room who he really likes talking to. Apparently she calms him down."

"It could be an old man pretending to be a young woman. You have to be careful. Like I was saying earlier, there are people who come to the chat room just to fight. What's he go by?" Julia asked.

"L-Z-9-9-O&O is how he signs. Have you ever come across that? I couldn't tell you what it stands for other than *L-Z* to mean landing zone, but that's just guessing."

Julia was quiet. It could be she was telling me she didn't want to betray someone, or perhaps she was shocked. It felt to me as if my asking had violated something private, and she was adjusting before answering. What was clear was she did recognize L-Z-9-9-O&O.

"It stands for Landing Zone 99 Over and Out," she said. "A helicopter picked him up there on his final tour. The answer to your next question is yes, I've talked to him, many times."

"Really?"

"Totally true. When did you learn this?" she asked. "I mean about keeping him stable."

"In the last few days, from the individual who knows him, although this is not someone we know well enough to trust."

"In the War Room we talk philosophy. We both agree that if a philosophy doesn't work in real life, it's not really a philosophy, so that's a big debate about pacifism."

"Have you ever given him your name?" I asked.

"I don't do that in any chat room."

"You've never given your name?"

"Never."

"What about where you live?"

"I have because sometimes I talk about Creech and Nellis Air Force bases being near me."

"What about the Alagara bombing?"

Asking that was in some way an invasion of privacy, and I felt lousy about it, but it had to be asked. Julia was quiet, then said, "Yes." That was enough for someone to put it together, I thought, but didn't take it any further with Julia.

"Supposedly, the young woman he's talked to about pacifism in a chat room has disappeared, and he really wants to talk to her," I said. "He told his friend he needs to talk to her."

"How could she keep him stable?"

"I couldn't tell you, but I know her moniker."

"Okay, what is it?"

"She signs as Peace Girl," I said.

"No, mostly she—I mean, I sign as PG. Only sometimes as Peace Girl." She ran her hands up her face and through her hair then asked, "Is this really happening?"

"It's happening."

"Are you surprised, UG?"

"When I heard about the young woman pacifist in the chat room, I wondered if it was possible that it was you. You may have been chatting with a former Army sniper named Jacob Corti that we believe is the cell-tower sniper we're looking for. How did you find that chat room?"

"Through Sam."

"I had a feeling you'd say that."

"I'm done with her, UG. I'm pretty much done with all of them if it's not too late."

"Have you damaged property? Have you hurt anyone?"

"Neither. One night in Long Beach we had a 'truth meet' outside at the fire pit, where three of the girls said they weren't comfortable with me. They asked if I was passing information to the FBI through you. I said no. I said I'd move out. So I did, and Sam talked me into going to the farm and getting my head clear there. She set it up so my car would be hidden near this artist colony, and no one would know where I was going. She said that would put me in control and let me reach out when I was ready."

"Ready for what?"

"I don't really know, but I was messed up by Nick posting that video, and a couple of the girls definitely didn't want me in the house. There was stuff. Sam has always wanted me to join up with whatever the other group is they won't talk to me about."

"So instead of trying to talk you into it anymore, she sent you right there where they were building the bombs."

She nodded, was quiet, and then said, "Still my mistake. We smoked some really strong dope, then they drove me there. I was out of it the whole drive. I didn't have my phone, my laptop, or my ID the next morning. Someone stole my wallet. I've made a lot of mistakes in the past year, but I haven't hurt anyone or trashed anything."

"Did you ever provide support for anything violent?"

She laughed. It was an older, more experienced laugh than I'd ever heard from her. It was close to a bitter laugh learned the hard way. But I had to ask. I had to know. I'd put my integrity on the line.

"Kind of hurts my feelings you're asking again," she said.

"But I am."

"I never wanted to know about or took part in any of their operations."

"What about the planning?"

"They would never talk with me in the room or anyone who wasn't part of the inner circle. I never heard anything. There were rumors, but I didn't believe them."

We drove in silence until I turned on the radio and listened to a report on the president's tour of the western states. Phoenix refugees who'd migrated to Salt Lake and were living in a tent city met with the president today. In San Francisco he would give a speech in Union Square.

"What else can you tell me about Mr. Over and Out?" I asked, then I realized I needed to show her a photo. I had an easily accessible one on my phone and brought it up as she talked.

"Certain people give him violent thoughts. I've asked him what about them does that, and we talk about it. Some people he has to avoid being anywhere near. He gets surges of hate. Some are people he knows, some are public figures."

"When we get to the Vegas field office and after we've met with my supervisor, would you be willing to try contacting him?"

"Sure," she said, "but it's pretty unbelievable. They're going to think I know him, aren't they?"

"Some will, for sure."

"It's chat rooms. Are there agents who monitor chat rooms for terrorists? Ask them. They'll get how chat rooms work."

"It'll be okay, Julia. Here take a look at this photo."

I handed her my phone.

"That's Jacob Corti, the cell-tower sniper we're looking for," I said. "This is who it could be."

"Cell-tower sniper? I don't know about that," she said.

I know you don't, I thought.

We arrived at the Vegas office. It was Mara's first look at Julia. She was eye to eye with him. Hers was a straight-ahead look, always had been. The insecurity and personal failure and shame that she'd revealed on the drive was nowhere in the room. I watched Mara look from the bruising around her cheekbone to her sunburned arms, scratched hands, broken nails, the raw physicality of youth. What we only have once.

That wasn't lost on Mara. He was a guy conscious of the passage of time and his devolution into later middle age. Halfway through the meeting he asked me to leave, which was fine. Mara would get to the same place I did. I wanted to take her to San Francisco with me. I wanted to try a different route to Corti that might lead to him giving himself up.

To my surprise, Julia accompanying me to SF was approved. After I was back in the room, Mara asked her to log in to the chat room on a Bureau laptop and reach out to Corti.

"Hey, it's PG. I'm back," she wrote. As we waited, Mara asked, "Does he always sign off 'over and out'?"

I forgot we hadn't told him, but Julia did now.

"He signs 'O&O' like 'over and out' and sometimes 'JC.'" She looked over at me. "Like Jacob Corti, I guess."

That sealed it for Mara.

"I'm going to log out. I don't have to answer right away if he picks up on that. Now at least he knows I'm back," Julia said. "He hardly ever gets back to me right away anyway."

In early sunlight the next morning, Julia and I descended into SFO. Jace picked us up at the airport and with a wry smile said, "Power went out in Saint Petersburg and part of Ukraine while you were in the air, plus about a dozen other Russian cities. Funny thing is, lights stopped flickering in thirteen US cities at the same time."

"Quite the coincidence," I said.

"True that. Some Brits seem to have heard about it first."

"Good on them."

Rumor had circulated through the FBI that the British separately concluded Russia was behind the US attacks. Allegedly, they had also warned Russia to expect retaliation after part of London and all of Bristol went dark three days ago.

The president will speak at Union Square for approximately twenty minutes near dusk. The lights of nearby buildings will grow brighter as he speaks. Jace got that from a Secret Service agent. The agent also said it's very important to the president's staff that surrounding building lights rise to full illumination as he talks so as to give the country confidence that things will soon return to normal.

Little of that mattered to me. Clearing Julia and finding Corti did. A few minutes after we arrived at the San Francisco field office, Julia logged into the War Room on an FBI laptop as I took a call from an Idaho number that turned out to be a Sheriff Summers, whose territory covered the eastern shore of Lake Coeur d'Alene.

"I'm holding a card with your name on it, Agent Grale."

"Where did you get it?"

"From the home of a William Mazarik."

"I gave it to him. Another agent and I visited him about a former Army sniper we're looking for."

"Who was that?"

"A guy named Jacob Corti."

"Mazarik was found dead of a gunshot wound four days ago. It was thought to be suicide, but his death may be murder."

"How did you get from suicide to murder?" I asked.

"Angle of the shot and solvent used to wipe the gun, which was left in a dog bowl full of water."

"So, inside the house?"

"Yes," Sheriff Summers replied.

"Someone he invited in."

"Or he opened the door and they were holding a gun." After a beat he said, "We believe it was someone he knew. Could it have been this Corti?"

"Anything is possible, but I doubt it, given Corti's movements."

"Ever hear the name Gary Farue?" Sheriff Summers asked.

"We're talking to him daily."

"If you're doing that, can you vouch for his whereabouts?"

"We can't. It's mostly cell conversations. I can give you his cell number but just so you know, he switches phones fairly often. He was in the Northern Star Freedom Brigade."

"And he tried to quit?"

"You got it. Here's his cell number."

I read it to him and he said, "We're going to want to interview him. He owed Mazarik money that Mazarik had threatened to sue to collect."

"How much?" I asked.

"Some portion of $50,000 loaned years ago to Farue so he could buy a place in Missoula. But all of this is up in the air right now. There was barely any solvent on the gun. It's possible the dog licked off Mazarik's prints while drinking water. But neighbors say Mazarik would never kill himself and leave his dog in there to starve. And between you and me, I've got a young crime tech here out to make a name. He's the one calling it a murder. I'm not so sure."

"I'm going to tell you something, Sheriff," I said, "something that goes absolutely nowhere. Not a word to anyone, but we hope to know more within a week. Stick with your young guy's theory for now because we're taking a really hard look at Gary Farue and not liking what we're seeing. I'll call you. Give me a week."

I laid my phone down as Julia called out, "He's here. He's writing me. He's here."

54

She'd written, Hey, what's up, JC? I'm back. Been gone. Didn't have Internet. Shoot anybody? Peace Girl.

 L-Z-9-9-O&O: Still hanging.

No harm?

 L-Z-9-9-O&O: Not yet.

Yet?

 L-Z-9-9-O&O: Got something going.

Want to talk instead?

 L-Z-9-9-O&O: Tried to find you for a while. Figured you were done.

Nope, on a farm. Hiding. No connection.

 L-Z-9-9-O&O: You okay?

Sorta. But worried. You?

It struck me that Julia's root honesty might be something he could feel and why he responded to her. She was forthright in a few words, which reminded me I only knew part of her.

L-Z-9-9-O&O: I've got head-tripping finger on the trigger type thoughts. Bad dude coming. Thinking of going over the falls.

She typed, Where are u?

L-Z-9-9-O&O: Norcal.

Me too.

L-Z-9-9-O&O: Where?

SF.

And just like that, we got to the hold-your-breath moment. We got there and he went silent. The laptop Julia worked from was tapped. As we waited for L-Z-9-9-O&O to respond, a tech agent walked in and announced, "He's here. He's right in this area."

He turned to Julia. "Can I use your laptop to pull it up?" She slid her laptop to him and he showed us. "Mission District, either on foot, bike, or slow traffic. I can't tell, but he's moving."

"How do we get more exact?" I asked.

"When he stops we can narrow it down."

But it didn't happen that way. He'd left the chat room and might have even disabled his phone. We lost him. I didn't see any reason for it in the exchange he'd had with Julia. I thought about it, then pulled a chair over and sat near her.

"Julia, on the flight here this morning, you said that the last time in the chat room he didn't sound like himself. It hasn't always felt like you were talking to the same person. Am I remembering that right?"

"It's one of the reasons I stopped talking to him."

"What about this morning?" I asked.

"This morning it feels like him."

"What's different? What feels like him?"

She replied, "He's like me in a way. When he's there, he's there, and gone when he's done."

"He left you with a cliff-hanger."

"He's not saying he's going to do it. He says he's thinking dark stuff. Sometimes he wants to bounce it off me."

"And when it doesn't feel like him, what's it like?" I asked.

"Like somebody prying. Where do I live? What do I like to do? How old was I really? That spooked me. I mean, it was him but not."

Julia turned slightly and pointed toward Jace, who'd finished a meeting and was at the far end of the conference table typing fast on her laptop. Jace had glanced at me a couple of times after coming back into the room, a signal she had things to talk about.

"I didn't think about this again until you introduced me to her," Julia said in a quiet voice. "It probably doesn't mean anything, but . . . okay, so he always signs off as JC or just types 'O&O,' you know, like over and out."

I nodded.

"Okay, so then once he said, 'Call me Jace since that sounds like JC.' Only it doesn't really, right? It was weird because he wanted me to *call* him Jace when we were in the chat room, so not just sign off with it. So then I thought I was talking to somebody else for sure and stayed away. Plus everything else was going on, and then I didn't have a computer. Coming here and finding out her name is Jace is freaky." She leaned forward and whispered, "It wasn't her, was it?"

"Definitely not."

But I immediately thought about Farue. How could I not? We had a tracking device on his vehicle after talking a judge into a wiretap. The judge had almost balked.

"An Afghan war vet, a go-to security consultant for several cell-tower companies and telecoms, and he's working with the FBI right now," the judge had said. "I'll sign it, but I'd never approve this if we weren't under attack. All you're giving me is a good reason to never approach the FBI and offer to help."

That last bit stung a little, but we got the wiretap. It might not do any good, and no doubt he would switch phones again soon, but we knew from the information he'd fed us that he was tracking places Corti contemplated renting in San Francisco. He claimed to be doing that for us. Perhaps he was. But he was also making calls to various vacation rentals. We didn't know yet what that meant. It could be that Corti was telling Farue about places he was looking at, as Farue claimed. Or Farue was gaming us and in truth the judge was right, we didn't have adequate proof of anything.

I walked back down to where Jace sat at the end of the table.

"Now what?" she asked.

"Bring up the photo of the second man at the American River cottage. I'm coming around to thinking the second man may have been Farue."

"Save it for a movie."

"No, I'm serious. Baggy clothes, his body covered, could have been. Where I'm going with this is he may be playing both sides. Farue brags about being able to hack into computers. That could fit here too. Hacking into a computer Corti owns. I'm thinking aloud here, but Julia says in that chat room she thinks someone impersonates Corti. Farue may know she's my niece. Could be he's targeting her at times when he's sure Corti won't be in the room. He's the one who told us about Corti and Peace Girl. He likes the thrill, likes living on the edge and flirting with danger, not to mention the money he's making right now."

Jace looked down the table at Julia then leaned closer to me. In a hushed voice she said, "Reasonable people might say you don't like Gary Farue."

"I don't, and you don't like the idea he may have played us. Hear me out. Farue went to sniper school. He got to be friends with Mazarik and Corti. He shot with them and got to know their shooting styles. When he saw the cell tower where we met him, he knew the one-two signature pattern. He knew from the skill level and I'd guess a half dozen other things it had to be Corti."

"What's your point?"

"I'd lay down money he contacted Corti before he called us. He's not playing both sides, but he's working both sides."

"What's the difference?" she asked.

"He's trying to manage the situation. He calls you, fishes for information, and passes on some of it. He wants Corti to keep shooting. He's kicking ass financially thanks to the cell attacks. He also craves the thrill, the dangerous game of working both sides. He finally feels appreciated. He can pick up his phone and call a telecom exec at nine at night. They're going to pick up."

I kept at it because often enough Jace and I will go back and forth with each other and get somewhere.

"Corti is still deep with the Northern Brigade," I said. "So maybe Farue sees a twofer. Make good with the Brigade by helping Corti, and make money mopping up behind cell towers Corti crashes."

"Cell towers aren't enough of a mission for the Brigade's leader, Croft," she said. "I've done more digging into his life."

"I want to hear about it, but say Farue is hooked up with Corti as well as feeding information to us and maybe feeding it back to Corti, and he's raking in the money. He's got a brand-new pickup in the carport at home. He's got a landscaper coming by once a week picking weeds at a house he's never at. Maybe he had a long period of scraping by and now with attacks underway, he can charge whatever he wants. So what if he points out a target or two to Corti? I mean, what's a cell tower or two between friends. What harm does it do? Nobody dies. Another project comes on line. It's win-win."

"That last is possible," Jace said. "The towers will get repaired, but the crisis continues. The money continues to flow, and Farue looks prescient in his warnings."

"There you go, that's the word, 'prescient.' Puff the ego."

"But it's not like the best days," Jace said. "It's not sitting legs hanging out of a helicopter bay flying somewhere to kick some ass."

"Right, he can't have that feeling again. But he's still living on the edge and making great money doing it. It's a temporary partnership and he knows it, so he's trying every trick in the book to monitor Corti. It's risky with the FBI close by, and then there's Croft. Farue gave up the church of Croft but Corti didn't, so Corti may be relaying back home that Farue is helping. If Farue is helping Corti, then maybe Croft can overlook the way Farue left the Brigade."

"That's buying into 'you can never quit.'"

"I guess it is," I said. "I'm going to jump to Montana. Have you talked with Farue about his cabin there?"

"He brings it up," she said. "It's where he wants to finish his days."

"He told me something like that too. Let's say we find Corti, he surrenders, and we tell him how much his buddy Gary Farue has helped us so we can work them against each other. Word of Farue's betrayal gets back to Croft. Corti, after learning Farue betrayed him, takes revenge and implicates him in the cell-tower shootings, which are now deemed terror-related crimes. I'm saying, Corti says to us, this is how Farue helped me. At that point it's all over for Farue. No more consulting business, no Montana retirement cabin, nothing but a long prison sentence. That's got to keep Farue up at night."

"And he knows we're looking at him."

I nodded. He does know. "So we're back to where we started with him," I said. "Why would he play both sides?"

Jace was quiet then said, "I like the money angle most. It fits with what I get from him, but I agree with what you said about the thrill.

Juggling it all while making the money. Pretty sweet but scary, and scary in a way he's addicted to. He gets something he needs."

I looked at her thinking it through, taking in her face as well, a strong, honest face with a gleam in the eyes.

Julia turned and looked our way. "Jacob's back," she said. "And doing something big today. He's telling me it's bad, so what he means is it's violent. If he's thinking that way, I want to stop him. Can I type I want to meet with him?"

"No," I said.

"What if he asks?"

"If the conditions are safe, we'll—"

Julia said, "He just asked."

55

Julia wrote Corti back, and as we waited for his answer, Jace and I went over the four short-term rentals in San Francisco where Corti had made deposits. Jace took us through it, as I got restless. A city map on her screen showed Corti's rentals with green dots and Farue's with red. She expanded the map and took us down to street view and still kept the identifying dot, a skill I don't have. *I'll age out,* I thought. That's what'll happen. Computer skills like this will become ordinary, and that'll be the end of agents like me.

"Metro cell towers aren't always obvious or easy to access, so if he's renting to be near them, where's he getting his information?" she asked.

"From his buddy Farue. Check on Farue again, let's see where he's at."

She switched screens. The GPS tracker showed Farue's vehicle south of Santa Rosa on 101 heading this way. We'd called him twice today, and the calls had gone to voice mail. I figured we'd try him again in half an hour. He could be heading here.

Jace took the map back to city view. At the other end of the table, Julia typed. When she saw me looking her way, she gave me a blank stare.

"Mission District. Nob Hill. Hunters Point. Glen Park," Jace said and then made a good case for four two-agent surveillance teams at the four spots rented.

"If any team spots Corti, the others converge and SWAT rolls from the SF field office. SFPD is backup. Game over. Corti in custody," she said. "What do you think?"

"If he's there, we bring an army."

I glanced at Julia again. Brow furrowed. Typing fast. Something she'd read she didn't like.

"If we look for towers related to those areas we get some targets but nothing spectacular. We know he's gathered base signal data, but his metro problem has been finding the cell towers. We're speculating he may get that from Farue. But when I switch to substations, take a look."

"Hunters Point has one, so does the Mission, the Larkin substation isn't far from Nob Hill, and Glen Park isn't far from the Bayshore. At least two of these are backbone substations, and each of his four rentals has two things in common: good lines of sight and parking. But I'm not saying he'll take the shots from the rental. Nob Hill has an underground garage with an owner pass. The garage has cameras, but he'll be careful. Take a look at Hunters Point, where the house is isolated. Look at the line of sight from the deck to the substation. That's an easy shot for him." She added, "I'm not off the wall with this substation idea."

Yes, you are, I thought.

"You're trying to make it all fit, Jace. I've made the same mistake myself many times."

Before Jace could respond Julia said, "Take a look. It's bad."

Both Jace and I walked down to Julia's end of the table.

L-Z-9-9-O&O: Hey, PG, bad day, struggling. No meet up today. I've done things I don't regret but wish I'd never done. It's the way life came. Did my best. No going back.

Julia had written back, Remember how we said, never too late.

L-Z-9-9-O&O: Too far along now, PG.

Lay down your gun forever.

L-Z-9-9-O&O: Suicide if I do.

Let's still meet up. Where are u?

L-Z-9-9-O&O: Wish I'd met you a long time ago.

Way too young for you. Eighteen!

L-Z-9-9-O&O: I know. Friend told me.

Was he the guy who bogus wrote me pretending to be you?

L-Z-9-9-O&O: Hope he didn't.

Think he did. Someone did.

L-Z-9-9-O&O: Still wish we'd met.

Still can.

L-Z-9-9-O&O: Later, PG

Don't go. Want to meet up. No violence. Other ways to get there. Call me.

I read that and saw at the end of her message Julia had typed in her new phone number.

"He signed out," Julia said. "What he wrote bums me out. I'm going to get out and take a walk along the water."

Julia headed for the waterfront and I said to Jace, "Let's go see these areas you're talking about."

I also wanted to see Union Square, where the president would talk. Jace drove. Hunters Point was the farthest out, so we saved it for last. We got on 101 south, looped around to the Glen Park house, then back over the hill and down to the Mission Street condo, and from there back across Market Street to Union Square. Jace pulled into a yellow zone and parked.

Carpenters worked on a wooden stage for the president that looked like something out of the past. A lot of prep was underway. The streets were already closed off. It was a pretty big buildup for a half hour speech at sunset, but that's my opinion.

"Orient me," I said. "Where from here is the Nob Hill unit he's rented? That's the first rental, the one that starts tomorrow, right?"

"Yes, and I think it's the one we can see, but it's back several buildings and up."

"And that's still Nob Hill?"

"Nob Hill area."

She pointed then guided me until I had it using the small binoculars she'd given me from her purse.

"I called the owner," she said, "and verified it starts tomorrow."

"Let's drive by it when we leave here," I said.

Once back in the car, Jace returned to the idea of Corti flipping to substation shootings. "Like Metcalf," she said. "Look how effective that was. He can get off the shots, break down, and be gone in no time."

"Substations are a big step up from what he's been doing," I said. "It's the kind of shooting that could lead to cordoned-off streets and a manhunt. I'm looking for why he'd take that kind of risk."

"To go out big like he's suggesting to Julia."

"He is saying that, isn't he?"

"That's the Nob Hill building straight ahead," she said like she'd just changed the channel.

"What's the unit number?" I asked, "And do you know which direction it faces?"

"No."

She looked at me and then in the direction from which we'd just come.

"The rental doesn't start until tomorrow, but good point," she said. "Let's double back on that. I'll give the owner a call. She said call anytime, so good chance she'll get back to us pretty quick."

She called, and I heard a phone ringing just before a voice-mail greeting. Jace left a message that included the question of the orientation of the unit, but we still went into the building, found a manager, and checked. It was a corner unit on the sixth floor. It did have a view of Union Square.

As we got back in the car, our world changed a little as I got a text from Carol Mann in the cyber division at headquarters. A rush of elation ran through me. I handed my phone to Jace.

"Read this before we drive away."

At 2:07 p.m. Carol had written, We found them and we're way into them. They're toast! C

"The cyberattacks?" Jace asked.

"Yes, and she would know."

Jace smiled in a big way. It leaked into the media within an hour that a condo high up in a new Dubai tower loaded with computers and servers was found some time in the last week and breached by the NSA, which then tapped in. Once in, it linked to servers in nine buildings in seven countries that ricocheted signals around the world. I don't know how it works at that point. I don't know how you track down the origin with signals bouncing all over the world, but I'd had enough conversations with Carol in the last year to know she wouldn't send this unless it was a done deal.

Jace and I picked up the Corti conversation again on the way back to the FBI office. I texted Julia as we bought a couple of sandwiches, but she'd eaten at the Ferry Building and had walked along the water down to China Basin and the Giants stadium, so we went back to work.

Then the Nob Hill condo owner called. I read the alarm on Jace's face.

She got off the phone and said, "Corti added a day. He took possession at three this afternoon. I'm going to get my supervisor and we'll get a SWAT team with us. I'll be right back."

56

As Jace left the room, I got a three-word text from Mara.

We got him.

I turned on the TV in the conference room, and the scene was a Shell station and mini-mart. A driverless white van at one island had a pump nozzle in its filler neck. Tracy Police and CHP cars had blocked it front and back. Other cars at the islands were also empty. Police were visible inside the mini-mart, but no customers. The CNN reporter said, "We've got a developing situation with a suspect locked in a bathroom."

We weren't on scene yet, except for two FBI agents diverted from their return to the Sacramento office. The man inside the restroom was believed to be John Daniels, aka Danny John. It was unclear whether he could detonate the van from where he was, so everyone inside was taking a very real risk. But good chance they knew something we weren't seeing.

As I watched, paramedics arrived, and now you could see through the windows and catch movement. They'd unlocked the bathroom door and gone in to find Daniels incoherent. He was lying in front of the toilet on his back with his arms splayed and his eyes dilated.

I called Mara and said, "I'm watching it on TV. He must have holed up somewhere and was bringing the bomb in today. Whatever hospital they take him to they need to know what his head injuries came from. It could be a blood clot, something like that. We're hoping he makes it."

"Why?"

"He's got a whole lot of information that could help us."

I didn't say anything about the situation here yet. We didn't know for sure. I didn't want to get into that. We ended the call as I watched paramedics bring him out on a stretcher. I couldn't tell it was Daniels, but it had been confirmed via two IDs he was carrying that Danny John was John Daniels, as Knowles had told me.

Jace came back in and said, "My supervisor and ASAC will be here in five minutes. We're a go."

I stood but didn't turn the TV off. I pointed at it.

"He told Julia this was his biggest bomb. He called it the mother of all bombs." I looked at her and added, "This is a very big break. It's lucky."

Her assistant special agent in charge walked in first. I muted the TV and shook her hand.

57

JULIA

May 10th

Julia stood near the Willie Mays statue and reread a text from a number she didn't recognize. It was JC. He'd changed his mind and wanted to meet after all. He'd sent an address on Bush Street with an elevator code, 6327, and condo number, 607, and wrote, Knock on the door or use code 02290. She had never seen a door with a code, but who cares about that? It just felt funny that the meeting wasn't at a place where they could get a coffee or something. Not the way she pictured meeting.

She texted him back, What about meeting for coffee?

No worries. Can't leave here right now, but I understand. Another time.

Are u okay?

Not really, but dealing.

Might come there.

No, I get it.

See you soon. Coming there.

She got an Uber. If she changed her mind on the drive, she could text him and go back to the FBI office or wherever. The Uber driver was not much older than she was and wanted to talk, and then took her by to see the crowd gathering in Union Square. He turned around and said, "They caught that guy."

"What guy?"

"The guy in the van with the bomb."

The driver dropped her off, and Julia went into the building. She was ready to enter the code when the elevator dinged and the doors started to open. She turned away but was aware of a man hurrying out. He went toward the doors to the street as she stepped into the elevator. She hit 6 and as the doors started to close, the man turned back.

He called, "Hold the elevator," but she didn't. She didn't want any-one else riding up with her. It was already spooky enough. UG would be all over her case for doing this, but she had to. Besides, the guy tried to get his fingers in and get the doors to open in the last second. Old elevator. Didn't work for him.

The doors opened on floor 6, and she hurried down the corridor to 607. Her hands shook as she reread the code number, 02290. She knocked twice, waited, then entered the code. She pushed the door open, then closed it quickly and went down a hallway to a big open room with a kitchen and a deck with a chest-high metal platform near a half-open sliding door. She saw a man on the floor on his side with blood around his head. Near him on neatly folded towels were what looked like parts of a gun.

She heard a soft knock, maybe a neighbor at the door. It stopped, but she didn't move. She froze for a moment, then texted UG,

JC wanted to meet at a building on Bush Street. If it's him he's dead.

A call came from UG. "We're almost there. Don't touch anything."

"I haven't. How did you know to come here?"

"Julia, can you see his face?"

"Half of it."

"Can you tell if it's Jacob Corti?"

"I'm not positive. I'm pretty sure it is. There are gun parts every-where like he broke his gun down like you do when you clean yours. The pieces are spread out on folded towels."

"How did you get in?"

"He sent me a code."

"Do you see a weapon anywhere near him that may have fallen if he shot himself?"

"No, but there's a metal stand. He was going to shoot from in here."

"Take a photo of the stand and of him and send them to me. Then go downstairs. There's an FBI SWAT team and San Francisco police on the way."

"I'm afraid to leave. There was a man who wanted to get in the elevator with me when I got here. The elevator doors closed before he could get in, but then there was a knock on the door here after."

"Okay, stay where you are, and when the police get there you'll hear plenty of noise. It'll be loud. It won't just be one person knocking. You'll know. Do you understand?"

"Yes."

"We'll tell them you're there and that you'll wait by the door."

In the background she heard Jace talking fast, relaying what she'd just said to other FBI agents.

"I'll take the photos right now," she said.

As she hung up, she heard sirens coming. She took the photos and sent them, then turned back to the man on the floor and thought about him as the JC who sometimes made her laugh so much. He was lean and long. He lay on his right side with blood dried on his neck. His dark hair moved with the wind through the open door. It was slick where he had been shot in his left temple. She saw his hands, and the boots that he wrote her about.

It was Jacob. She was sure it was Jacob, and waves of sadness came through her. She knelt and touched his arm and cheek, though she knew she shouldn't. She had to. She stepped back and looked again at the gun pieces so exactly laid out. The parts arranged on the towels with the bullets lined up must mean something. His phone must be here but she didn't see it. She felt nauseated and stepped out on the deck and saw in the distance the little rectangle that was Union Square. The crowd had spilled off the square into the street.

"You were going to shoot the president," she said, and just then she heard knocking, then pounding on the door, voices yelling. She hurried to the door. "Police. Open up!"

She opened the door with her heart pounding and saw the man from the elevator she'd seen earlier. He grabbed her and pushed a gun against her head.

"Do exactly as I say or you're dead."

He half dragged her down the hall. They went down the elevator and out the lobby. He lowered his gun but still held her, though not tightly anymore.

"I'm sorry. You must be Julia. I'm working with the FBI. I work with your uncle Grale. I'm very sorry to put a gun to your head, but a lot is going down right now, and we had a report of an armed young woman as part of a sniper team. She may still be in the building or right outside, so we don't want to attract attention as we leave here. Do you see the black SUV at the curb?"

Julia had seen other FBI vehicles like that. She nodded, and he gave her a kind of a hug and said, "Hey, I'm really sorry. I know what it feels like to have a gun to your head. I'm going to look around another few seconds here, and then we'll just walk normal and get in and drive away. You ready?"

"Sure," she said, not sure she believed him.

"Okay, here we go."

The Suburban unlocked with a loud click. She opened the passenger door after he'd hurried up the other side and got in. He slid onto the seat and as he did, he said, "Get in—what are you doing?"

She shut the door and ran from the SUV. She ran around the front of the building and down the street, pulling out her phone without slowing. And still, he caught up to her so fast she couldn't believe it. The street was steep, but he caught her left arm and held it, then pushed the gun against her skin under her shirt.

"Do anything and you're dead. Walk back up and around the front of the building, and we'll get in on the driver's side. You'll slide over. I have no problem with killing you. I have zero problem. If you look at anybody and they ask if you're okay, I'll kill them too. You look down at the sidewalk. Start walking."

When they were back where it was flat, she dove to her right and rolled. She yelled. She scrambled away, and he kicked her. She started to get to her feet, but she was down again, and when she saw the barrel of the gun she knew it was over.

58

When we drove up the hill, I could see Farue frog-walking Julia up the sidewalk. I didn't see a gun, but I could read his posture, and Julia resisted each pull forward. We were almost there as they reached the corner, but got blocked by a car. I saw Farue's black Suburban and Julia switch from resisting to lunging forward. When she fell onto the pavement, I saw Farue's gun and said, "Jace, I'm out."

I swung the door open, cleared it, and shot him. It didn't drop him, but it interrupted his aim. Two shots from his gun struck pavement near her head, kicking up chips and concrete dust. My next shot dropped him and should have killed him, but first responders got there fast enough to save him.

FBI, SFPD, and Secret Service converged on the building. Julia, Jace, and I went up the elevator before Farue was in an ambulance. Julia's elbows were skinned and she was still catching her breath as we got off on the sixth floor. FBI SWAT arrived but waited in the lobby. Two SF homicide inspectors came up to the condo. Secret Service followed, and unit 607 became a homicide scene. A dozen FBI agents and more Secret Service fanned out into adjacent buildings after Corti's weapon was identified as a sniper rifle.

Late sunlight slanted through the tall windows. A breeze blew in through the half-open sliding door. On the deck were plants in two cerulean blue pots that resembled urns. From the folding metal platform, the shot would angle down over the top of the wire railing. I looked at Corti's body again and tried to see how it went down.

I turned to Julia and asked, "What are you seeing?"

"He said he was going to do something that could get him killed."

"Shooting the president would do that."

"That's not what he meant."

As she pointed at the gun parts I could see her right palm was raw and scraped.

"Jacob took his gun apart. He came here to shoot the president, then decided not to and that he was done. Sometimes he would write about breaking down a gun and cleaning it. He once wrote me that he wanted to get to the place where he broke his guns down and left them disassembled forever. He said it was a way of coming to terms."

"With what?"

"I don't know." Then she asked, "Did the guy who grabbed me kill him?"

"Good chance he did."

"Do you know who he is?"

"Yes. Do you know him?"

"No."

I checked her face, wondering if she understood how close she came to getting shot. If Farue died he'd be the third person I'd shot and killed in my career. That's a high number for an FBI agent, but with each there was no other obvious choice. With Farue I felt lucky. I'm a decent shot but not great and could easily have missed him.

The more I looked at the body and the quasi-ritualistic arrangement of the gun parts on white towels, the more I came around to the idea that Corti took apart the gun and Farue interrupted him. Corti may have been doing just what he'd talked to Julia about, breaking it down and walking away. But Farue wouldn't have any interest in assassinating the president. If he did, I couldn't see it. The Northern Brigade I could picture sending Corti here. Farue said Corti would rant about corrupt politicians and the deep state. And Farue once told Jace that Corti spoke through his gun. That rang true to me.

My phone rang after we were back in the lobby. Outside, the street was filled with media vans. The call was from the head of the presidential Secret Service detail. He handed me off to one of the president's team, who said, "Agent Grale, the president very much wants to give this speech in San Francisco. It's information the American public needs to hear. We understand the shooter is dead. The president wants to thank you."

"He was dead when he was found, and we're not certain who killed him. It doesn't appear he was going to shoot. His gun was broken down."

"But he is dead."

"Yes, he's dead."

"If there's no further risk, the president can still make his speech from Union Square."

"That's a Secret Service decision."

The caller knew that better than me. I looked at the cameras outside wondering what the news stations had pieced together.

"Do you know of any more shooters, Agent Grale?"

"I don't, but you might want to make sure the vice president is somewhere safe before the president starts speaking."

"Thank you for your time."

The president's venue got moved. He no longer would stand on the wood podium at dusk with the lights rising in the buildings surrounding him. They put him upstairs in the Ferry Building, where he was safe. But it didn't diminish the information he was delivering.

He said, "We have identified Russia as the foreign actor behind the cyberattacks. They deny this. They will continue to deny this, but we will show the world the proof we are sharing with allies. We are in negotiations with the Russians, and our negotiations include reparations. We do not expect this to be a rapid process.

"Over the course of the past few weeks, we have dismantled a sophisticated network of hackers. This network spanned seven countries. Some of those hackers are no longer with us. Some we will extradite. All will be tried here in the United States.

"As I speak, power is out in Moscow. Several large turbines have destroyed themselves. The Russians are experiencing power outages in other major cities: Novosibirsk, Samara, Nizhny, Saint Petersburg, to name several. It is a reminder of how interconnected the world has grown and how dependent we are on the goodwill of each other.

"It is the intent of the United States to avoid a larger war. To do that, it is necessary for the people in both countries to remain calm. It is also necessary for the people of the United States to see the immediate cessation of all cyberattacks by Russia, after which deaths and economic losses can be assessed. If reparations are agreed to and paid, we believe a comprehensive understanding can be reached to avoid a future war."

Many had varying takeaways from the speech. What I heard was that the Russians would not admit to the attacks, and we weren't going to officially admit the counterattacks. A rough eye-for-an-eye scenario was playing out. Some level of parity would be agreed to behind closed doors. But there was no going back. A new form of warfare was emerging, drying its scaly wings in the sun.

The next morning Julia flew back to Las Vegas, where she was met by Jo. She'd stay at Jo's house. I flew in late in the afternoon and talked to Jo as I drove to my house. Inside, it smelled like new paint. I tore back the red-brown paper covering the hardwood floors. They hadn't looked this good since Carrie and I bought the place. Maybe that meant something. There were decisions to make in the kitchen, but the bathrooms were back together, and a hot shower sounded better than food. I met up with Jo and Julia after, and we went out to dinner, where I got a text I thought was from the Secret Service but turned out to be Dan Jenkins, the carpenter, sending me photos of Ikea cabinets.

The next day Jace and I worked through a timeline of Corti's and Farue's moves. One more day and the intubation tube would come out, and soon Farue, if he wanted, could talk. I planned to fly back to SF as soon as the tube was out, but if anyone could get anything out of him it would be Jace.

Two things changed my plans. The first was a message from Samantha Clark via her lawyer that she wanted to talk. The second was a seventeen-year-old kid from Idaho driving day and night with his Northern Brigade father. They arrived at SF General, where Farue was, and the young man sold the night-shift nurses a story of driving from Idaho to see his father, Gary Farue. He showed ID with the name Theodore Farue and teared up when they relented. The charge nurse said no more than ten minutes with Dad.

He didn't need ten. He needed less than two minutes to bury a seven-inch hunting knife up to the hilt in Farue's right eye. Jace, with her dark, dry sense of humor, asked, "Do you think Farue saw it coming?"

But that was to cover our frustration. I canceled my flight to SF and flew from Vegas to LA the next day, after the discovery of a gun.

In a reaction to Jody Gavotte hiding Julia's car under debris and trash in the former commercial space, Max Tona had, at the owner's expense, hired a crew to clean out all but the leaking barrels of chemicals. They used a Bobcat tractor to scoop debris and carry it outside. There, it was loosely sorted and broken up before being loaded into trucks.

During the sorting, a waterproof bag was found. Inside the bag were a modified assault rifle and $7.62 \times 54R$ steel-core bullets that matched those used to kill the security guard in the Tehachapi and destroy the transformers.

Gavotte disappeared the same day after hearing a gun was found. A warrant went out in his name when fingerprints on the gun matched his. Hofter and I questioned Gavotte's distraught father, who said he had no idea where his son would run, then added, "It won't be far enough."

He was right, though I'm not sure that's what he meant. Jody Gavotte was arrested that night in Laguna Beach after breaking into a house owned by the parents of a former girlfriend. The parents were in London, where the father responded to an alert on his iPhone when cameras in the house detected movement. He'd called Laguna Police, who arrested Gavotte without incident. If I can be there when he's arraigned on murder charges, I promised myself I will.

59

Century Regional Detention Facility

Clark was held without bail in LA, and terrorism charges were pending. With the Long Beach terror cell, FBI investigators kept working it, doubling back, reinterviewing, making certain everyone associated was arrested and that anyone peripheral not charged had provided testimony. The soon-to-be-charged were sweated in hopes they'd give up more.

Both the Bureau and the DA's office kept circling Julia. The business of playing those held without bail pending terrorism charges, one against the other, would spin on for another month, maybe more. Among those repeatedly questioned was Samantha Clark. Her answers on Julia hadn't wavered. I'd listened to the following tape of Clark.

She stated, *"Julia Kern was not involved in any bomb making at the Tulare farm or anywhere else. She was never briefed, never rode with a bomb team or participated in scouting. She had no access to the site in the dark web. She was never in planning meetings. She was purposely kept in the dark due to her FBI uncle and her pacifism."*

When I got to the LA County jail, a sheriff's detective named Greg Johnston was waiting. He wasn't working terrorism. He was here about the Signal Hill officer slayings. He got out of his car after I had parked and started for the door. He was clearly tipped I was coming and called to me before I got in the door. He shook my hand like we knew each other.

"We've worked hard on this case," he said.

"You really have, and I heard you've narrowed it down with phone records."

"We haven't made an arrest. Let's just get right to it. What does Clark want with you? We can't wrap our heads around it. We liaised with two agents out of the LA FBI office, but you're out of Vegas, right?"

"I'm not here about Signal Hill," I said.

I stared at him a moment. He knew Samantha Clark was from Las Vegas, but maybe he didn't know much about Julia.

"Clark knows my niece."

"Wasn't your niece the girlfriend of one of the terrorists?" he asked.

"Where are we going with this?" I asked.

"I'd like to be with you when you talk with Clark today."

"I'm here about my niece."

"I hear you, but I'd like to be in there with you."

"What are you worried about?" I asked and was genuine.

"I hear you're trying to get your niece to skate through without charges. What are you giving Clark this morning? What's the trade? What brought you here?"

"There's no trade. If that's why you're here, you can leave. If you want me to ask her something, I will. If she wants to talk, I'll come get you. Pop off any more about my niece on things you know little about—no, make it zero—that you know nothing about then I'm going to turn my back on you."

He shook his head and turned away, but he'd wait. I left him and went inside. They brought her out and into a small room so we could talk face to face.

Clark's face had paled, and her eyes dulled in just the short time she'd been jailed. Her lawyer hoped that what she'd created with Witness1 would foster goodwill with a jury. That, and how Russian foreign agents who operated undercover manipulated them. The pair of Russian agents arrested had been in the states for a decade. To at least three cells they'd provided money and expertise. They were how the farm was purchased. They were patient. Their operation had been designed to take years. They became enablers and empathizers, but that wasn't going to sell to juries looking for revenge.

"I want to thank you for being truthful about Julia," I said.

"You don't need to thank me."

"I want to, and I want to say Witness1 is a strong idea. Fix its flaws and keep it going. It may give you strength."

"I can't do anything from prison."

"You can do more than you think."

"No, you're looking at a wasted life."

"You took a wrong turn. Get back on the road."

"It doesn't matter what the lawyer comes up with, now or ever," she said. "It's over for me. I'll never walk along a beach again. I'll never wake at night, reach over, and touch the one I love. I'll never have children. We were careful not to hurt or kill anybody, but then Tehachapi and Los Banos happened."

We talked about that, and then her voice trailed off. She was going away. Before she withdrew, I asked, "What about Signal Hill? There's a detective outside who wanted to come in with me."

She looked back at me a long time. She had nothing to gain, only more notoriety.

"Why do you ask?"

"I've seen a lot, Sam. I've lived around it. I think it's better to get it all out."

She stood, perhaps to say she was done. She looked past me and said, "I wasn't part of any planning. I was told to circle around in the Signal Hill area. I would get a call. I think he thought up the idea on his own. Something was going down, and he knew about it but couldn't tell me."

"It was someone you know?"

"Yes, and you do too, you know him. I thought you'd already figured it out."

I had.

"When I got the call, he said to go to the Black Bear and get a table by a window. I wasn't told what would happen, but he did say 'We're going to make you famous.' So I went. I didn't quite put it together before I went. I saw those two officers get out of their car. They were tired, and happy their shift was winding down. You could see it in their faces. They were trying to joke with each other. I could see that from where I was without hearing anything they said. They were fellow human beings, and I realized as I was watching them that the call was about them, but I didn't move. I betrayed them."

She shook her head.

"I betrayed them, but it's not like I knew what was going to happen. I didn't know Nick would shoot them. Now I don't know how to make amends. I don't know that there's any forgiveness for that. But you need to know that's why I'm standing up for Julia. The others are being offered better deals if they can name more terrorists and deliver testimony. I'll keep standing up for Julia. She was never involved. If they charge her, don't listen to them. There wasn't a single operation she took part in, either in planning or execution. I won't let them trade away her life."

"I thank you for that."

"I know you do, and I know you mean that. Tell the county detective I'll tell him Nick Knowles was the killer. I still find it hard to believe. But Nick once told me his father routinely beat him and he ran away when he was sixteen. Maybe it all comes from that physical abuse. I don't know. I don't understand."

"He was nineteen when his parents died. They had retired from the State Department and were living in Africa. Police there think a young white man nailed the doors to their house shut, then doused it with gasoline and burned them alive. Every year they try to extradite Nick Knowles. It might have driven him to find new identities."

She froze upon hearing that, and I said, "I don't know when we'll see each other next. Most likely at trial, unlikely before. I'll find the LA County detective now and tell him. Start a fund for the children of those officers after this is over, after the trials. After everything, Sam. Do it for them. Do it for yourself."

"I might do that."

We left it there. Outside, it was hot with a wind blowing. Human nature is a contradiction.

60

Corti was dead and the Long Beach cell dismantled. Fourteen people associated with the Long Beach house were arrested, Julia among them. Yes, Julia. I still couldn't accept that. None were allowed to post bail. When I saw Julia next, she was in an orange jumpsuit with her hair cut and her face looking much older. There was nothing I could do to help.

After she was arrested, I worked alone more. In western states, attacks dwindled to near zero. More arrests were made, and more would be made, but physical attacks on infrastructure had all but ended by Memorial Day. On June 3, an American surveillance plane and a Russian fighter jet collided, and it felt as if we came close to war. Cyberattacks resumed, but tapered off within a week. Not in Russia, though—they continued there, some doing serious damage, then stopped altogether in the third week of July.

There was never an "official" end, just an end. Maybe that means something about future war, though I couldn't tell you what. That a cell of fourteen young people in the Los Angeles area was able to go undetected also means something. To me it suggests sympathizers. In that, what I hear is that we need to get it together as a country, and I don't mean just security. We're getting factionalized, too tribal. We need to talk more.

I kept my contact with the Vegas office to a minimum. I volunteered for the investigations that kept me out on the street. I resented

Mara—he had known Julia would be arrested and charged and hadn't told me, though I knew he couldn't. It wasn't rational to resent him, but it's how I felt. I'm not saying I was sullen or hard to work with, and Mara and I never said a word about it, but there was an unspoken undercurrent in every conversation we had.

Few of the domestic-terror-cell cases were as strong as Long Beach, yet the trial was still months away. I was told to plan for three to four days of testimony. I stayed in close touch with Erica Roberts, Julia's lawyer, although Roberts didn't need me. She was driven and vocal. She knew courts favor those who keep up the fight. At any media opportunity she raked the prosecutors for delay and for cynically charging her client with crimes she didn't commit. But for the public, I think that talk is just noise, and common sense seemed to say Julia Kern should have known better and gotten herself away from them.

An image of my niece I like is her straight-backed on a hard chair after her escape and night in the orchard, facing down Mara, answering his questions. I take comfort in that memory. I see my sister in her. I see her father. What I see tells me she'll survive and endure. She's got the fire.

Jo and I kept each other close. We made time. We took small trips and found some peace in the quiet together. In late June, I checked out keys and returned alone to the bomb factory at the farm in Tulare County. Mara and Fuentes knew I was going. No one else did. Ostensibly, it was to make notes and prepare myself for trial.

I walked the outbuildings and the bomb factory, with its sheet-metal bins that had stored up to five tons of ammonium nitrate. At least two tons were still here. The smell was strong when I came in the door. I smelled that as well as a damp that must have come from a spring or welling from the creek, now dry, or the pond. I thought of the bomb at the Olin substation, weakened by moisture content.

I videotaped and took photos I'd review before I testified. A rat or squirrel scurried somewhere in the back of the bomb factory as I left and relocked the door. Then I walked the farm, the rows of dead tomato plants, dried shrunken bush beans, a small dope grow field that was doing just fine on its own. The sun was hot on the porch, and the house smelled musty and unused inside. I tried the lights. The power was off. I thought about the two others who'd lived here and were facing terror charges yet claimed they knew nothing about the bomb making. But the question again, how could they not?

With Hofter I'd made a last visit to the Long Beach house, which was about being clear on what we'd investigated together, no collusion, but a necessary talking through as we prepared for trial. Inevitably, we got to Julia, or I made sure we did.

"Should we even have that conversation?" he asked.

"No prosecutor is going to call me to testify about her role. They already know where I stand. It'll be you and others. What do you think the charges against her hang on?"

"Testimony from the others."

"I agree."

"And they're all trying to make deals through their attorneys, so you know where that leads."

I did. It leads to trying to please the prosecutors by providing damning testimony. With Julia I believed it would come down to the night of the move and whether she had any active role in negotiating storing her car to make it seem she'd disappeared. That would work against her with a jury, and yet, blood is blood, I simply believed Julia.

Jace and I keep a banter going. We're simpatico that way. It's our way of dealing with the dark places. Casewise, we had less and less to talk about. I did go to Missoula and, with an agent out of Helena and a locksmith, got into Farue's cabin. I talked to Jace from there as the Missoula agent worked from his car.

Unlike the sterile house in California, the cabin had mementos. I sifted through those and learned more about Farue, though nothing that clarified his association with the Northern Brigade. The teenage boy who killed him had never met him, nor had his father, but Croft had made Farue into an immediate threat to the Brigade after the media reported him as the suspected killer of Corti.

In a leather album, Farue had photos of himself and what looked like a girlfriend in Santiago, Chile. He looked tanned and happy. She looked young and vibrant as they toasted with two glasses of champagne.

"You should have stayed there," I said in the empty cabin.

In July, Julia and two of the others were released on bail with the condition they wear ankle bracelets. That system was modernized recently, and bracelets were now tracked by satellite. The bail was backed by her inheritance, an outcome Jim and Melissa could never have seen. To my surprise, a judge allowed Julia to accept an invitation to move to red rock country in Utah, to an old town some young people were trying to reinvigorate. They were growing crops and Julia said many of them also had online jobs, part time or otherwise.

Recently they'd bought inexpensive solar panels at a Home Depot, along with other components, and storage batteries from the new Tesla factory in Nevada. A welder in the community used scrap aluminum to put together frames for the panels after a young guy studying electrical engineering at an online school and a local retired astronomer figured out the best orientation and the most efficient system.

They installed the panels on a Saturday, then had a barbecue and drank craft beer from a new microbrewery in town. That all happened the day after a decision was made at the Justice Department that would forever affect Julia's life. Mara called me in. He got it from way up the chain, and they left it for him to tell me. It wouldn't be official until next week, but she could be told. Not just told, but a judge had allowed another step.

"You get to be the one," Mara said. "It should come from you, not her attorney, and Erica Roberts, her attorney, agrees. She called me. She feels the same."

From Vegas, it was a three-and-a-half-hour drive to Saint George then east to red rock country. Julia had invited me out for a Saturday "power party," as they called their solar-installation celebration. I arrived late as usual. Julia exuded energy. Her face was lit up. Gone was the pale, anxious blinking into bright sunlight when she first walked out of jail. She wore shorts and a white cotton top, and the heavy ankle bracelet like it was a piece of jewelry.

Blue smoke rose from the barbecuing underway, with chicken and burgers grilling on oil drums sliced lengthwise then fitted with grills and welded-on legs. They were cooking over sustainable mesquite charcoal someone in the community had made.

"I'm so glad you came, Uncle Grale. I wanted to let you know I signed up for that online school. No matter what happens, I'll get my degree. Want to take a walk? I'll show you the solar panels. Almost everything is sustainable here. It's so cool."

"Yeah, let's go see them and talk."

The panels were bright in the sun.

"You wouldn't believe how cheap they've become," Julia said.

"I've read about it. How are you doing?"

"Much better. It'll be very hard, but I'll deal with it."

She was talking about trial and prison, and a surge of emotion flowed through me. When you're young, you don't quite see how short it all is, how precious. I had to look away at the line of the mountains. That's me, the old hard-bitten FBI agent getting soft. Or maybe it's just that as we age we know more.

"I've got news from the Justice Department, Julia."

"Don't tell me yet."

She frowned and bowed her head. I knew she was thinking good news would be lesser charges, but she also knew even those would carry a ten-year minimum sentence. I watched her take a deep breath and look out at the mountains studded with pine and fir and strung with red rock. She turned, faced me, and said, "Okay, tell me. I'm ready."

"Charges have been dropped against you and two others."

"I'm not going to prison?"

"You're not going."

They'd given me the key to the ankle bracelet. "Put your right foot on that rock."

"Why?"

"Just do it."

She did so and I leaned over and unlocked the bracelet. It was heavy, but she'd made a point of walking like it wasn't there.

"I've got to take this back with me," I said.

"I'm really not going back to jail?"

"You're not going back."

Her eyes clouded with tears, and emotion rose again in me. All I could do was nod. She closed her eyes and tears ran down her cheeks, then a smile started and got larger.

"UG, really?"

"Yeah, so take it like a second chance. Make the world a little better."

"I will. You know I will."

I put the ankle bracelet in my car and we sat in the shade and ate burgers, and I drank the beer they made in town. It was pretty good, but nothing was as good as hearing Julia laugh again.

Acknowledgments

Once more, many thanks are owed former FBI supervisory special agent George Fong. Check out his crime novel, *Fragmented*. Thanks go to Rick Jackson, longtime LAPD homicide detective, now retired, and Elvis Chan, FBI supervisory special agent on Squad CY-1, where the focus is cybercrime and national security. When you embark on writing a crime novel, it's very lucky to be able to reach out to those who've lived law enforcement.

Thank you, Megha Parekh, my editor at Thomas & Mercer, and to all at T&M for easy communication and openness. Thanks to Philip Spitzer and Lukas Ortiz of the Spitzer Literary Agency—let's go to a baseball game sometime. Thank you to Kevin Smith for that first look, and many thanks to Peggy Hageman for a keen eye and knowing insight.

About the Author

Kirk Russell is the author of numerous thrillers and crime novels, including *Shell Games*, *Redback*, *One Through the Heart*, and *Signature Wounds*, his first book in the Paul Grale series. His book *Dead Game* was named one of the top ten crime novels of 2005 by the American Library Association. Russell's novels have garnered many starred reviews. Among them, *Library Journal* referred to his *Counterfeit Road* as "an addictive police procedural on speed." Russell lives in Berkeley, California.